Sweet Second Chances

Lorelei Tiffin

authorHOUSE®

AuthorHouse™
1663 Liberty Drive
Bloomington, IN 47403
www.authorhouse.com
Phone: 1 (800) 839-8640

Published by AuthorHouse 09/17/2018

ISBN: 978-1-5462-5939-8 (sc)
ISBN: 978-1-5462-5938-1 (hc)
ISBN: 978-1-5462-5940-4 (e)

Library of Congress Control Number: 2018910616

Print information available on the last page.

Acknowledgements

No author writes in a bubble, and no book gets written without support from someone somewhere. I've had encouragement all along the way, from beta readers who told me what was good and bad in what I was writing. And I've had a higher level of support from a few people who pushed me to get books finished and then more importantly, pushed me to find a publisher. People who scoured local newspapers to see what seminars and writer's workshops were coming up.

DJ, you were the first to read my work, and at a point when I was about to stop writing, you gave me the encouragement to keep going.

Laura, you've provided so much support and editing feedback, you're the best beta reader a girl could ask for. I owe you so much.

Cinnamon, you were so enthusiastic about reading my books, and gave me so much feedback along the way, I kept going when other people urged me to stop writing.

Pat, I can't say enough about your support along the way. You disliked a character's name in another book so much, I started looking for alternative names, and Chase and Coco came to life along the way. This book is all because of you.

And what can I say about family. You never made me feel uncomfortable about how I write or what I write, I love you all.

And of course, the people at authorHouse, we're on this journey together. Thanks for helping me find my way.

Prologue

January 1981, Myrtle Beach, SC

The music continued, but the dancing had stopped abruptly. "Mr. Buckingham? Mr. Buckingham!!" *Coralee, he's the customer. You have to be nice. Don't scare him off with that bitchy tone of voice.*

"What? I'm sorry, Miss Brighton, what did you say?" *Chase!! Dude! Focus!! You're wasting time.*

"Mr. Buckingham, you're letting me lead again. If you're taking dance lessons to impress a young lady, I don't think your current skills are going to cut it." *He's so cute! You've always been a sucker for tall, blonde and handsome, Coralee. Too bad he seems to have two left feet – and he can't seem to focus worth a damn!*

"I'm sorry, Miss Brighton. I'm having trouble concentrating tonight. There's a marriage proposal in my near future and I guess I'm more nervous than I thought." *Or maybe you're just befuddled by how good this juicy tidbit smells and how soft she feels in your arms. Dude, where the hell did that just come from?!? You're going to propose to the woman you love in two weeks, you can't be thinking like that about this little ball of fluff who's trying to teach you how to dance!! And why are you still holding her?*

"Mr. Buckingham, perhaps we should separate and review the steps side by side again. Are you sure you want to learn all these dances in three lessons? Arthur Murray Dance Studios have an excellent program but that's a lot to absorb in a short time." *Certainly too much for you, gorgeous!*

Chase, you can't dance with your head in your ass, dude!! "No, I'm good. I can do this. I only have this week in town so I'm up against a deadline. Let's go again. I lead!! Come on, we're burning class time!"

February 1981, Columbia, SC

The restaurant ambience is just right, dinner was fabulous, we've had just enough wine and I danced like Fred Astaire. It's been a perfect night, Chase, don't blow the fucking finale! "Gail, we've known each other for a while now, and I think you know how I feel about you. We're perfect for each other. I love you and I think you love me as well." Chase stood up, walked around the small table, got down on one knee and reached into his pocket for the ring. "Gail, I'm sorry I'm not more romantic, but I adore you. Will you marry me?"

"Oh my god, Chase. Why do I feel like this is sudden?"

"I don't know, Gail, I've been dropping hints for a month. I know you've been distracted with mid-terms but I think it's time for us to move forward with our relationship. We can be engaged, get married even, and still finish school."

"Do you really love me, Chase?"

"Of course, I do. More than my next breath."

"Then yes, I'll marry you."

Chase slid the ring on Gail's finger, wrapped her in a hug and kissed her passionately. The patrons of the small, exclusive restaurant all applauded, the waiter tore up their check and wished them well, and off they went to Gail's parents' house to tell them the wonderful news.

May 1981, Chapel Hill, NC

"Gail, I don't understand. I don't want your ring back, I want to marry you. Why are you doing this?"

"Chase, I can't marry you, I'm in love with someone else. It was wrong for me to accept your proposal, I knew it right away. I've been trying to convince myself for three months that marrying you is the right thing to do, but it's not, and I can't string you along any longer. I'm so sorry. Please don't hate me."

"Gail! Wait!"

"I have to go, Chase, I'm so sorry, I have to go."

And she was out the door, leaving him standing in the doorway of his apartment, wondering what the hell had just happened to his world.

Four hours later he was drunk, puking up the dinner he shouldn't have eaten, sobbing so hard he couldn't breathe. Chase drunk dialed his parents' home phone and when his dad answered, Chase cried so hard he couldn't talk. His dad kept yelling into the phone, "Chase, is that you? Son, what's wrong? Are you hurt? Are you sick? For god's sake, Chase, talk to me."

Finally, Chase took a deep breath. "Dad, Gail gave my ring back. I don't know what to do. Can you come?" Hell had well and truly come to earth for Chase Buckingham.

June 1981, Myrtle Beach, SC

Chase was in his parents' house, in his childhood bedroom, reliving too many recent painful conversations. His dad walked in, surprising him and pulling him out of his waking nightmare. "Chase, Son, what the hell? Your mother just told me you enlisted in the Army? Chase, I know you've been really upset about Gail breaking off your engagement, but that's no reason to throw away everything you've worked so hard to accomplish. You have two years of pre-Law under your belt, and summer internship offers out the ass. You'll be practicing law with me in just five years. Don't do this."

"Dad, I know you mean well, but I've made up my mind, and nothing you can say will change it. I know now that Gail wasn't the one for me, but neither is the path I'm on right now. Everything just feels wrong, out of control. I need to take a big step back and rethink what I want out of my life. The Army, hopefully the Rangers, will give me the opportunity to do that. My recruiter was very enthusiastic about how far I can go if I apply myself. I report in two weeks."

"Chase, Son, please…"

"Dad, you're an Army veteran yourself. Hell, you served in Nam, Dad! Look, I already returned the engagement ring. I need to put that past behind me. Please don't try to talk me out of this, just support my decision, and help Mom and Grandma support me too."

"Okay." Father and son embraced, crying for lost chances and hoping for safe opportunities. "I love you, Chase."

"I love you too, Dad."

April 2013, Myrtle Beach, SC

Coralee Brighton walked through the front door of her little cottage Friday evening feeling dog tired – it had been a really long week. She'd thought semi-retirement would make things easier but it certainly wasn't feeling like it. She had expected that moving back home to Myrtle Beach to start her own web design business would be a breeze, but so far, she was working more than full time hours, and thinking she'd made a huge mistake.

Coralee had started her web design business slowly, gaining clients from among the family and friends who had known her and her parents best. Luckily there were quite a few people among her friends and family who had small home based businesses – and who were in desperate need of eye catching, well placed web sites to draw in their own clients. Success breeds success, and local word of mouth was giving her the boost her business needed to make a name for itself. If her own business continued to do well, she would have to hire someone to help with the demand. But in the meantime, she was seriously overworked, and glad the week was finally over.

She kicked off her heels, turned on the TV, and changed the station to her favorite conservative talk show. Nothing made her feel better about herself than to see a rehash of whatever the latest Capitol Hill disaster had been that day. She threw the mail and her cell phone on the coffee table and went to the kitchen for a much needed glass of wine. Coralee had been drinking a lot of wine lately. She carried her very large glass of Riesling with her to her bedroom, changed into some comfy Friday night sweats and went back to the living room, wine in hand. She plopped down on the sofa and took three large swigs from the wine glass, closed her eyes, went to her safe happy mental place, and took some deep cleansing breaths. When she opened her eyes again, she had put the week's crap behind her and started to relax. She decided maybe yoga wasn't such a bad thing after all, if she could learn to relax that fast. The added bonus of yoga keeping her 50 year old body toned and fit was a big plus.

As she scanned the day's mail, tossing junk mail into one pile, and bills into another, one envelope stood out from the rest. It was large, square and heavy, and had a return address she didn't recognize. She threw the rest of the mail to the other end of the sofa and opened the mysterious envelope, thinking that the red color of the envelope lining reminded her of someone. She pulled the contents out of the envelope, noting it was a wedding invitation, and took two seconds to read the beautiful engraved words – before she screamed for joy!! "FINALLY!" They were really going to do this!! With happy tears in her eyes, she read the invitation again aloud –

THE CHILDREN OF
Gabriella Marie Gomez
AND
Robert Glenn Davis
Invite you to celebrate with them the
marriage of their parents
Saturday, June 15, 2013 at 6:00 pm at Kingsley Plantation
Myrtle Beach, SC

Without even thinking what she was doing, Coralee picked up the phone off the coffee table and hit speed dial 2. Four rings later, she was talking to one of her two best childhood friends, her closest confidant, sharing more happy tears with the woman she'd known longer than anyone outside her family. Beautiful Gigi, as Gabriella was known to her closest friends, had finally agreed to marry the love of her life, the stunning Robert Davis, and Coralee couldn't be happier for them both. This marriage was long overdue. Naturally Coco – as Coralee was known to HER closest friends – needed every detail of the lead-up to the proposal, the acceptance and the planning.

The conversation started out with a little recrimination – "Why the hell didn't you tell me about this, Gigi? What were you thinking, keeping this a secret??"

"We wanted it to be a surprise for everyone. And by the tone of your voice, I'm glad we did!!"

Two hours later, Coco's wine bottle was empty, she had locked up the house and turned off most of the lights, and she had moved to her bedroom to recline in bed and let the room spin all it wanted. She had all the details she wanted from Gigi, at least for tonight, and it was time for a little sleep. She knew she'd have a hangover in the morning, but a short run around the track at the high school down the street – the one she and her friends had graduated from more than 30 years before – would make her feel better and get her weekend off to a productive start. At least that was the plan as she faded off to sleep.

Hours later, one eye popped open and squinted toward the clock radio next to the bed – 8:30 AM. Coco really needed to find a way to sleep longer on weekends!! The hangover she had anticipated the night before was in full force, and even with the blinds drawn and the curtains pulled closed, the early morning Myrtle Beach sun was brightening her bedroom more than she could stand. Morning sun? In a bedroom? What the hell had she been thinking when she bought this house? Blackout curtains would have to be one of her next purchases! Sure that she would not be getting back to sleep, Coco threw off the covers and dragged herself into the bathroom, searching for and finally finding the Ibuprofen that would help to fix her head. From there she moved to the kitchen and grabbed a glass of juice from the fridge, groaning at the sight of the empty wine bottle in the kitchen sink along the way. She questioned briefly whether she had developed a drinking problem – this would not be the only wine bottle in the recycling bin from the past week – then put the thought out of her aching head. Wine – and a good vibrator – were a single woman's best friends. No drinking problem there!

After finishing her juice and two cups of coffee, along with a chocolate fiber bar, and reading the mail she had ignored the evening before, Coco headed for the high school track down the street. Her planned run turned into a moderately paced walk, but she was able to manage 30 minutes of movement without vomiting before she allowed herself to walk back home. A quick shower made her head feel much better, and by the time she had dressed and forced down her usual breakfast of scrambled egg substitutes, turkey sausage and some fruit, she was ready to make her next phone call. It was time to check in with the third leg of Myrtle Beach High School's infamous Gang of 3 – Class of 1980.

Even at 10:30 AM, Coco knew her other best friend had been up for hours already. Maggs. She couldn't wait to talk to her and as she dialed the number she knew as well as her own, she walked to the bookcase in the living room and glanced at her picture of the Gang of 3 – Coco, Gigi and Maggs – Coralee, Gabriella and Magnolia – the day they graduated from high school. Maggs, tall and slender, Gigi, voluptuous even at 18, and Coco, the runt of the litter, short compared to the other two, always 10 pounds overweight, no matter how hard or how long she ran around the track. They had their whole lives ahead of them that day. None of them knew what the future would bring, but they knew as surely as they knew their own names that they would be friends forever. They were three friends who would never let go of each other. And they had been true to each other through thick and thin, comforting each other through all of life's disasters.

The call connected with one scream followed by another – "Coco!!!!" "Maggs!!!!"

And simultaneously – "They're getting married!!"

For the next hour, there was laughing, crying, saying the same thing at the same time – friends who were so in tune with each other, even a separation of six months hadn't come between them. Just as they both were in tune with Gigi. By the end of the call, they had planned every detail leading up to the wedding, right down to what they would wear for the big day. Maggs was sure that somewhere on Gigi's wedding dress, there would be her signature red color – the red that matched the envelope lining of the wedding invitation – the red that made her auburn hair glow. Maggs would be dressed in the classic jewel tone green that set off her red hair spectacularly. And Coco would be dressed in the cobalt blue she had always thought brought out the best of her coloring, brightening her normally mousy brown hair and making her blue eyes pop with color. They would look like three jewels standing next to each other in the photo they planned to take – older versions of the three girls that smiled at the world on graduation day.

Coco would mail back her RSVP immediately – a sad little '1' in attendance, as there was no guest she would want to bring to this particular event. But Coco was in such a good mood by the time she had finished talking with Maggs that she decided to clean the house. The whole house! And as she labored in each room, tidying and cleaning, listening to her favorite old time swing music, her mind drifted back to a week more than 30 years before, three dance lessons, and a young man she had never been able to forget.

2

Wedding Day, June 15, 2013, Myrtle Beach, SC

Saturday morning, Chase Buckingham woke up quietly, not exactly sure where he was or who he was with. And he had a hangover that wouldn't allow him to go another minute without some kind of pain killer. He popped one eye open and looked to his left, toward the soft snoring sounds next to him. His bed mate's back was to him, a mop of blonde hair exploding across the pillow. He realized that he was not in his own bedroom, but there was little recognition beyond that. He had no recollection of where he had picked up this person, his last memory of the night before was going into his favorite neighborhood bar and ordering a scotch neat.

Then the person next to him rolled toward him, and he said a silent pray of thanks that it was a 'she' next to him, and she looked to be somewhere between 18 and 30 years old. He had a sudden uninvited memory of waking up a few weeks prior in bed with a 15 year old girl and a 25 year old man. Chase shivered and had a sudden urge to vomit at that particular memory, vowing once again to change his evil ways. If he wasn't careful, he was going to end up either in jail, or a father, or both. And dead was also a possibility. Mass quantities of alcohol and sex with barely legal young women weren't making the demons go away, and his current lifestyle was going to get him into real trouble if he didn't get his shit together. Time to get back into group therapy again.

As he slid out of bed, the still nameless young lady reached for him, meaning to pull him back into her arms for another round of whatever they had done the night before. But Chase knew he needed to make a quick getaway, or he'd never make his best friend's wedding.

As he found his jeans and shirt, and started getting dressed, he put on his best playboy smile and said "I'd love to stay, baby, but I really have to go. Last night was incredible but I have a lot to do today."

"Case, baby, you said last night that there was nothing in the world you'd rather do than fuck me blind, over and over again. I only got one fuck last night, you still owe me for that great blow job I gave you in your car!! Please come back to bed, baby, it's so early, we have plenty of time."

He said another silent prayer for the fact that she didn't remember his name either, and said "Sorry, darlin', but I really have to go. Maybe I'll see you again some time."

And he blew her a kiss from across the room as he all but ran out the front door. He jumped into his Jeep and tore away from the curb, eager to put his latest indiscretion behind him.

Wedding Day, June 15, 2013, Myrtle Beach, SC – the other side of town

In Coco's world, the big day had arrived, the day her dear friend Gigi would become Mrs. Robert Glenn Davis, with the full support of her children, his children, and their closest friends and family. Coco, Gigi and Maggs had treated themselves to a spa day earlier in the week – mani-pedi's, facials, hot rock massages, everything waxed so smooth, a hair wouldn't dare to come back any time soon!! Coco had found the perfect outfit to wear to the wedding – chic but comfortable, perfect for a beachside wedding ceremony and reception. The Kingsley Plantation was a very formal setting, but Gigi and Robert were just this side of too casual – a little surprising for a Physical Therapist and a Pension and Trust Attorney. The dress code for the wedding was whatever felt good. The only rule Gigi and Robert had set was NO JEANS, which was more for the younger generation than for their 50-something friends, and mostly for all of the photos that would be taken that evening.

White Capri leggings fit Coco's curvy hips and toned legs perfectly.

Her yoga and miles running around the high school track every week really paid off keeping her fit and trim. Her leggings were topped with a satin and chiffon sleeveless tunic with plenty of cobalt blue satin layered with floaty chiffon swirled with lighter blues, pinks, purples, even a touch of green – the perfect top to hide the extra 10 pounds she could still never seem to shed from those curvy hips. This was exactly the look Coco had been going for – casual but with a sexy edge. Her one new extravagance – the cobalt blue crystal studded Manolo Blahnik stiletto sandals – matched the outfit perfectly and made Coco feel like she was the hottest thing Myrtle Beach had ever seen. Diamond studs and platinum hoops, an extravagance from her past, along with her platinum Chanel watch and matching bracelet, were all the jewelry she needed. A little pink blush, mascara and some shiny pink lip gloss and she was out the door, ready for a fabulous evening, celebrating with her best friends.

Coco was just dropping off her car at valet parking when she saw Maggs and her husband – Dr. and Dr. Russell Corson – pulling up behind her. Who knew when Maggs was called to do her first emergency appendectomy 20 years before, she would be teamed with new Anesthesiologist Dr. Russell Corson, and it was love at first cut – or stitch – or something. Maggs looked gorgeous in her emerald green low cut silk shantung sleeveless blouse with matching Capri pants. She had her own extravagant Manolo gold stilettos and showy gold jewelry to match.

Coco hugged Maggs and then Russell, exclaiming "Russell, I can't believe you let her wear that blouse – it's pretty risqué!"

And Russell agreed – "Yes, it is. But I don't think I had any say in 'letting' her wear this outfit. And I figure these muscle bound beach bums can look all they want. She'll be going home with me!"

And he wrapped his wife in a tight hug, finishing with a juicy kiss. They all laughed and walked through the main entrance of the Kingsley Plantation, to be directed to the event space of the Gomez/Davis wedding.

Coco, Maggs and Russ found their assigned 4 person table, then left Russ to get himself a drink and hold down the fort, while they went in search of the bride. They wanted one last hug and two minutes with their best friend before she became a 'Mrs.' again. Unfortunately, they located the bride's room, but couldn't get past the determined little door guards who were Gigi's twin daughters, Grace and Mimi, no matter how much they begged, pleaded and threatened. The girls both looked lovely in their pink taffeta bridesmaid dresses, perfect young adults, but they were absolutely stubborn about not letting Coco and Maggs in to see their mom.

Thinking it best not to cause a big scene right before the ceremony, Coco and Maggs leaned against the door, shouted "We love you, Gigi!!", hugged the girls and found their way back to their table – with one small detour to grab a glass of wine from the bar. At the table, Coco and Maggs found that Russ had gotten drinks for them as well – an almost dusty dry martini for Maggs and a White Cosmo for Coco. Russ never forgot any girl's favorite drink.

The room where both the ceremony and the reception were being held was lovely – beautiful deep red and white flowers everywhere, tables decorated flawlessly. The double French doors on the far end of the room were open and offered a spectacular view of the patio, and the beach and ocean beyond it. The sounds of the waves on the shore were low but hypnotic.

Coco and Maggs had barely started chatting about the last six months in their lives when a harpist started playing a beautiful melody – one that sounded vaguely familiar. The small crowd began to smile and laugh, almost in unison, as everyone recognized the opening notes of Robert and Gigi's favorite AC/DC song, *Hells Bells*. As the harpist played, the minister took his place before the open doors, and Robert and his groomsmen – his sons Brock and Thad, and Gigi's son Harper – appeared from a side door, moving to stand in front of the minister. The music stopped for a split second, and then the harpist began again, this time playing a livelier tune – the Rolling Stones classic *Jumpin' Jack Flash*. The crowd rose to their feet amid tears and applause as the bridesmaids danced the bride from the other side of the room to her place next to Robert. Sure enough, the skirt of Gigi's beautiful white wedding dress had an overlay of deep red chiffon with sequins that sparkled under the bright lights. Her Jimmy Choo wedding white stilettos were quintessential Gigi.

The music stopped, the crowd was seated, and the wedding ceremony began. The minister spoke of the gift of love and the support given by family and friends to the happy couple. He also spoke of the importance of timing – knowing that Robert and Gigi had known and loved each other for years, but they never felt the timing was right until the last of the kids were out of high school, leaving them no more excuses for postponing this wedding. Robert and Gigi recited the vows they had written from their hearts, exchanged simple, stunning wedding bands, and received the blessings of the minister and the State of South Carolina, before they shared the longest tongue twisting kiss the Kingsley Plantation had ever seen. No quick, chaste kiss for Gigi and Robert! They intended to inhale each other! The minister cleared his throat twice, and finally tapped Robert on the shoulder to let the bride and groom know that the honeymoon hadn't started yet – they were in a room full of people, including some children!! The newlyweds finally came up for air and the room erupted in applause, cheers, whistles and confetti. All in all, a beautiful ceremony – long awaited by everyone in the room, nearly 10 years in the making.

When the ceremony was done, the bridal party formed a casual receiving line outside on the patio. The crowd had 15 minutes to hug and kiss and congratulate Robert and Gigi while the wait staff set up for the dinner buffet. During that 15 minutes, a few guests who hadn't made it in time for the ceremony drifted in, including a single man who found himself seated at the table with Coco, Maggs and Russ. The mystery man was tall – well over 6 feet – and broad shouldered, with curly dark blonde hair, dazzling green eyes and a smile that lit up the room. And he was dressed in a spectacular black suit that fit him extremely well. The total package. So attractive, Coco couldn't help but stare and hope she wasn't drooling. She reached for her wine, and kept drinking.

When dinner was ready, the bridal party made their way to the long table at the front of the room and were served their meals first. Then the small crowd was invited, table by table, to go through the buffet line, get their food and return to their tables. Wait staff were ready to take additional drink orders – Coco ordered another glass of wine and another White Cosmo. The stranger ordered Scotch neat. Russ ordered another beer, and Maggs switched to water.

With everyone back at their table, including the very dashing newcomer, and more alcohol served, everyone started sharing memories of Gigi and Robert, followed by hysterical laughter. Maggs shared a story about Gigi's infamous wardrobe malfunction during a swim meet their Senior year of high school, and Coco talked about Maggs and Gigi getting chased up a tree by a bear cub during a junior high class trip. In retaliation for the bear cub story, Maggs shared about Coco coming out of the bathroom at her and Russ's wedding reception with the back of her dress tucked in her pantyhose, her curvy – and unpantied – ass on full display.

Coco decided there had been enough stories about the bride and her friends, and she asked the newly arrived – and exceedingly good looking – man at their table whether he was a friend of the bride or the groom. He didn't look familiar to her and she jumped to the immediate conclusion that Mr. Hot as Hell was an old friend of the groom. In response to Coco's question, the stranger simply replied "Both", and continued eating.

To keep the handsome stranger talking a little longer, Coco asked "So how did you end up at this particular table? When we arrived, there wasn't a place card at that seat."

"The wedding planner lady put me here. Is there a problem?" The smirk on the stranger's face said he was happy to be right where he was.

"No, not at all." And Coco took a long drink of her current glass of wine and shut up.

By the time they had finished dinner, Coco had already had several glasses of wine and two White Cosmos, and she no longer had the ability to be discreet or tactful. Her attempt to draw the delectable stranger into the conversation again started out shamelessly – "You're a very attractive man, if you don't mind my saying so."

"No, I don't think I mind at all."

"I see you're not wearing a wedding ring, I assume that means you're not married."

"A fairly safe assumption."

"Assuming that you're actually a friend of the groom, you must not live around here because Gigi would have tried to throw you and me together by now. She sees herself as the ultimate matchmaker, and she's always trying to hook me up with some friend or other."

"You're right. I haven't lived around here for a long time. Until now, that is. I'm just moving back here from Columbia – South Carolina, that is. But I've known Robert for more than 30 years. We met in college and have been friends ever since. So naturally I know Gigi as well."

"I can't help thinking I know you from somewhere. Have we met before? I'm sure I would have remembered a stud like you, but I just can't place your face. Or those shoulders!"

The stranger laughed and Maggs yelled – "Coco, you're embarrassing yourself!! Perhaps we should visit the Ladies Room and have a chat about appropriate wedding reception etiquette! Come with me!" Maggs laughed as she pulled Coco out of her chair and dragged her out of the room.

Russ simply looked at the man, shook his head and said "You'll have to excuse Coco. The drunker she gets, the flirtier she gets, and then she just passes out. My name is Russ, by the way. I don't think I caught your name."

"My friends call me Chase. And I think your friend Coco is adorable. And she's right, actually, she looks very familiar to me too, but I just can't quite remember where we met." And as men will do, Russ and Chase shook hands and then headed for the bar to get more drinks for themselves and the women at their table.

Ten minutes later, Coco and Maggs were back, just in time to greet the newlyweds. Gigi and Robert had been making the rounds in the room after dinner and had just arrived at their table, chatting with Russ and Chase. Coco and Maggs made a beeline for Gigi and got more hugs and pictures with their best friend, while Robert shared some man talk with "the boys". Coco and Maggs still hadn't been formally introduced to Chase, so Gigi did the honors. When Gigi got to introducing Coco and Chase, she had that little matchmaker sparkle in her eyes, saying "You two might have something in common." But she couldn't elaborate because the bride and groom had just been called to the dance floor for their first dance as husband and wife.

Soon other couples had joined the newlyweds dancing, including Maggs and Russ, leaving Coco and Chase in awkward silence at the table. Ever the gentleman, Chase asked Coco if she would like to dance, and after hesitating for just a moment, she threw back half the wine in her glass and said yes. Chase led her to a quiet corner of the dance floor, took Coco in his arms, and started to dance like a pro. Within ten seconds in his arms, Coco had that spark of recognition and so did Chase. With one voice, they shouted "Mr. Buckingham, you're letting me lead again!" And they both laughed.

Coco caught a glimpse of Gigi across the dance floor, laughing and smiling, looking right at Coco with that "Gotcha!" look on her face. When Coco looked back at Chase, he said quietly "When you said I looked familiar, I had the same feeling about you. Now we know why! How do you suppose Gigi knew about the dance lessons? And how coincidental is it that one of my best friends ended up marrying one of your best friends? I guess life is full of strange twists and turns, isn't it?"

And Coco responded just as quietly, "It certainly is." And they danced in silence, Coco looking at Chase like she could eat him up, and Chase staring at Coco, reflecting the look back at her.

3

*A*n hour of dancing later, Maggs and Russ headed out to the patio for a little quiet time together. As the last song had finished, Chase had taken Coco's hand in his, kissed it, and thanked her for the dance. Then he guided her back to their table for a drink and a rest. Their conversation while dancing had been light and fluffy, sharing nothing of consequence, only snippets of stories about the bride and groom, and the briefest information about current careers.

But back at the table, just the two of them, there was another awkward moment or two of silence. Then Chase kicked off the conversation by saying "You still dance very well. It was my pleasure to lead you around the floor." And he smiled so brightly, it took Coco's breath away.

She responded with a coy smile of her own and said "Thank you very much, it was my great pleasure to be led around the floor by you. There was a time I wasn't sure you would ever learn to dance, but by the end of that week, you were quite accomplished. As I recall, there was a marriage proposal planned. How did that go?"

Chase looked away for a second, as if remembering something unpleasant, making Coco feel suddenly very sad. To make amends, she said "I'm sorry, that was very nosy of me. But I was a little nosy back then as well. I saw your engagement announcement in the newspaper, but I never saw anything about an actual wedding. And I didn't hang around long after college. I couldn't wait to get out of the 'Home of the Grand Strand' and start my career."

"That marriage wasn't meant to be. I don't see a ring or even a ring tan line on your finger. No one ever captured your heart?"

Coco looked at the ring finger on her own left hand and reflected on her own sad memory, but then smiled and said "No, I was too busy building my career, and then life sort of got in the way."

"I have to admit to being a little nosy once myself. I was home on leave just before my first re-up, and I tried to find you. You weren't at the dance studio anymore and it took me awhile to find someone who knew where you had gone first when you left town. I found out you weren't there either. I thought about tracking down your parents to see where you were but I decided that might be a little bit like stalking so I didn't bother them. Then I had to report back to base, and things got a little busy – war in the Middle East and all that."

"So I heard Robert tell Russ you left college and enlisted in the Army – the Rangers no less. I also heard him say you're a lawyer now. How did you get from the Rangers to a Law career?"

"I gave the Army 20 years and then got out. Law school came after that."

Coco reached out and placed her hand gently on Chase's arm and said "I'd like to thank you for your service to the country."

When he gave her the typical 'don't thank me' look, she scolded him. "No, don't look at me like that, I'm serious. While I was out globetrotting through my career, you were in scary places protecting my right to be a sassy girl."

Coco's hand didn't move and Chase reached over and placed his free hand on hers. "No thanks necessary, sassy girl. The Army was there at a critical time in my life, and I learned a lot – about myself, about life, you know, the Universe."

As if they both noticed the intimate contact at the same time, their hands separated and Coco said "You're a lawyer now – very impressive. Did you know you wanted a Law career when you were in the Rangers?"

"I knew I wanted to be a lawyer when I was six. But since I quit college to enlist, and then ended up staying in the Army for awhile, I had a little catching up to do before Law School. I had one stateside assignment before I left the Army and I finished my pre-law online. Then when I retired from the Army, I went back to UNC and lived there for three years while I went to Law School."

"So how was that? Being a mature student going to Law School with all the kids? I really am impressed by your drive and determination."

"Don't be – the law is kind of in my blood. My dad's had his own practice for all the time I've been alive, and when I graduated from Law School and passed the Bar, I started practicing with him. His office has always been here in North Myrtle and I opened a branch in Columbia, so that we could be more involved in statewide issues."

"What kind of law do you practice? Your last name sounds sort of familiar now for a different reason."

"I'm an environmental lawyer, just like my dad."

"Oh no, you're a tree hugger!?!"

"Yes, I am! And I'm enjoying myself. I find I'm not quite as jaded as other attorneys my age. They've all been practicing longer than I have, they're a little beat down by the system. I still have a little enthusiasm for the work. And I've been pretty successful so far."

"Your dad is on the North Myrtle City Council, isn't he? He's a Democrat!"

"Yes, he is – City Council and a proud Democrat!"

"And I suppose you're a Democrat too?"

"Through and through. Sounds like maybe you're NOT a Democrat."

"Guilty."

"Independent?"

"Hardly. I'm a staunch Republican. As a matter of fact, I'm involved in the fight against some statewide legislation your dad is working on – marshland protection."

"So you're against protecting marshland?" And a shocked and disgusted look crossed his face.

And Coco countered with her own disgusted face. "Of course I'm not against protecting the marshland, but I think the legislation is so sweeping and so top heavy it's going to be impossible to fund – except by raising my taxes. Again. But I think you're working on this case with your dad, and we shouldn't talk about it, should we?"

"We just took on a new partner to run the Columbia office so that I could move back here and work with Dad on this case. And no, we probably shouldn't talk about it." And Chase smiled a sweet, almost devilish smile and Coco started to melt.

Just about then, a few of the wait staff passed through the reception room announcing that while the room and the bar would stay open for another hour, and patio access to the parking lot would be open all night, valet parking was about to close. Maggs and Russell had just left to head back to their hotel, and Coco headed across the room to give Gigi and Robert one last hug and head for home herself. She thought she needed to sober up and get some sleep before seeing everyone for brunch the next day. But Chase clearly had another idea.

Coco had just said goodbye to Gigi and Robert when Chase came up behind her and said "Coco, why don't you give me your valet claim check and I'll get your car and park it next to mine in the parking lot. The lot will be open all night so we can take a walk on the beach and not worry about the time."

"Are you planning on offing me and dumping my body somewhere? Because that would be bad for the environment, you know."

"As tempting as it would be to eliminate the opposition, no, I'm not planning on anything that drastic. I'd just like to talk a little longer, maybe get a little kiss goodnight before I lose track of you again."

Tired as she had thought she was just a moment before, Coco was now wide awake again. She only hesitated a split second before she reached into her clutch purse and pulled out the claim check along with a $5.00 bill for the tip. Chase took the claim check, but handed the Fiver back to Coco with a definite frown on his face and said "Don't do that again. I think I can afford the cost of a valet tip to spend a little more time with such a fascinating – and sassy – woman."

Chase winked at Coco, then turned and walked toward the door. As he reached the door, he turned around and yelled to her, "Meet me on the patio in ten minutes." And he was gone. And Coco was as aroused as she had been in years.

Coco took the opportunity to hit the Ladies Room, and then grab a plastic glass of water from the bar on her way out to the patio. She thought that if she was going to walk on the beach with the enchanting Chase Buckingham, she'd better try to sober up a little. Even environmental lawyers could get a little handsy on a moonlit beach and, with Chase, she would need all the control she could muster.

Coco had just walked out onto the patio when Chase walked up the patio steps from the parking lot. He saw the drink in Coco's hand and decided that would be a good idea. A minute later, he was back beside her with his own plastic glass of water. He had managed to change out of his suit into a pair of faded jeans in the parking lot, and with the top button of his now untucked white dress shirt unbuttoned, he looked deliciously casual. A pair of well worn flip flops completed the wardrobe change, and he looked considerably more comfortable than he had in his suit.

Chase stared at Coco for just a few seconds and then said "You haven't changed much in the past 30 years. It would appear that the years have been good to you."

"Oh, honey, if you only knew. Looks can be deceiving."

"So what do you do to stay in such great shape?"

"I try to start every day with a run around the neighborhood, sometimes around the high school track down the street from my house. And I started doing yoga last year. I try to do three or four 30 minute sessions every week. It's a great stress reliever and it really helps with my arthritis."

"Rheumatoid or osteo?"

"Osteo. Running relieves my stress and yoga keeps my joints limber. The combination keeps me off the pain killers." And she laughed to ease the slight tension that had come between them.

Chase smiled and said "Let's take a walk."

"Okay."

But as they moved toward the steps down to the beach, Coco realized that her very substantial shoe investment was in jeopardy – her Manolo's could not walk in the sand – and she stopped abruptly. "Wait! My shoes!"

"Oh, of course. We can't let anything happen to these fine stilettos. There's nowhere to sit out here. Give me a foot."

She was still just drunk enough to giggle and grab hold of the patio rail, lifting her left foot in his direction. Chase unbuckled the offered shoe and slipped it off Coco's foot, but held and caressed that foot ever so gently before letting it go. Which sent a visible shiver down Coco's spine. Chase demanded the other foot, and Coco presented it. Ten seconds later, the second shoe had been removed and her right foot had been caressed and squeezed ever so lightly, making Coco pant for just a few seconds, and hoping Chase hadn't noticed.

Without her four inch heels, the height difference between Chase and Coco was considerable and he chuckled. He took her in his arms as if they were going to dance and said "Yes, that's the Coralee Brighton I remember."

"I'm afraid I only wear flat shoes when I have to. You don't know what's it's like to be so vertically challenged!!" And they both laughed.

Since Coco was already holding her clutch purse and her drink in one hand, Chase took her shoes and his drink in one hand and held out the other hand to her. She put her free hand in his and they headed down the steps to the beach. Once they were down on the beach, the breeze was stronger – the satin and chiffon of her tunic top fluttered, allowing the night air to reach underneath and cool her overly warm skin. She wasn't sure if she was overheated because of the temperature inside the reception room or the fact that she was holding Chase Buckingham's hand, but she was grateful for the cool breeze regardless.

When she looked up at Chase, his curly hair was waving a little in the breeze, making him look younger than his 50+ years. Just as sexy as he had been that week in 1981, maybe more so now that his hair was a little darker and he had that little bit of grey at his temples. Sexy. Distinguished. And unfortunately, a freaking Democrat!! Such a shame! Images of Mary Matalin and James Carville suddenly floated through her mind. But she put them away – talk about the cart before the horse!!

They walked hand in hand in surprisingly comfortable silence for a short while, and then Chase asked "So I know what you're doing professionally now, but how did you get from high school graduate dance instructor to web site designer?"

Coco launched into her professional life story – how she got interested in IT in junior high, before it was even called IT, and decided that Information Technology would be her life's work. She talked about her career path – the technical certification that brought her computer hardware repair jobs, some programming classes at the local junior college, clawing her way to her Bachelor's degree in Computer Science, taking night classes when she could. She explained some of the technical certifications she'd gotten along the way, how and why she got her Master's degree in

Business Management instead of IT. Coco rambled on about all the places she'd lived nationally and internationally, how she still couldn't converse in any foreign language other than to ask for the nearest bathroom, despite her international jobs, how the '.com' bubble had burst around her and changed her career path a little. And she talked about how hard she had worked to become a lioness of the IT industry, only to find out that she wasn't really leadership or even management material after all. And how that realization had brought her to web design – something she enjoyed, that she was good at, and that required no personnel management for as long as she worked alone.

What she didn't tell Chase was how losing both her parents in a horrible holiday car accident had brought her back "temporarily" to her home town – to settle their affairs – and how that one event had eventually brought her home for good. Coco had finally sobered up and was enjoying spending time with Chase – she didn't want her family tragedy to cloud their conversation.

By the time Coco finished the tale of her professional odyssey, two hours had passed and they found themselves somewhat farther down the beach than they had planned. Chase suggested taking a break on a convenient beachside bench, and Coco wholeheartedly agreed. For twenty minutes, they both rested and talked about how they had met Gigi and Robert, told a few more funny stories about the bride and groom, finally commenting on the passionate kiss that had completed the wedding ceremony.

The thought of that kiss, the one that Chase had seen from the door of the reception room on his way in, stopped them both – stopped them from talking, stopped them from even breathing. They stared into each other's eyes for a few seconds, with the almost full moon shining down on them. And then Chase took Coco's face in both his hands and pulled her to him – their lips were millimeters apart and their breathing was shallow, almost panting – and then he kissed her. Gently at first, just lips touching lips. And then their passion began to grow. Chase licked at the seam of Coco's lips with his tongue, and a little moan escaped his throat as she opened her mouth and let out a low moan of her own.

As their tongues explored each other, so did their hands, unconsciously fisting hair, grasping shoulders, touching any exposed skin they could find on each other. The kiss paused – they both pulled away gasping for air. Chase stared into Coco's eyes and saw his desire reflected back at him, and the kiss resumed. For several minutes, they were all lips and tongues and hands and hot breath, and things were about to get X-rated as Chase's hand moved up under Coco's top toward her breasts, and Coco's hand started moving down Chase's steel abs toward his zipper and what was waiting for her there.

And then there was a loud rapping noise on the back of the bench they were seated on. Chase was about to get all beastly with whoever was interrupting his amorous activity, and then he noticed that the interruption was a police officer with a disapproving look on his face. The officer said one thing – "You can't do that here – go find a room somewhere!"

And Chase and Coco slid apart from each other on the bench like they were opposing ends of two magnets. Coco flushed with embarrassment and without making eye contact with the police officer, said "I'm so sorry, Officer, I haven't seen my friend for a long time and we got a little carried away. It won't happen again." The officer made some kind of grunting noise and walked away, and Coco and Chase laughed so hard, Coco snorted – twice. Which just made them both laugh harder.

Still chuckling a little, Chase looked at Coco and said "Maybe we'd better head back. I'd hate to think I was responsible for getting you arrested in the middle of the night."

"It would certainly be a first for me. My record is clear so far!" They refilled their plastic glasses from a public water fountain and walked again in silence for a short way, both of them laughing spontaneously from time to time, thinking about their brush with the law.

Then Coco started the conversation again – "So now you know everything there is to know about the professional Coralee Brighton. But I don't really know much about you between the time you took those dance lessons and the beginning of your Legal career. How did you decide on the Army? And what did you do when you were a Ranger?"

"Not much to tell really."

"Because you don't want to talk about it or because you're sworn to secrecy? I know a number of retired military people who refuse to talk about their time in the service because they just don't want to be reminded of that time. I know a few others who really are sworn to secrecy about things they did and places they went."

With a slightly haunted look in his eyes, Chase replied "A little of both, I guess. You were right before, I was in some scary places. I saw and did some ugly things in 20 years. But I'd do it all again, because I feel like I made a difference, we did important work."

Coco took Chase's hand again and said "I'm sorry, I don't mean to dredge up bad memories. So tell me about all the times you made the little law students at UNC pee their pants with that kick-ass look you get in your eyes. I bet you were intimidating as hell in moot court arguments."

Chase laughed loud and said "I was a little intimidating, maybe a lot intimidating, back then. I had some serious PTSD issues when I came home. When I got settled in Chapel Hill for Law School, my dad hooked me up with an old friend of his, a psychiatrist who worked with returning military. He didn't take on a lot of patients at a time and he made himself available to us 24/7. He got a lot of calls from me in the middle of the night in those early days, and he was always there for me. He set me up with group therapy and it was good to share experiences with other men and women who had seen and done the same disturbing things I had.

"Doc retired a few years ago and his son Chet took over his practice. I still see him at group now and then. Chet served in Iraq and Afghanistan around the same time I did, and I think he gets as much help from us as we get from him. Even psychiatrists have problems with PTSD. I'm glad I was able to get private help with my problems; I wish the VA was able to provide the same help to all veterans that I've been able to get privately."

Coco didn't respond, but she squeezed Chase's hand a little just to let him know that she appreciated the years he'd dedicated to the military and to his country.

"Anyway, in a nutshell, I served in Grenada, Libya, Panama, Columbia – the country! – working that war on drugs, you know. Then my unit was deployed in Desert Shield and Desert Storm, and we spent some time in Somalia, plus a few other places we probably weren't supposed to be.

"I had just separated a few months before 9/11, and when it happened, I tried to re-enlist, but the recruiter said thanks anyway, I had already done more than my fair share. I think once he saw my age and my service record, he decided the Army had abused me enough. I hooked up with a mercenary group and we spent six months following the money trail back toward the 9/11 planners, but I finally decided I had some personal issues I needed to deal with and it was obvious the Middle East wasn't the place for me to be.

"So I came home and let my mom and dad take care of me for awhile, and started getting my head together again. I got accepted to UNC Law School in the class that started the fall of 2003 and once I was settled in

Chapel Hill, I started working with my dad's shrink friend. By the time I graduated and passed the Bar, most of my nightmares had stopped. I've been a little lax about attending group meetings lately, and I've been having some problems because of it. I know I need to get back to the group, as much to help myself as the new men and women coming in. We all help each other. It's all good."

Coco was glad it was dark on the beach, so Chase couldn't see her tears, but he could hear her sniffles and finally stopped under the light from the Indian Hill Pier. He brushed away her tears with his thumbs and said "I'm sorry, I didn't mean to make you cry. It wasn't that bad."

"No, I'm sure it WAS that bad, and I feel bad that you and everyone else who served and sacrificed, endured life in hell to keep me safe so that I could do stupid things."

Chase kissed Coco on her forehead and held her close for a minute, and then they started walking again. But they didn't have to walk far – they were back at the Plantation in just a few minutes. They walked back up the steps to the patio, and headed for the parking lot, but didn't get far before Coco realized she needed to put her expensive shoes back on or step on a lot of stones with her bare feet. But she was hesitant to put her Manolos on sandy wet feet.

Once again the gentleman, Chase picked her up and carried her to the parking lot and set her down gently next to her car. Coco got her keys out of her purse, opened the trunk of her Cadillac ATS and pulled some cobalt blue flip flops out of a box full of shoes. She took a towel from the trunk and brushed the sand off her feet, then put the flip flops on. Then she took her stilettos from Chase, put them in a plastic grocery bag, and deposited them in the box. Chase stood beside her and stared with a 'why do you have so many shoes in your trunk' look on his face but never said a word.

When she had closed the trunk, she looked at Chase and asked "What?"

"I don't think I even want to know about that box. There are more shoes in your trunk than I own in total! So I'm going to pretend I never saw a thing." And he laughed. And she huffed a little, and then she laughed also.

Chase said "That was a really long walk we took. I'm starving!! Could you eat?"

"I shouldn't."

"Oh, come on. It's been hours since we had dinner."

"Okay."

"Yeah? Great!"

"I don't have much willpower, do I?"

"I certainly hope not." And he wiggled his eyebrows and grinned an evil little grin. He said "I know a great place that serves breakfast 24/7."

"I'm in!"

"Excellent. It's pretty close to here, only about 10 minutes. Just follow me."

"Don't be running any traffic lights! And don't drive too fast – I'm not good at following people."

"Don't worry – I won't let you lose me, sassy girl."

Chase reached up and brushed a lock of hair off Coco's face and gave her a sweet kiss on the lips. He walked her around to the driver's side of her car, opened the door and helped her in, then closed the door for her. He got into his Jeep and headed out of the parking lot, with Coco following right behind him. She knew she should be headed home to bed – alone – but there was just something about this guy and she wanted to see where this would all lead.

5

Coco and Chase met up in the parking lot of his favorite little all night restaurant – obviously a mom and pop joint that employed all the kids and a lot more relatives. A neon light on the street blinked "Mama's Myrtle Beach Kitchen" in yellow, red and blue. Coco rolled her eyes a little when they were met at the register by a very attractive, very young lady with a wink and a seductive "Good evening, Mr. Buckingham, what brings you out in the middle of the night?"

"Your brother's 5-way special! It's been a whole week since I've had one so I'm way overdue. Is my usual booth available?"

"For you? Always. Come right this way." And Coco rolled her eyes again.

The young lady led Chase and Coco to a booth in the back next to an open window looking out over a covered porch and the beach. The sound of the waves from the beach was hypnotic, and under the outside lights on the back of the restaurant, the view of the waves was spectacular. The view was pretty impressive inside as well. Chase was in a very good mood and it made him look so young and so hot, Coco suddenly felt a little like a "cougar." But she continued to stare and hoped she didn't make him feel uncomfortable.

The young lady handed them menus and took their drink orders – Dr. Pepper for Chase and water with lemon for Coco – then walked away to give them a few minutes. It was a huge menu but Coco zeroed in on what she wanted quickly. If she was going to chow down in the middle of the night, she was going to eat what she really wanted. By the time their owner-waitress – Jesse – came back with their drinks, she had already written down Chase's order – the renowned 5-way special.

Coco gave Jesse her order and then excused herself to visit the Ladies Room. By the time she got back to the booth, business taken care of – face and hands washed, hair brushed and pony tailed, lipstick reapplied – their very early breakfast orders filled the table.

Chase had ordered something that looked like it would feed a small town – a huge plate with home fries on the bottom, covered with 3 over easy eggs, topped with cheese, a thick layer of salsa, and crowned with sour cream – indigestion made to order! With toast and bacon on the side, and a second Dr. Pepper already on its way, Coco could only stare.

Her own breakfast was large enough – cheese grits, real scrambled eggs, hash browns, sausage and an English muffin – she was sure she wouldn't finish everything but planned to give it her best effort. Just looking at all the food made her realize she really was starving!

They had just started tasting everything when Tony, the "chef", stopped by the table. He shook Chase's hand and greeted him like an old friend. They chatted for a few minutes about a legal matter that Chase had handled for the family recently and Tony thanked him for being such a good lawyer, loyal customer and true friend. The look on Chase's face told Coco that he really liked these people, and would do just about anything to be of service.

For the next hour, they ate, talked and laughed about funny things that had happened to them during the past 30 years. They talked about their favorite music, their favorite movies, found out they had a few of those in common. They talked about growing up in Myrtle Beach, and how they never planned to live in their home town in their retirement, but wasn't it funny how plans changed.

They were just finishing breakfast and Chase had paid the check, and the conversation got a little quiet. Chase finally broke the silence by saying "I had no idea when I went to that wedding reception that I was going to have such a good time. All because of you. You're way too easy to talk to, I feel like I have totally spilled my guts tonight. I've talked about things I haven't ever talked to anyone about. I'm not ready for the night to end. I know you're probably tired but… I only live three minutes from here. I have a house on the beach. We could take a blanket out on the beach and sit and watch the sunrise. Please come home with me."

"I shouldn't – I'm supposed to be at Gigi and Robert's house at 11:00 for a post-wedding brunch."

"I'm supposed to be there too, but I still want you to come home with me. Please don't say no. We can always sleep later."

Coco heard the quiet pleading sound of his voice, and in her quiet voice, said "Okay."

"Yeah?"

"Just know that I'm very surly when I'm tired and it will be all your fault."

"I'll take all the blame – no problem."

"Okay. Lead the way."

Chase said goodbye to Jesse and Tony and he walked Coco to her car in the parking lot. One quick kiss on the cheek and she was in her car, following him out of the parking lot and down the street. Sure enough, just a few minutes later, Chase pulled into the driveway of a lovely looking bungalow and Coco pulled in next to him in the driveway. He helped her out of the car and escorted her into the house.

Chase took Coco on a short tour of the living room, kitchen and bathroom, grabbed two bottles of water from the fridge and a blanket from the back porch and led her out the back door down to the beach. Coco helped Chase spread the blanket and they sat down in the dark. Chase's house was in a neighborhood where the houses were spread out and there weren't many lights on the street or on the beach.

The lack of light was a little disconcerting to Coco, but in the dark, they had a spectacular view of the moon and the stars. They didn't talk for a few minutes, just enjoying the sound of the waves and the view of the night sky, and then Chase broke the silence with a slightly strained voice. "I Googled you earlier, when I went to move your car. I was being nosy again."

With a guarded tone of voice, Coco replied "Did you, now? And what did you find?"

"I found lots of things about your career... And I saw your parents' obituaries. I'm so sorry, Coco. Losing them so suddenly must have been devastating. Is that why you came back home?"

"It's been five years since the accident and not a day goes by that I don't think about them or pick up the phone to call them and then realize they're not there anymore. I still feel so guilty, living so many years away from them, and then losing them like that – I wasted so much time I could have spent with them if I'd only known. I did come home for a few months to settle the estate, take care of a few legal issues with my dad's share of the drug store, spend some time with the rest of my family, and then I went back 'home', thinking my life would continue as if nothing had changed.

"Phoenix just seemed so cold after that, it wasn't home anymore. My job wasn't fulfilling anymore, every day was just a battle to survive. I stuck it out for three more years, and then decided home was here and I needed to come back. It took me awhile to get out of my contract at work and hand everything off to my replacement, but I finally packed everything up and moved back to Myrtle Beach.

"I had been renting out my parents' house and it happened to be empty at the time. I tried living there, but there were just too many memories, I was sad all the time. So when a very young newlywed couple made me a ridiculously low offer on the house, I took it. I bought the house I have now and moved in – just this past Christmas. My aunts and uncles and cousins have been great since I moved back, they've helped to fill the void.

"And of course, Gigi and Maggs have been there for me every step of the way. My girls. You never appreciate friends until something happens and you really need someone to lean on. I owe them both a lot. I know I'm old enough, I should be able to pull my big girl panties on and get over losing my parents, I'm really trying, but some days are still harder than others." A huge sob escaped Coco's throat and the tears rolled down her cheeks unchecked.

"Chase, enjoy the time you have with your parents. The time you have with them is too precious. Don't waste it like I did."

Chase wrapped her in his arms, whispered "I know. I'm so sorry", knowing how lost he would be when it was time for him to say goodbye to his own mom and dad. And he held her tight while she cried.

Coco didn't know how long they sat together like that – she had gone to a safe, quiet place in her mind. What brought her back to reality was the motion of Chase laying her down on the blanket, and lying down beside her. She opened her eyes just enough to see him, and to see that morning light was just beginning to bring the world into view again.

He noticed her barely open eyes and said quietly "I'm sorry, I didn't mean to wake you. You looked so peaceful but I thought you'd be more comfortable lying down."

Coco opened her eyes a little more so that she could study Chase's facial features, see the smile wrinkles around his eyes, see the tiny flecks of brown in those eyes that she'd originally thought were the deepest green. Chase had leaned close to her, and she stared at his lips – they were so soft and full, the most beautiful shade of rose pink, lips any woman would kill for.

Coco couldn't resist the urge to touch those lips again and she raised her hand to his face, running her thumb along his lower lip. Without realizing she was actually speaking aloud, she murmured "So soft, so perfect." And Chase closed the space between them and put those soft, perfect lips on her own.

Chaste kiss morphed into passionate, desperate, devouring kiss – taking them both back to that hungry kiss on that other beach that had been so rudely interrupted. Hands searched for any contact they could make, and the two would-be lovers were quickly engulfed in the flames of desire again. Chase's lips and tongue attacked Coco's, and she responded in kind. Little sparks seemed to fire between them and breath was coming in fits and starts. The kiss continued as their rising passion threatened to consume them.

There was enough space between their bodies that Coco was able to reach up and unbutton Chase's white dress shirt, exposing a spectacularly muscled chest, lightly covered with the softest blonde curly hair. Her hand moved down to Chase's jeans, stroking the huge erection hidden behind the zipper.

At the same time, Chase's hand had moved up under Coco's blouse, caressing her left breast, teasing her nipple through the lace of her La Perla bra. The nipple responded just like Chase had hoped it would, growing tight and distended. Their moans were becoming louder and more frequent, their minds focused on only one thing, their hands becoming more insistent as the tension of their desire reached new heights.

Coco's hand moved to pop the snap on Chase's jeans and her fingers started slowly moving the zipper down, realizing Chase was going commando. Chase had abandoned Coco's breast and his hand was headed south, under the waistband of her leggings, moving toward her own commando promised land.

And still, the kiss continued, their bodies engulfed in flames of desire, blocking out everything around them.

Gasping breath filled the next minute. Coco's hand made contact with the soft, hot skin of Chase's substantial steel hard cock!

At the exact same time, Chase's hand came to rest on Coco's Brazilian-waxed pussy!

At the exact same time, the neighbor's huge Golden Retriever jumped on their passionate pile, wanting to play!

At the exact same time, the neighbor yelled at the dog to get off the pile, and yelled at Chase, "For god's sake, Buckingham! Take it inside!"

Chase chuckled a little and rubbed the dog's head before sending him back to his owner, shaking his own head sadly. Frustrated eyes met frustrated eyes as Chase looked down at Coco and said "The Universe is cock-blocking us! I don't understand it, but I guess we shouldn't try to fight it anymore. This just isn't supposed to happen right now."

Forehead touched forehead, and they started to laugh – so hard, Coco snorted – again – and again! One last chaste kiss, lips to lips. Then they pulled themselves together and sat up. Just in time to see a glorious golden sunrise that they would have otherwise missed.

*C*hase and Coco stood in the driveway next to her car, knowing she
needed to leave, both hesitant to let that happen. They both knew
that once Coco drove away from Chase's house, the spell would be broken
and they might never get it back again. But they were both expected at Gigi
and Robert's house at 11:00 AM for the big post-wedding brunch – barely
5 hours away – and Coco needed at least an hour of sleep before she had
to make herself presentable again.

Chase tried to talk her into staying – "Come on, you can take a nap
here, I'll make sure you wake up with more than enough time to get ready.
I can wash your clothes and you can shower here and look fresh as a daisy
when we get to Robert's house. It just doesn't make sense for you to drive
all the way to your house, sleep, get ready again, and drive all the way back
down here, when I only live 15 minutes from their house."

Coco laughed and said "Oh, no. The last thing I need is to show up
at brunch wearing the same clothes everyone saw me in last night. That
would live in infamy, just like my dress mishap at Maggs and Russ's
wedding reception. I don't need any more stories like that, there are more
than enough as it is. I'll go home and take a quick nap, shower, put on
DIFFERENT clothes and meet you there. Put my cell number in your
phone and call me at 10:00 to make sure I'm back up again and out of
the shower."

"Your cell number is already in my phone, on speed dial 3 by the way.
That's a place of honor, right behind my dad and my mom."

"How did my cell number already get into your phone? Never mind, I don't think I want to know."

"Please stay."

"No, I have to do the responsible adult thing."

"But I want to do the irresponsible adult thing with you and the Universe seems to be getting in the way!"

"I think that's a sign, Mr. Buckingham. Now give me one last kiss, then go take your own nap. And make sure you call me at 10:00."

"Very well, Coralee, as you wish. I'll call you at 10:00." One last quick but lively kiss, and Coco was in her car, headed down the street toward her own home.

Chase called Coco right at 10:00 and she had already napped, showered and was mostly dressed, a little ahead of schedule. Chase felt the need to chat for a minute – "I took a nap, and I dreamed about you. Actually I dreamed about this morning on the beach, only with a more benevolent Universe, and no damned neighbor's dog to interrupt us. I can still feel your hand on my cock, baby, and I can still feel my hand on your smooth, soft pussy."

"Chase!!"

"What? You know that's what happened, I'm not reinventing history. But I would never have taken you for a Brazilian kind of girl. Is that the sassy part of you?"

"That's part of the sassy part of me. And that's not something you need to share with anyone, okay? Now I have to go and finish getting ready. You've made me all hot and sweaty again and I don't have time for another shower." And she laughed a little at the memory of the two of them on the beach earlier. "I'll see you in a little while, gorgeous."

Coco pulled up in front of Gigi and Robert's house at 11:00 on the dot and noticed that Chase was outside, waiting for her. He opened the car door and helped her out, then wrapped her in a hug and planted a sexy kiss on her pink glossed lips. "I love this dress you have on, baby. It's so satiny, and just the right amount of short, it makes your legs look a mile long. And a perfect pair of little kitten heels? Were they in your trunk?"

"How do you know about little kitten heels? Never mind. Again, I don't think I want to know. No, these shoes were not in the trunk of my car. And I wore this dress just for you, gorgeous."

"Thank you, I appreciate the gift. Although it's giving me another gift that's really just for you!" And he hugged her close and rubbed against her so she could feel the 'gift' he had for her inside his jeans.

"Chase!! You're making me all hot and bothered again!"

"Come on, let's go inside before I throw you down on the lawn and have my way with you."

Half way up the front sidewalk, Coco noticed that too many people, including Maggs, Russ, Gigi and Robert were watching through the front window, laughing. Coco presented a middle finger salute and Chase followed her through the open front door to the party, where they both enjoyed the brunch, and each other's company, very much.

The afternoon flew by, but at 6:00 PM, Coco decided it was time to go. There weren't many people left other than immediate family – Russ and Maggs had already left to return to their home in Columbia – and Chase walked Coco out to her car. He put his arms around her and said "Can I see you sometime this week? I'd love to take you to dinner – any night other than Wednesday, I have a meeting – that is, if you want to see me again."

"Oh, gorgeous, why wouldn't I want to see you again? You're smart, funny, sexy as a Greek god – and tall! Have I mentioned how tall you are?? And have I told you how well you dance? Someone must have taught you really well." And she smirked at him just a little as he laughed about who had taught him how to dance. "Unfortunately, gorgeous, I have a really busy week ahead of me. But I'm not planning on working Saturday, I could make dinner for you at my house. You could bring a nice bottle of wine. I could show you my shoe closet!!"

"Well who could resist dinner and a tour of the shoe closet?"

"I'm glad you're interested. I'll plan on dinner Saturday. Around 7:00 PM? Maybe you should take a nap that afternoon, I wouldn't want you to be too tired. In the meantime, I'll be done working by 10:00 every night this week. You could call me one night and talk dirty to me while I lie in my bed and you lie in yours. Kind of like porn pillow talk. That would be fun."

"Yeah? I'm really good at the dirty talk, but I'd rather we were both lying in the same bed while I do it. The dirty talk, that is. And the other thing. I'm really good at that, too!"

"Kiss me, Mr. Buckingham, and then let me go. I told you I get surly when I'm short on sleep, and I feel a grumble coming on."

Coco got her kiss, along with another close hug showing off Chase's "gift", prompting a few moans from both of them. Then Chase opened the car door for her and helped her in. As she drove away from the house, her face was split almost in half by a huge yawn – she was incredibly tired. But she had already decided that spending the previous night with Chase, even the way it had turned out, was worth every minute of sleep she had missed – maybe more so BECAUSE of the way it had turned out.

Coco was barely home again when her cell phone rang. Chase had called to make sure she got home okay, and to start the dirty talk a little early. Coco went to her bedroom and reclined on the bed, letting her hands roam all her pink parts while Chase told her a few things he intended to do to her on Saturday.

"Coco, I want to tell you a little about what I plan to do to you Saturday night. I think you should wear a dress that night, and I can't believe I'm saying this, but I would love for you to wear some sexy black underwear – maybe a matching bra and panties. And some stilettos, of course. You won't have them on long but just the thought of you standing in front of me in black underwear and stilettos is cranking me up right now." Coco couldn't stop the little moan that escaped from her throat at the thought. But Chase continued.

"I'm starting to sweat just thinking about it, baby. Just like you're going to sweat when I put my lips on your nipples and start to suck, maybe a little bite just to hold your attention. Keeping your attention won't be a problem when I reach down and cup your pussy with my hand – thumb your clit until you're all wiggly and juicy for me. I'll put one or two fingers into your cunt and rub some of that juice all over my fingers and then put them in my mouth and lick them clean. I bet you'll taste so fucking good. Fuck, I can't wait."

"You're right, gorgeous, you're pretty good at the dirty talk!"

Ten minutes later, the call ended and Coco headed for the bathroom with her favorite vibrator to take a shower and get rid of Chase Buckingham and her aching hornies for just a little while.

*T*he next two days crawled by. The down side of working with family and friends was Coco had to work with family and friends! One of Coco's favorite cousins turned out to be her worst nightmare as a client. Cousin Angela had a gourmet bakery and was trying to start up a catering business, and there were too many things she didn't like about the web site Coco had designed for her. Every time Coco sent her a link to the latest design, there was something else the cousin/client from hell wanted to change or something new she wanted to add.

In addition to Angela's constant demands for changes, Coco had four new clients she needed to get prototypes set up for, along with routine maintenance for fifteen or twenty other existing clients. Monday and Tuesday turned out to be 6 AM to 10 PM days, barely getting in her morning run each day, not even stopping for lunch or dinner. By the time Coco crawled into bed Tuesday night, the last thing she wanted to hear was her phone ringing. But there it was.

Coco had hoped maybe it would be Chase calling with a little more late evening dirty talk, but no, it was someone else entirely. Joshua Barkin was a young attorney, looking to make a name for himself in the South Carolina state legislature, one of her partners in opposition to the proposed marshland protection legislation Chase and his dad were championing.

"Coco, please, you have to do this. The meeting tomorrow evening is too important for you to miss. If we can't even get County buy-in to our changes, we don't stand a chance at the State level. You have to at least come and provide moral support for the rest of us. You're always the voice of reason amid our combined insanity, and we need you there."

Shit – this would be the meeting that Chase had referred to on Sunday. There was no way she was going to put herself in that nightmare situation. "Josh, I can't. I'm absolutely swamped with work right now. I do have my own business to run, you know."

"Coco, if you don't come to this meeting, you know we'll fuck everything up and our arguments will all go straight down the tubes. You have to come."

"I can't, Josh, I have a conflict of interest right now."

"What kind of conflict of interest could you possibly have? Even if you were fucking the opposition, you wouldn't... Wait, you're fucking Chase Buckingham? What the hell, Coco? You don't even know Chase Buckingham! Where did you run into him that you could put yourself in this position? I don't believe this! You're going to sink our whole argument for the sake of a quick fuck? I've heard he's good in the sack, but give me a break, Coco! I thought you were more responsible than this. This is pure teenage behavior. If you need to scratch an itch, I'll fuck you! Stay the fuck away from Chase Buckingham!"

"First of all, Josh, I'm not fucking Chase Buckingham. Second, if I was, it would be none of your damned fucking business. Third, you don't have the right to speak to me like that, and I'm not taking any more verbal abuse from some snot nosed kid who hasn't got a clue how life works. I'm hanging up, Joshua, and we're going to pretend this conversation never happened."

"Coco, wait. I'm sorry. We just have a lot on the line right now and so much of it depends on you. At least come to the meeting. You can sit in the back, you don't have to say a word, Buckingham will never know you're there."

"No."

"Please, Coco, I'm begging."

Coco paused for most of a minute, running through all of the horrible possible consequences of attending the meeting, but she finally said "Josh, you are going to owe me big time! Huge! I'll come to the meeting, but I'm not going to say a word. Do you hear me?"

"Loud and clear, Coco. Thank you so much. I'll see you tomorrow night, 7:00 PM at the Government Center on Hicks Boulevard."

"Good night, Josh." And she hung up. Maybe now was the time to start smoking again! She felt like she'd just screwed herself royally, and a cigarette would be the perfect accompaniment. Coco turned out the bedroom light and tried to sleep, but her mind was moving a mile a minute, imagining all the horrible things that were going to happen at that damned meeting.

Wednesday turned out to be almost as bad a day as Monday and Tuesday had been. Coco's 5 AM run around the neighborhood turned out to be slow and short!! And the thought of attending a meeting where she would be on the opposite side of an argument from Chase was like dread growing inside her. Whatever happened at the meeting, she was sure that things would change between her and Chase on some fundamental level. But if there was one thing Coco had learned in more than 30 years in the business world, it was how to manage disaster. She just hoped it wouldn't come to that.

Coco got to the Government Center a few minutes early so that she could stash herself in a dark corner in the back of the room. Josh and the rest of her colleagues barely acknowledged her presence when they walked in. They took seats in the front of the room, on the right side, facing the main table, and ignored that fact that she was there.

Chase didn't seem to notice her when he and his dad walked into the room and took their seats on the left. The meeting started on time, opened by the Head of the County Department of Planning and Zoning, who explained the purpose of the meeting. There were three issues on the agenda, the Buckinghams' proposed legislation being the last.

Coco sat through the first two agenda discussions, not really listening, thinking about her newborn relationship with Chase Buckingham and wondering what effect this meeting might have on it. The whole Democrat/ Republican thing was bad enough, but being on opposite sides of an issue that they both obviously felt so passionately about could prove to be a relationship killer. Coco was a little depressed by the time the second agenda discussion had finished, and she was grateful for the 15 minute break to hit the restroom and hide for a few minutes.

Coco had been keeping an eye on the time, and was trying to get out of the restroom and back to her shadowy seat without being seen but her timing was a little off. As she was coming out the restroom door, she turned right toward the meeting room, directly into the path of her opposition – Chase and his dad – coming out of their own restroom. If Chase hadn't been so quick, she would have bounced off his beautiful chest and fallen on her ass on the floor. His accidental embrace made her tingle all over.

Once Chase had settled Coco on her feet, on solid ground again, he said "Miss Brighton, I'm not sure why, but I'm a little surprised to see you here tonight. Did you just arrive or have you been lurking in the back of the room? Dad, this is the woman I was telling you about. Miss Coralee Brighton. Miss Brighton, this is my father, John Buckingham."

"Mr. Buckingham, it's a pleasure to meet you. I'm somewhat familiar with you professionally, and after talking with Chase, I feel like I know a little about you personally as well. And I really am just here as an observer tonight, Chase, I don't intend to participate."

And the elder Mr. Buckingham smiled and said "I feel I know a little more about you also, Miss Brighton. I believe the meeting is about to get a little lively. Shall we all go in?" And the three of them walked back into the meeting room – Chase and his dad taking their seats in front and Coco moving back to her seat in the dark back of the room. She still planned on not participating in the meeting, and she hoped her colleagues wouldn't screw things up so badly they couldn't be recovered. Famous last words.

Once the meeting reconvened, the senior Mr. Buckingham addressed the board, and explained the basics of the proposed legislation, including what he expected by way of support from the County. Coco was in the back of the room taking furious notes, hoping that her colleagues in the front of the room were doing the same. She wanted to make sure that they addressed all of their arguments against the legislation as it was currently written, noting some of the changes they wanted to propose.

Coco took her mind off the meeting for just a moment – at least she thought it was only a moment – and when her focus returned to the night's proceedings, a lively debate has descended into hell. Even though John Buckingham had the floor, Josh was arguing loudly against John's comments, trying to drown him out. Finally Mr. Buckingham shook his head, smiled, and stopped talking, letting the little baby lawyer ramble his way into oblivion.

Finally Coco couldn't take it any longer. She wrote a quick note on a piece of scrap paper, got up from her seat in the back of the room and moved to sit in the row behind her colleagues. She reached over the seat in front of her and handed the note to the young lady who was seated closest to the podium where Josh was standing, ranting. Coco was trying desperately to mitigate the damage already done, by bringing Josh back to the center of his argument, but he refused to be tamed.

Coco grew angrier and angrier as Josh continued his rave – "Ladies and Gentlemen, can you not see what Mr. Buckingham is trying to do here? He's trying to lull you into a false sense of security by outright lying to you about this legislation! The scope of this proposed bill is so far beyond what he has described, it's almost a fairy tale he's spinning for you.

"This bill would take control of county land and move it under the jurisdiction of the state, and leave us absolutely no recourse for damages or recompense in the future. Democrat that he is, he would wrap every bit of county property in a web of state control, leaving us no say in disposition of the land in the future but saddling the residents of this county with the cost of maintenance in perpetuity! It's a typical Democrat ploy and it's absolutely criminal!"

Josh stopped to take a breath and was about to continue his tirade, when Coco couldn't take it anymore – she stood in place and yelled "Josh, for god's sake, shut your mouth and sit down – NOW!!"

The meeting room became deathly quiet and everyone turned to stare at Coco, including Mr. and Mr. Buckingham. Everyone else in the room had the decency to look horrified, but senior and junior Buckingham just looked slightly arrogant, which pissed Coco off royally. Coco took a deep breath, moved to the podium, pushing her colleague out of the way, and turned to the members of the board. With a very contrite look on her face, Coco began to speak – "Ladies and Gentlemen, please allow me to apologize for my colleague. And please allow my colleague to extend his own apology for his behavior."

She turned to Josh, who stood and said "I apologize for my behavior, Ladies and Gentlemen, Mr. Buckingham. I lost my head in the heat of the moment."

Josh sat down with his own little smirk on his face, and Coco was very tempted to smack that smirk right off his face. But instead, she turned back to the board members and continued – "The rest of my group does not share all of our colleague's opinions, at least not out loud. My group is young, driven, and passionate about the issue. They attempted on several occasions to make contact with Mr. Buckingham to set up a meeting for discussion of this proposed legislation, but were unsuccessful, leading them to request this meeting before the full board."

At this last comment, Coco looked directly at John Buckingham and his gloriously sexy son with a look that implied "If you'd just met with us, we could have avoided all of this."

Coco returned her attention to the members of the board one last time and continued – "Ladies and Gentlemen, if you would allow me just 5 minutes to raise our most serious concerns, we will leave you to deliberate as your time permits."

The chairlady nodded and Coco spoke again – "Obviously, our greatest concern is that this legislation would wrest control of County property from the jurisdiction of the County and place it in the hands of the State of South Carolina, with no say in the future disposition of that property. Our second concern, almost as critical, is the statewide scope of the legislation. Every county and municipality would be bound by this legislation, whether they are financially prepared to bear the cost or not, that cost being considerable in many cases.

"My colleagues and I feel that the legislation would be more appropriate if it was structured to begin with our own county only. It would be easier to fund, easier to manage, and the land most at risk could be taken care of more quickly. If we can be successful at the County level, other counties might take a page from our play book and pass their own similar legislation to address their own counties' land management issues.

"Over time, it might be possible to roll up to an overarching bill at the State level, but let's not force undue financial hardships on our neighbor counties who don't have similar issues, but would be forced to assist with funding. All we ask, Ladies and Gentlemen, is an opportunity to meet with a member of your board along with the gentlemen to my left, to discuss options and alternatives before it's too late. We thank you all very much for your time and attention." Coco returned to her seat in the second row, but not before shooting a look at Josh that should have killed him on the spot.

After the meeting adjourned, Coco waited until all of the board members had left the room, as well as John and Chase Buckingham, before she tore into her little group of conniving idiots. "I know you staged that whole fight, just to pull me into speaking tonight. I had every intention of walking out and leaving your asses hanging, but I – unlike all of you – take my civic duties a little more seriously than that.

"I don't know if I can ever look any of those people in the eye again, you made us all look like junior high assholes. If you ever behave like that in my presence again, I will kick your collective ass to the curb and then I will walk away and never look back. Am I understood?"

Coco was met with groans and nods and accusing looks aimed directly at Joshua Barkin – and she left the room without another word. Luckily it appeared that Chase and his dad had already left the building, so Coco walked to her car as quickly as her 3 inch heels would permit, and headed home, furious at her colleagues and in tears, thinking she had just ruined her relationship with a wonderful man.

Ten minutes after arriving home, working on her second large glass of her favorite Riesling, Coco picked up her cell phone, found Chase's number, and dialed it with trembling fingers. She was suffering from emotion overload – anger, embarrassment, fear, sadness – it was all there and bubbling quickly to the surface, manifested in the tears falling across her cheeks.

Chase didn't answer her call and she ended up in his voice mail – the first thing he would hear in her message was a loud sob, followed by her heartfelt apologies to him and his father for what had occurred at the meeting – "Chase, I am so sorry about what happened tonight, I know there's nothing I can do to make amends, please extend my apologies to your father, he was nothing but charming and composed and didn't deserve any of the tantrums he was subjected to. I'd still love to have you over for dinner on Saturday, but I'll understand completely if you've changed your mind. Please call me when you get a minute. I hope to talk to you soon."

Twenty minutes later, Coco was in bed, crying into her pillow, her 'I'm sad' play list pouring out of her iPod in its docking station. When her cell phone rang, and she saw it was Chase, she was almost too embarrassed to answer the call, but she really wanted to talk to him. She pushed the button on her phone to pick up the call, but before either of them could say anything, she sobbed again, loud and hard.

Chase took pity on her – "Coco, baby, please don't cry. It wasn't your fault, and you handled the whole thing admirably. My dad was very impressed. He thinks you're quite a girl. So do I."

"Tell him thank you for me. Lord knows I'll never be able to look him in the eye again." And she sobbed again, but then managed to calm herself down a little.

"Coco, it will all work out – don't worry about it. Now why would I not want to come to dinner on Saturday? I would be a pretty shallow guy if I let something like that silly meeting come between me and my sassy girl."

"Do you know how wonderful I think you are right now? You're a really special person."

"Stop, Coco! You're making my head swell!"

After a short pause, she asked "Which one??" And she snort-laughed just a little.

"Both, you dirty little girl! And you're drinking, aren't you? You snort when you laugh when you've been drinking."

"What's your favorite meal, gorgeous? Or maybe I should ask if there's something you really don't like. I wouldn't want to make something for dinner that you didn't like."

"If it's food, I'll eat it. Why don't you make something you really like and I'm sure I'll love it."

"Okay. Chase?"

"Yes?"

"Thank you for calling. And thank you for being you."

They talked for a few more minutes and wished each other sweet dreams, then ended the call. Coco slept fitfully that night, but every time she did fall asleep, she dreamed of Chase, naked, sitting in her hot tub filled with bubbling strawberry Jell-O, pineapple and miniature marshmallows, topped with whipped cream.

*T*hursday and Friday sped by – by the end of the week, Coco had Cousin Angela's web site finished and approved, and she had found two new clients along the way. Saturday morning found Coco at the supermarket early, pre-empting her early morning run so that she could buy all the ingredients she would need for the dinner she was making for Chase that night. Everything was prepped and ready by 11:00 AM so Coco ran a 30 minute lap around the track at the high school, came home and ate lunch, and then settled in for a quick nap.

She woke up before the alarm, checked and answered a few emails, then went out to the deck to check on the hot tub. Finally she changed the sheets on the bed and started getting herself ready. She was nervous about seeing Chase again after the infamous meeting, but he had been so sweet – and so dirty – on the phone each of the last two nights that she was as much excited as nervous. She said a silent prayer to the Universe, asking for no cock-blocking, checked her condom stash and hoped for the best.

At 6:30, Coco put their entree in the oven along with her special cheddar biscuits, and prepped the side dish to cook on the stove top. Then she went to her bedroom to finish dressing – putting on something special that she thought Chase would like. Coco had just finished buckling the straps on her black patent leather stiletto sandals when the doorbell rang – 7:00 – right on time. When she went through the living room, she could smell dinner cooking and she was instantly hungry. But when she looked through the window of the front door and saw Chase standing on the porch, looking edible himself, she was suddenly a different kind of hungry, and something clenched tight, deep inside her.

Coco opened the front door and unintentionally whispered a breathy "Hi.", then recovered herself and held the door open for Chase to come inside. He was wearing a pair of black chinos, just the right amount of tight to get a peak at all of nature's gifts, with a pale green, fitted button down shirt that made the green color of his eyes pop. His black flip flops were the perfect casual offset – so sexy Coco couldn't help commenting.

With a hungry look on her face and a sparkle in her eye, Coco said "You look spectacular, Chase. Do you always look this good? Do you ever just look normal? Like the rest of us mere mortals?"

"You're one to talk there, Sassy Girl. You in this floaty black chiffon dress should be illegal. And those shoes! You can't imagine what this little outfit is doing for me right now. Then again, maybe you can already see what it's doing for me. And before I forget to say it, if dinner is half as good as it smells in here right now, I'm moving in! You will be forced to cook for me forever!" And he kind of growled at her, making her step back a few inches, before she reached for him and gave him a quick kiss hello.

Chase held up the bottle of chilled White Zin, and Coco led him to the kitchen to turn off the oven timer that had just gone off. She pointed Chase in the direction of the cupboard where he would find wine glasses and a corkscrew while she pulled the biscuits and the stuffed pork chops out of the oven. She covered the pork chops with foil to rest and put the biscuits in a linen lined basket to keep warm, then turned the heat on low under the olive oil drizzled green beans and almonds.

Chase handed Coco a glass of delicious wine and then wrapped her in a hug, sniffing at her neck, murmuring his approval of her perfume choice. "I don't think I've ever been sniffed in this kitchen before, Mr. Buckingham. I rather like it."

"I'm glad you like it because I'll probably do it again sometime and I wouldn't want to make you uncomfortable in any way."

"You're a tease, Mr. Buckingham. But I rather like that too. Now I feel like I need to distract us for a little while. We have 15 minutes before dinner is served. Would you like a tour of the house?"

"As long as the tour includes the shoe closet, I would love one."

Coco took Chase by the hand and led him out the back door to the deck, showing off her hot tub, complete with wood lattice walls and roof to ensure their privacy and provide some shade from the South Carolina sun. "I wouldn't have taken you for a hot tub girl, Miss Brighton."

"Maybe we can take a little dip later, Mr. Buckingham."

"Dipping outside? I didn't bring any swim trunks. Is that another part of your sassy side?"

"You ain't seen nothin' yet, Mr. Buckingham."

They went back inside the house and downstairs to the finished basement with the old fashioned turntable stereo and vinyl album collection, along with the 65 inch flat screen TV hanging on the wall opposite the row of four recliner theater seats.

"Coco, I hate to tell you this, but I'm never leaving. You can bring my dinner down here and feed me while I watch wrestling and boxing and bad Japanese TV while I listen to all of your old vinyl."

"Feel free to stay down here, Mr. Buckingham, but you'll miss the tour of the shoe closet if you do."

"Lead the way, baby, I can't miss the shoe closet."

Coco led Chase up the stairs and toward her master bedroom, pointing out the guest bathroom along the way. As they entered the bedroom that took up the far end of the first floor, Coco explained that she had taken half of another bedroom to create a larger bathroom with a Jacuzzi tub and separate huge shower, and to make a larger closet space for the bedroom. What had been left of the second bedroom had become her little office.

Coco led Chase to a closed set of double doors and said seductively "Here it is, baby, my shoe closet. Don't let it get you too hot and bothered."

And she smiled and opened the doors – revealing rack after rack, holding Coco's 47 pairs of shoes, many stiletto heels, with plenty of room for future shoes if she found a pair she couldn't live without. Chase looked at all those shoes, imagined Coco naked, standing in front of him wearing each pair, and the thought went right to his cock.

But as impressed as Chase pretended to be with the massive number of shoes in the closet, something else caught his eye. "Is that a gun cabinet in the corner? It's really big!"

"Yes, that's another part of my sassiness. Right now I have a Remington 12 gauge that I use for clay shooting, plus three hand guns – a Browning 9mm, a Remington .45, and a Ruger LC380. The closet door has a triple lock on it, the whole closet is Kevlar lined, and when the doors close, the interior is sealed and ventilated through the roof. I keep two burner phones in one of the drawers in case I'm trapped inside – it won't protect me much from a hurricane, but it should keep me safe from intruders. I can't have someone coming in here and stealing all of my shoes!"

"Fuck, girl, that's some protection you have there. I don't think you're just paranoid though, so something must have happened somewhere along the line. In the meantime, that's a damned sexy closet!!"

"Yes, there's a story there, but we don't have time, because dinner is ready. I hope you're hungry."

"I'm hungry – and I'm hungry! First we'll take care of one hungry, and then hopefully we can take care of the other." Chase grinned his evil little grin and nuzzled Coco's neck again, running his hands down the back of her silky chiffon dress, cupping her ass cheeks and making her giggle. She grabbed his hand and led him toward the dining room, where she sat him down with another glass of wine while she busied herself serving dinner.

Forty-five minutes later, they had finished eating and were half way through a second bottle of wine. They were both stuffed, and a little tipsy. "Coco, this meal was incredible. The stuffed pork chops were outstanding – was that apple in the stuffing, and maybe some bacon or pancetta? You're an outrageous cook."

"This was a specialty of my mother's, my favorite when I was growing up. It's my go-to dinner when I want to impress someone."

"I'm honored – and duly impressed. Now can I help you clean up the dining room and the kitchen while we digest our fabulous dinner?"

"Yes, I think you can. I love to cook but I'm a little light on clean-up. What I really need is someone following behind me when I'm in the kitchen, cleaning up the messes as I make them."

"I'd love to follow behind you anywhere, baby, so let's do this and then we can relax – or something."

They carried their dishes to the kitchen and while Coco worked on putting left-overs in containers in the fridge, Chase loaded the dishwasher with just about everything but their wine glasses. Coco washed the few things that either couldn't go in or wouldn't fit in the dishwasher and Chase dried them. In no time, the kitchen was clean and Chase was getting handsy – and chatty.

"Coco, you really look lovely tonight, and dinner was excellent. You've really spoiled me. I'd like to return the favor." While Chase whispered in Coco's ear, his hands caressed her body. His fingertips started at her shoulders, tickled their way down her back, and ended up on the cheeks of her ass, just the slightest amount of pressure along the way, so that she barely knew his hands were there until he reached his destination and gently squeezed those cheeks with his big hands. Coco had been sighing as Chase's hands slid down her body but when he started lightly massaging her ass, she let out a moan that could only mean one thing – he had just lit her pilot light and he'd better be ready for the bonfire.

Barely able to speak aloud, Chase whispered "Coco?"

And she whispered back, "Yes, Chase?"

"I really love your ass, I can't seem to keep my hands off."

"I noticed."

"Coco?"

"Yes, Chase?"

"Let me make love to you tonight."

"Yes, Chase."

She placed a kiss on Chase's chest, over his heart, took his hand, and led him to her bedroom. They stood in the middle of the room for quite some time, holding each other, nibbling on each other, enjoying the taste, the scent and the feel of each other. There was no conversation and no rush, but plenty of sighs, murmurs and moans from both of them. They were both happy to enjoy the quiet, gentle connection they had developed, both knowing that the urgency and the desperation would come soon enough.

Chase eventually reached up to the top of Coco's dress and slowly started lowering the zipper. When the zipper pull was almost to her waist, Coco decided a quick conversation needed to take place. She met his gaze and said "Chase, wait."

"What's wrong, baby? Did I do something?"

"No, gorgeous, I just need to tell you something. I should have told you before now but there was never a good time to bring it up."

"Tell me, Coco, what's bothering you?"

Coco continued to hold Chase's gaze and confessed "Ten years ago I was diagnosed with breast cancer. I was working in Japan at the time, and would have taken care of things there, but my parents insisted I come home for my treatment. The doctors did everything they could, but eventually I had to have surgery."

"A mastectomy?"

"No, they were able to get everything with a lumpectomy, but it took two separate surgeries to get clear margins around the cancer, and they had to remove a sizeable chunk from my right breast. It looks like someone took a big bite out of my boob. It's quite noticeable and I didn't want you to be surprised by how different it looks compared to the other breast."

"Are you nervous about me seeing you naked?"

"Very."

As if proving her point, Coco's breathing amped up just a little, almost a little pant, and a solitary tear slid down her cheek. Chase reached up with his thumb to wipe away the tear, and kissed her cheek. To make her feel a little better, Chase offered a confession of his own.

"Coco, would it help if I told you I'm not quite the same as I used to be either?"

"Yes, gorgeous, I think it would."

"Well, fifteen years ago, I was injured during a fire fight in one of those places we weren't supposed to be. One of my buddies stepped on a mine and I took some shrapnel, between my thighs, as it were."

"Oh my!"

"Yes, 'oh my' is right. Everything works just fine – better than fine, actually – but I'm missing a testicle these days and I don't look like I used to look either."

"Do you miss it?"

"My testicle?"

"Yes. Do you ever look at yourself and wish that nothing had ever happened and you were still the same as you had been before?"

"No, Coco, and you shouldn't either. We're survivors, baby, and that's sexy as hell. But I won't be able to tell you just how spectacular your remodeled breast is until I can actually see it… touch it… put my mouth on it. Can we make that happen?"

"Yes, I think we can. Chase?"

"Yes, baby?"

"I'm sorry about your buddy."

"Me too."

Chase pulled Coco to him for one of those hugs that said so many things, and then he finished lowering the zipper on her dress. He stepped back a pace, grasped the shoulders of her dress and slowly lowered it down her arms, past her breasts, off her hips, and let it drift to the floor in a black chiffon cloud, which Coco stepped out of and kicked away. The sight of Coco's translucent black bra and matching thong panties, with her standing in front of him in those stiletto sandals, made Chase moan, and his breathing became shallow and quick. Hearing that sound from him made Coco shiver and bite her lip.

"You wore this outfit just for me, didn't you, baby?"

"Your wish is my command, Mr. Buckingham. At least for tonight."

"Then do a slow turn for me, baby, I don't want to miss the view of those luscious hips before we get carried away."

She turned in a small circle, very slowly, panting a little as she did, knowing Chase was seeing a close up view of her thong clad ass. And Chase moaned again as he captured the full view, and bent to give her a quick kiss on each butt cheek as she twirled.

And their panting continued. As she finished her sexy little turn, Chase captured Coco's gaze with his and said "Are you ready, baby? For the big reveal?"

She was suddenly mute, and her eyes were a little teary, but she managed to nod yes. Chase pulled Coco close, reached around behind her and unhooked her bra, slowly pulling the straps down her arms and off, releasing her breasts for him to see – and touch – and taste.

There was a sudden, loud intake of breath as Chase stood back and stared at Coco's naked breasts, her nearly naked body. And then there was a little smile and a look of carnal appreciation. "Magnificent – you're magnificent, Coco. I don't mean to tell you what to do, but please don't ever be ashamed or reluctant to show off your beautiful body."

Coco had been right, her breasts weren't the same anymore. But there was something so sexy about the scar and the dimple that it formed on the top of her right breast. He couldn't stop himself – he reached up and gently ran his fingertips over the scar, watching for Coco's reaction to his touch. When she didn't back away or turn her face away from his, and both her nipples continued to harden and distend, Chase leaned down and licked the scar, kissed it, almost worshipped it. And then he moved slightly and wrapped his lips around the erect little nipple on that breast and lavished it with a tongue full of affection.

Coco clutched Chase's massive biceps and moaned loud, arching her back to bring Chase closer to her breast. Her breathing grew more shallow and rapid, making her the slightest bit light headed – she was feeling the fire inside begin to blaze. And Chase was just getting started.

Coco nearly leapt off the floor when Chase continued to suck her nipples like a nursing baby, and at the same time, reached down and slipped his hand inside her panties, wanting to recapture the feel of her smooth, waxed pussy on his hand. His lips returned to her lips, his free hand on her lower back pulling her closer, that magic hand inside her panties, brushing her swollen clit with his thumb, caressing her already wet pussy with big fingers.

Coco was panting like she'd just run a mile, but managed to whisper "Chase, if you keep doing that, I'm going to come, really hard, and I'll probably fall down when I do. Maybe we should lie down?"

Chase laughed into Coco's mouth, and mumbled "Maybe that would be a good idea. Let me help you out of these panties, baby, you don't need them anymore. But can we keep the stilettos on for awhile? They're just so fucking sexy. I haven't been this hard in a very long time."

Coco just nodded and laughed a little, leaning on Chase's broad shoulders to keep her balance as he knelt down and helped her out of her sexy – and soaked – black thong panties. While he was on his knees, he took a moment to stare at her smooth, pink, wet pussy and do a little panting of his own. He leaned toward her and placed his hands on her ass cheeks to hold her close. When his tongue slid over her swollen clit slowly and gently, they both groaned and her legs shook.

"Chase!"

"Okay, baby, but once you're in a reclining position, you're mine to do with as I please. Feel free to scream out my name any time you need. I intend to make you need a lot."

He stood again, kissed Coco hard one last time, her essence still on his tongue, then slid his arm under her legs to pick her up and place her gently in the center of the king size bed.

"Spread your legs for me baby, I want to see all of you." Coco flushed a little and then pulled her knees up and spread her legs. Standing at the end of the bed, Chase didn't breathe for most of a minute, almost startled by the amazing view Coco was giving him. Then he started a slow striptease for her, slowly unbuttoning his shirt, pulling it lazily off his shoulders and dropping it on the floor.

When Chase had removed his shirt, Coco caught sight of something she'd not seen before, and it took her mind off his huge erection. She couldn't stop herself from yelling "Holy fuck, what is that?!?!"

"What is what, baby?"

"What do you mean, 'what is what?'! That gorgeous ink on your chest!"

"Oh, my tattoo. I usually forget it's there. Do you like it?"

"Oh, gorgeous, I want to lick that! You have to come up here so I can get my tongue on it!"

"Not right now, baby, there's plenty of time for that later. Right now, I want to free this big cock from my pants and lick YOU!" And Coco growled without even knowing she was doing it.

Chase unbuttoned the waistband of his chinos and started unzipping, a scant half inch at a time. Every inch or so, he would stop unzipping and rub his hand over his cock through his pants. Every time he rubbed the outside of his pants, the line of his cock got longer and thicker, and Coco got wetter, moaned louder.

"Fuck, Chase, you're killing me! You've got a fucking Chippendales body and you're teasing me with it!"

Coco was just about to get up and help Chase out of his pants and give that tattoo a little lick when he finally finished unzipping. Never losing eye contact with her, he slid those pants ever so slowly off his hips and kicked them off when they dropped to the floor, showing Coco that he had again left his underwear at home. His cock was rock hard, nearly vertical, waving at her like a flag in a strong breeze, and Coco, unaware that she was even doing it, reached out and started flexing her hands and fingers as if she couldn't wait to get her hands on him and pull him closer.

Chase's heated gaze still on Coco, he reached down and slowly started stroking his big cock, making them both pant. He gave her a warning – "Baby, I'm going to let you have three minutes with my best friend here, just because I really miss the feel of your hand on me, but then those hands go up over your head and stay there. I intend to make a meal of you, and

I don't want anything distracting me from my feast. I'll tie you down if I have to – don't think I won't do it. But feel free to make all the noise you want."

"I have rope and toys in a drawer in the bathroom, if you find you need tools to get the job done."

And she smiled a coy little smile. And Chase just shook his head and smiled back at her – "I don't think that will be necessary right now, but I'll keep it in mind for round three or four." Coco's pupils went dark as her eyes darted back and forth between his eyes and his stunning tattoo and that big beautiful cock, reduced to making little whimpering noises and nothing else. She was too choked with desire to speak anymore.

9

Chase climbed onto the bed and crawled toward Coco, stalking her like a wild animal would do. He stopped at her pussy for one quick sniff that made him growl, one gentle kiss on her exposed clit that made her moan, and continued crawling. When he stopped, he was straddling her, his thighs across her ribs, with his huge erect cock resting between her breasts. He looked at Coco and said "You have three minutes to grip, lick, kiss, suck – whatever you want to do. And then it's my turn. Have at it, baby."

Coco's hands were on Chase instantly. She clutched his cock in her left hand, and reached up to gently brush her fingertips over his tattoo with the other, making his nipples pucker at her touch. But the tattoo wasn't as tempting at the moment as his erection. She continued to stroke his cock with her left hand, and pulled her right hand down to palm the head, swiping at the small stream of pre-come she saw there. Still gripping him firmly, she raised her right hand to her mouth and licked his essence onto her tongue, getting the taste of him. Chase's eyes rolled back in his head and he moaned loud at the sight of her shamelessly carnal behavior.

Coco put her hands on Chase's ass cheeks, trying to move him nearer to her mouth, saying "I need you closer, gorgeous." He scooted up a few inches, just enough for Coco to get her tongue and lips on the head of his cock, enjoying her own little feast. And then her three minutes were up.

Chase started scooting away from her, toward the foot of the bed, and she squeaked "No, I'm not done!"

And Chase's voice went deeper than she'd ever heard when he said "Yes, you are, baby. I gave you your three minutes, just like I promised. And you made me harder than I've ever been in my life, brushing your fingers over my tattoo, licking your hand like that. Now it's my turn. Do like I told you – hands above your head, no touching me while I'm enjoying my Coco feast." And he gave her a look that said "Don't argue with me!"

"I can't guarantee I'll be able to do what you want me to. I'm pretty handsy myself, and I haven't had anywhere near my fill of touching you, anywhere I can get my hands on you."

"Then I guess I need to visit the toy drawer and get that rope now, just in case I need it before I'm done."

"Don't go! I'll try to be good!"

"Don't worry, baby, I won't be gone long."

"Fuck, I shouldn't have said anything about rope."

And he laughed as he climbed off the bed, disappearing into the bathroom, leaving her panting at that view of his luscious ass. Coco could hear the sound of drawers opening and closing, and then a long, low growl, as Chase located the drawer he was looking for. She heard the sound of him rummaging through the drawer, heard him say "Coco, baby, is that a fox tail butt plug in this drawer?"

"Umm…"

"Baby, you are one dirty, dirty girl, and I love it."

Chase found the silk rope he was looking for, left everything else in the drawer, and made his way back to the bedroom. Still a few feet from the bed, he leered at Coco as he started playing with the rope, coiling and uncoiling it in his hands, tying and untying little knots, teasing her with the rope skills he'd learned in the Army – the ones that translated so erotically to the bedroom.

Watching Chase playing with the rope got Coco moaning and panting again, feeling like she was making a freaking puddle on the bedspread with all her juices flowing so freely. Chase laid the coil of rope on the pillow near Coco's head, saying "Just in case." and then climbed back on the bed between her legs again.

Chase sat between Coco's legs, with each of his legs pinning down one of hers, opening her completely to his touch, and he let his hands play freely in her pussy. His thumbs tormented her clit, driving her mad with slow, light swirls. Just about the time Coco got his rhythm and started to breathe and move her hips a little in time with the motion, Chase would stop and pinch that little swollen nub between his thumb and forefinger, coaxing another little dribble of juicy goodness from her cunt.

The first pinch made Coco scream his name, and Chase smiled and said "That's one. Let's see how many more times I can make you scream my name before I let you come."

Poor Coco couldn't keep up with the changing sensations and her head was starting to spin. "You're a fucking bastard, Buckingham!! You're killing me! Oh, holy FUCK, do that again!! CHASE!!" And he laughed again.

"That's two, baby. Let's see what this does."

And he sank two big fingers as far as he could into her pussy, pointing toward the front, slowly, methodically stroking the ultra sensitive G-spot he found there. The combination of Chase's left hand torturing her clit again, and his right hand still mercilessly stroking the most sensitive internal inch of her whole body was too much to bear. Coco's breathing became labored, spots formed before her eyes. With her last ounce of energy, Coco pulled a pillow free and clutched it over her mouth with her hands. And she heard Chase's evil laugh again.

The orgasm started deep in her core and as it move out in all directions, her whole body trembled. Her pussy clamped down on Chase's two fingers so tight he didn't think he would get them back again, and even with the pillow over her mouth, Chase could hear Coco scream his name again. By the time Coco recovered, Chase was lying on top of her, gazing into her eyes, ready to start on round 2.

"You're absolutely stunning when you come, baby. Has anyone ever told you that before? You looked up at me right before you came, and I swear the look on your face was almost blissful. I can't really explain it. It was breathtaking."

"I admit to having a few really good sexual partners in my time, but even when I was in Japan, with men who were supposed to be legends in their own time, no one was ever as good as you were just now. I think I'm lucky I survived it."

"I'm glad you enjoyed it, but we still haven't gotten to my favorite parts. That was just appetizer sex, baby. But if you need a little more recovery time, we can just lie here and cuddle."

"Fuck that! We can cuddle later. I really need to spend some time with that sexy tat! And I want to suck your cock dry – really bad! When do I get my turn tasting you again?"

"When I'm so spent, I can't move off the bed."

"Well let's get at it then, gorgeous. I'm a hungry girl!"

Chase had started sliding down Coco's body, stopping for a few minutes to lavish her breasts and nipples with a little love, and Coco's hands were suddenly in his hair, twirling and clutching the dark blonde curls. He looked up into her eyes with a slight frown and asked "What are you doing? What did I tell you about your hands?"

"I didn't think you meant that indefinitely. I want to touch you. I want to memorize the feel of your skin on my hands, on my fingertips."

"I meant until I told you otherwise, which I haven't yet. I'm beginning to think I can't trust you to do what you're told." As he caught sight of the rope on the pillow out of the corner of his eye, he got another evil grin on his face and said "I think you need to be restrained."

"No, Chase, I think you need to give me another chance to prove myself trustworthy."

"No, baby, maybe next time. But right now, I think you need to be taught a little lesson."

"Chase, I don't like being restrained. Really."

"But you have the rope – and the perfect headboard for a rope restraint. This wrought iron ivy pattern is just begging me to put you where I want you."

And she begged "Chase, no."

Chase's voice went all gentle as he got close to her face and stroked her cheek. "You can trust me, Coco, nothing bad will happen and maybe you'll even find you like it just a little. If you find you just can't handle it, I'll have you out of it in 5 seconds. Okay?"

"So if I let you tie me up, I need something from you in return."

"What's that, baby? What do you need?"

"The stilettos have to go. You don't want to have to stop in the middle of something highly erotic just to rub a cramp out of my calf. If I keep these shoes on any longer, that's what you'll likely be doing."

"Ok, I promise, the shoes will be gone soon. But I want one opportunity to see those babies on my shoulders before we lose them. They make your legs look a mile long and just the thought of that is making me so hard I could pound nails with my cock."

"You are such a dirty boy, I wish I'd known you when I was a little more limber than I am now."

"Coco, I think eventually we will reach and even exceed your limber limits. Are you up for that?"

"Do your worst, Mr. Buckingham. Let's see if I can take it."

Chase crawled back up Coco's body, grabbed the silk rope, and within 15 seconds, had her hands tied together, and secured comfortably to the wrought iron ivy of the headboard. She wasn't going anywhere. He leaned down into her face, seeing a little fear in her eyes, and said "It's okay, Coralee, I won't let anything happen to you. Now close your eyes, take a deep breath in through your nose and hold it for three seconds. Good. Now blow it all back out again."

When Coco had inhaled and exhaled like Chase had told her, she opened her eyes again. Chase could see the fear had receded some but he wanted to make sure she was no longer afraid of him and what he might do. "Coco, baby, are you okay?"

"I'm good, gorgeous. Thanks for taking such good care of me."

"Any time, baby. Are you ready? Because I'm ready and a half!" She nodded and took another deep breath, smiling at the thought of what Chase was about to do.

Knowing that Coco was okay, Chase gave her one last tongue-filled kiss and started crawling and kissing his way back down her body – gentle, playful licking kisses that tormented Coco just the way she liked it. He paused for a few minutes to play with her breasts, tease her nipples just a little, a little bite here, a little bite there, loving the soft moans he got from her. Finally he headed south again toward Coco's pink, swollen promised land, and Coco's moans of anticipation increased in volume. Chase loved oral sex, was really good at oral sex, and wanted to show Coco how good he really was. He settled himself on his knees between her legs, pulled her knees back up and out to the sides, pinning her legs securely in position with his forearms.

He leaned his face down so that his nose and lips were almost touching Coco's pussy. Almost. He was close enough to see that his warm breath on her exposed skin was having the desired effect – he could hear her panting, see the lips of her pussy starting to tremble, see another stream of juice dribble out. And he couldn't hold off any longer. He took that first slow lick, gathering her juicy essence on his tongue as he moved up toward her clit.

"Fuck, Coco, you taste so good, I can't describe it. I've never had another woman taste so good before."

"CHAAAAAAAASE!!"

Chase had started flicking her clit fast with just the tip of his tongue, making her back arch so high off the bed, he thought she might hurt herself, causing that high pitched scream of his name. But he didn't stop. Not until he thought she'd stopped breathing. He lifted his head up high enough to see that her whole body had flushed the loveliest shade of pink, and she was indeed breathing. She was actually sucking in so much oxygen, he thought she might lose consciousness and he didn't want that – he wanted her aware of everything he did.

Chase paused, waiting for her to settle a little, and when her breathing was a little more normal, he said "So you liked that, did you?"

A barely audible "Uh huh" squeaked out of Coco's mouth.

"Shall I continue?"

Another hushed "Uh huh" answered his question.

It was obvious Coco's clit was ultra sensitive and might need a short break, so he spent a few minutes delving into her pussy with his tongue, which suddenly seemed about a foot long to Coco. That tongue was devilish, a serpent that speared into her pussy over and over, driving her insane. Chase could make Coco feel gloriously dirty with that tongue, and he soon turned that tongue's attention back to her clit, just because he could.

When he had sucked and nibbled at Coco's clit for a little while longer, and had licked up all of the juice oozing out of her pussy, he decided it was time to change direction. His cock was rock hard and getting more painful by the minute – and he didn't want Coco to come again until he was inside her. He placed one last nibbley kiss on Coco's clit, his teeth just barely scraping her sensitive flesh, causing her to moan low and deep in her throat. He took one last lick through her mega-wet pussy and then he took his forearms off her legs and sat up on his knees.

Coco was so loose she couldn't even move her legs anymore, and Chase chuckled a little. He straightened both her legs and massaged each one a little, then took her left leg and propped it up on his right shoulder, eyeing that stiletto with a hungry look. Holding her leg in the air, he started at the edge of her pussy and placed light, teasing kisses and licks on that leg, all the way from the inside of her thigh to her ankle. He let his hands run slowly up and down that leg, gently, loving the softness and smoothness of her skin against his hands. More little moans escaped Coco's throat as he proceeded up her leg, as if his kisses and his touch had a direct line to her pussy.

He removed her stiletto sandal from her foot, licked across her instep, making her toes curl, and then rubbed her de-shoed foot for a minute. He laid that leg down gently on the bed and then he went back to her pussy, and started the process again with her right leg, accompanied by more of Coco's sweet little moaning sounds that went straight to his steel hard cock. When he was done, both of Coco's stiletto sandals were on the floor, her legs and feet had been gently massaged, and Chase was ready to rock and roll.

Two fingers inside her pussy assured Chase that Coco was more than wet enough for his favorite bedroom activity, and just the act of him checking caused another little downpour from her cunt onto the already soaked bedspread.

"Oh, baby. My cock is so hard. I just can't hold him off any longer."

Coco had pulled her knees up again, opening herself as wide as she could, making a place for him close to her. "I haven't done this for awhile, gorgeous, but I'll do my best to take everything you've got. Don't stop until you're balls deep, baby. I want it all. I need you to rock my world!"

"Ok, sugar, it's show time!"

Chase leaned over and placed a kiss on Coco's belly button, letting his tongue sink in and swirl around just a little. He crawled forward until his hands were at Coco's shoulders, her hands still tied and resting above her head, the head of his cock pressed against the opening of her pussy. He had expected the fit would be a little snug, but as Chase pushed up and into the warmth of Coco's body, he was surprised how tight the fit was.

Coco whimpered a little, started to pant a little, her hands clenched into tight fists. But this wasn't her first dance and she knew what to do.

"Coco? Are you okay?"

"Just give me a second, gorgeous, I'll make it better for you."

As Chase watched, Coco closed her eyes and took a deep breath in and out, forcing herself and those tight little vaginal muscles to relax. Almost immediately, Chase felt the grip on his cock ease a little, and he whispered in her ear "Okay?"

And she nodded and continued to breathe in and out, relaxing a little more. Chase started to move again, tentatively, tunneling further into Coco's pussy, pulling back an inch or two, then charging forward again. Soon Coco was clutching the headboard, thrusting with him, and Chase began to move faster, harder, deeper with every thrust. Her pussy was still like a velvet glove squeezing his cock but he could move without feeling like he might be hurting her.

Coco needed more contact with Chase – normally she would have left some claw marks on his back or on his ass by now – but with her hands tied above her head, she needed alternative contact. She curled her legs around Chase's waist, settling into the new position, and suddenly started to laugh.

Chase could feel the sensation of her laughter – he stopped thrusting and said "I'm not sure that laughter is what I need right now, baby. I need to know what you find so funny in this highly erotic moment."

"I need to mark you, gorgeous. I want to dig my nails into your back and those hotter than hell ass cheeks of yours, but I can't because you insisted on tying me up. So my next best thing would be to wrap my legs around your waist and leave a few stiletto marks in your ass – but I had you remove my shoes! So now I have no way to mark you except maybe to bite your lip, but that would show too much. So when we're all done with this, you won't have anything to remember me by. And it made me laugh. But now I think it makes me a little sad."

"Well, baby, just so you know, you don't have to mark me to make me remember this – this is one night I'll remember for the rest of my fucking life. I'm not crazy about the laughter, but we can't do sad either. So let's just do this." And he reached up and untied the slip knot that was holding her to the headboard.

Coco immediately pulled his head to her, intent on inhaling him. The kiss inflamed both of them. Chase started thrusting again with renewed vigor and Coco matched him stroke for stroke. He shifted his hips this way and that with each thrust, hitting different spots in Coco's pussy until the one stroke that made her scream into his mouth and he knew he was right where he wanted to be. He continued thrusting in that one same spot over and over, hearing Coco's raspy throated screams, getting exactly the reaction he wanted from her.

Coco broke off the kiss, throwing her head back and gasping for air. Her nails dug into Chase's back like her life depended on it. Chase thrust faster and harder, crying out "Come on, baby, give it to me!"

Coco screamed "Yes! Yes!! Oh god, yes!!!" as Chase's thrusts hit both her G-spot and her ultra-sensitive clit. The new orgasm hit Coco like a speeding car into a brick wall, and Chase exploded as all the tiny muscles of Coco's pussy caught his cock in a stranglehold like he'd never felt before. Their bodies continued to thrust at each other for a few minutes, moving slower and slower, like an amusement park ride coming to a stop. And then Chase collapsed on Coco, their two heads resting on the one pillow side by side, gasping for air until they could think and breathe again.

When Coco found herself again, Chase had pulled his satisfied cock out of her well fucked pussy, and was lying beside her, holding her close in his arms. They were silent for a minute or two, and then Coco said "Chase?"

And knowing exactly where she was going, he said "I know."

And in unison – "We didn't use a condom."

And Coco said "So, I guess we should have that conversation."

"The one about how many sexual partners we've had and how much unsafe sex we've had and how long it's been since we've been tested? That conversation?"

"Yeah, that one."

The 'conversation' was easier than either of them had anticipated. Coco confessed that she hadn't had sex at all in the past year, and the times she'd slept with men before that, she had made sure she was well protected against an unplanned 'change of life' pregnancy. The physical she had right before she moved back home had included tests for all the usual STD's, plus a few unusual ones, since she had been living abroad in the five years previous.

Chase admitted to having a boatload of sex in the past two years, but swore he always wore a condom. He had been sleeping with considerably younger women and he also refused to risk an unplanned pregnancy, or be tricked into a marriage he wasn't interested in, by the threat of fatherhood. The physical he had three months before had also included tests for all the usual STD's and everything had come back clean.

"Coco, I'm so sorry. I don't know what happened, it just never occurred to me to reach in my pocket and pull out a condom."

"You're not the only forgetful one, baby – I have a full box in the drawer right next to the bed. Of course, I'm not sure my condoms would have fit that super sized cock of yours, but at least we would have tried."

"I hate to ask but is an unplanned pregnancy a possibility? I know you're a little older, but things still happen."

"No, sweetheart, lucky for you, you just missed the nightmare of my menopause. One of the things my doctor checked during my last physical was my hormone levels. If I'm suddenly pregnant, it's a bona fide miracle and you're a bigger stud than I originally thought."

"Do you hate me now?"

"Oh, gorgeous, why would I hate you? Because we didn't think to use a condom? No, it's all good."

"Coco, I have to tell you – I've been fucking way below my age group the last few years. I guess I was trying to recapture a little of my youth. But all those 20-something and 30-something women have NOTHING on you, baby. You are an amazing woman."

"Yes, I am. Now how about a dip in the hot tub? I could use a little soak after all that exercise. And I need to spend a little time with this spectacular tat you've got!"

"Lead the way, baby."

10

They crawled out of bed, stopping for a quick leer at each other and a tonsil deep kiss. Coco caught sight of the huge wet spot on the bedspread, shook her head and laughed a little.

"Chase, help me with this, please." And they pulled the bedspread and top sheet off the bed onto the floor. Coco felt the bottom sheet to make sure it was still dry and said "I guess I'll be going to the laudromat tomorrow. I hope I have enough quarters!!" And she laughed again. "How did you do that to me? I've never had a problem with 'wet' before but this was ridiculously wet."

"Stop, Coco, you're making me blush! But, fuck, you are just so responsive. I was going to ask if you're always like this, or if it was my legendary lovemaking skills."

"I'm thinking you'll always be legendary in my mind, gorgeous. No man has ever done that to me – made me respond like that – made me scream like that. I fear the neighbors will be circulating a petition to boot me out of here. Do you suppose it was as loud outside as it was inside?"

"Are you asking if maybe your screams rattled windows down the street? Yes, I think so." And Coco looked horrified! And Chase said "I'm joking, baby, you got a little loud a few times, but the police haven't showed up yet, so I think we're good."

Chase pulled Coco to him for a hug and a kiss on the forehead. After a quick pit stop, they headed for the hot tub on the deck. Coco stopped in the kitchen, asking Chase if he was in the mood for dessert. "I thought you were dessert, Coco. But I can always eat. What have you got?"

"It's a surprise." She reached into the fridge and pulled out another bottle of wine and handed it to Chase. "Why don't you take the wine and two glasses out to the deck. There's the corkscrew by the fridge. I'll be out in a minute with dessert."

After he had grabbed the corkscrew, the wine and the glasses, he headed for the door. "Where's the light switch for the deck?"

"Oh, wait, you can't go out like that. You'll frighten the neighbors."

"As if we haven't already frightened them enough?"

Coco laughed and went to the closet by the back door and grabbed two towels. She threw one on the kitchen table for herself and wrapped the other one around Chase's waist, reaching up for a quick kiss to his tattoo. "There. You're at least PG-13 friendly now." One more lively kiss that tented Chase's modesty towel a little and he was out the back door. Coco flipped on the deck lights and the paddle fan over the tub and took a minute to enjoy the view. His toweled ass and exceptional shoulders, and yet another tattoo over his left shoulder blade that she would have to examine later, left her a little breathless. So she turned back into the kitchen and got to work on dessert.

Five minutes later, Coco was standing next to the hot tub holding two large dessert glasses and spoons, admiring the fact that Chase had figured out how to turn on her temperamental Jacuzzi. He'd also lit a few citronella candles that she had placed around the deck. Chase was already seated in the tub, enjoying the pulsing of the jets, sipping his wine. Coco's wine was waiting for her on the bench next to the hot tub, along with the re-corked bottle. She put the dessert glasses next to her wine, did a little striptease for Chase while removing her towel, and then she climbed in. She motioned for Chase to move over next to her and she handed him his dessert. He eyed it suspiciously and asked "Is that what I think it is? Jell-O?"

"Yes, it is. Strawberry Jell-O with pineapple, pecans and miniature marshmallows, topped with whipped cream. It very recently became my favorite dessert."

They started to eat their dessert and Chase continued his impromptu interrogation. "And why has this become your favorite dessert? I would have taken you for a Chocolate Decadence kind of girl."

"Well, there's always room for chocolate, but this is special."

"Because?"

"Because I had a dream about it the other night."

"You dreamed about Jell-O the other night? Tell me more."

"Well, Counselor, it was Wednesday night. The meeting from hell made me so depressed, and then you called and you were so sweet, you made me feel better. But I still didn't sleep very well. I would drift off into a dream and then wake up suddenly. And then I would fall back into the same dream, and then wake up again. That probably happened five times before I finally got up and went to my desk."

"The same dream? All night long? What was the dream?"

"This hot tub featured prominently in my dream."

"This hot tub? Really?"

"Yes, and you were in this hot tub."

"NO!"

"Yes, and the hot tub was filled with bubbling strawberry Jell-O."

"Shut up!"

"And pineapple chunks."

"No fucking way!"

"And pecans and miniature marshmallows."

"Was there whipped cream?"

"Gorgeous, you were covered in whipped cream."

"I just got hard all over again!"

"I think I just came a little myself. I'll have to sanitize the hot tub tomorrow!!"

"So, were you in the hot tub too, or was it just me in the Jell-O with the pineapple and the nuts and the marshmallows?"

"No, I got into the hot tub, and I ate a path to you through the Jell-O and the pineapple and the nuts and the miniature marshmallows."

"And what happened when you ate your way to me?"

"Your cock was sticking up out of the Jell-O, covered in whipped cream."

"Fuck, you're killing me!"

"And when I finally reached you, I opened my mouth and stuck out my tongue to take a lick."

"And?"

"And I woke up. Every time. Five fucking times. By the time I woke up that fifth time, I was exhausted and horny and damn near cross-eyed. And I had a sudden craving for strawberry Jell-O with pineapple chunks and pecans and miniature marshmallows and whipped cream. And you. I had a very strong craving for you."

"Fuck, Coco, you are such a dirty girl! I'm so glad I ran into you again!!"

"Me too, gorgeous. So I've finished my dessert and now it's my turn to have a bigger taste of you. The first thing I need is for you to come down here into the light so I can check out your tats. You have to tell me about them. While I lick them."

Chase caught a moan in his throat as Coco put her tongue to his chest and started licking an outline of the tattoo on his chest, then finally managed to speak. "I was in the Army for 20 years. There was no way I was coming out with no tattoos, but I knew my mom wouldn't be thrilled if I came home covered in them. So there's just two, to remind me of special things."

"This one on your chest is rockin'. An eagle holding an American flag in its talons? I love how there's a space between the claws exposing your nipple. That's so sexy. And the detail in those spread wings is impressive, but it looks like you've had it for awhile. Have you ever thought about touching it up, bringing the color back a little?"

"I actually like it better now than I did when I first got it. I like the subdued color, it shows through my white dress shirts a little less than it did originally."

"So what was the special thing you got this tattoo for?"

"After my buddy got blown up, and I got injured, I got evac'ed to Ramstein for a few weeks to recover, and get some shrink time. I was having trouble with the big picture – why we were there and all that. Since we were technically somewhere we weren't supposed to be. But I spent a lot of time talking with some other wounded guys at the base hospital, and decided the world would be a worse place if we weren't doing what we were doing, so I needed to celebrate my buddy's life a little. He was a great guy and he had flag tattoos all over his body. So right before I was set to return to my unit, I got this tat. I went to see his family when I got home and told them what little of the story I could tell them, they seemed pretty pleased with the tat."

"That's a beautiful tribute, gorgeous. I'm sure your buddy is somewhere watching over that tattoo and the man who wears it." And Coco sniffled just a little, showing some unplanned emotion.

Chase leaned in and kissed Coco's forehead and said "I sure hope so, baby, since I have a new reason to be optimistic."

"And what's that, gorgeous?"

"You. You know that other tattoo? The one on my shoulder blade?"

Coco moved around behind him to get a better look at the tat in the light and said "Yes, it looks like… a man and a woman in silhouette… dancing?" And her finger tips started to trace an outline of the tattoo, very gently.

"Yes, that's you and me. All those years ago. When I got 'unengaged' so abruptly, and joined the Army, my head was all over the place. But there was one memory that always picked me up when I was down. No matter where I was or how bad things were, I could think back to that week and know that someone special was holding my hand. And now here you are again. Robert and Gigi's wedding turned out to be my lucky day."

As she slid back around to face him, she said "Thank you, Chase, that's a beautiful sentiment and an exceptional tat. That week was special to me too. For 30 years, I've been cleaning my house listening to Swing music and thinking about a stud college man who couldn't dance but took my breath away."

"But I learned how to dance that week, you taught me to dance, just like I wanted you to."

"Yes, you did learn very well. I was very proud of both of us at the end of that week. But now I have to change the subject and the tone because your 2XL cock is starting to poke me in the belly. And I'm claiming my taste time. So I want you to sit up here on the edge of the hot tub and spread your legs so I can eat MY fill."

"I think I need more wine, and I'm sure you do too."

Chase stood up, reached over and grabbed the wine bottle, and filled both their glasses again. Then he sat down on the edge of the hot tub, right where Coco wanted him. He spread his knees wide and showed off that big beautiful cock, which was definitely hard again. Coco knelt between

Chase's legs, on a soft chair cushion that she had placed on the hard plastic seat in the tub. She took a big gulp from her glass of liquid courage, grasped his cock and held him lightly, amused when he jumped a little at her touch.

She carefully lifted his cock so that she could see where his injury had occurred, visible in the lights from the deck and the hot tub. In addition to the scar in place of his missing testicle, she could see a small scar on the underside of his cock about an inch from the base. She couldn't resist running her thumb gently over both scars, feeling Chase shiver when she did.

"Is that sensitive? Does it hurt? I don't want to do anything that will make you uncomfortable."

"No, it doesn't hurt, it's more numb than sensitive, even after all these years. I can feel pressure there but not necessarily any actual feeling."

"My breast is the same way, although sometimes when nerves reconnect, I get a feeling like lightning for a few seconds – not altogether pleasant."

"I get that, too, and I agree – not altogether pleasant."

"Is it okay for me to do this? I want to, but not if you don't want me to. I'm just not sure if I'm any good at this. It's been awhile."

"I would love for you to do this. You may be only the second or third woman who's wanted to go down on me since the injury occurred. Most women have been gracious about me having an injury, but they haven't actually wanted to look at it. You seem very interested – I'm a little surprised you don't have a magnifying glass down there looking around."

"I'm very interested in everything about you. Not sure why, but I am. So if you're up for this, just lean back and enjoy. And stop me anytime you need."

"I have to say, you examining my cock so intently is really hot. So have at it, sassy girl. I'm all yours."

Coco emptied her wine glass in one gulp, knelt up at the edge of the hot tub, grasped Chase's big beautiful hard cock and slid her hands down and back up the shaft several times, ending every slide with a lick across and around the large head. Every lick gifted her with a little taste of come, seeping out from the head. After three little licks, and three moans from Chase as he watched her, Coco decided she needed more – more touch, more taste, more Chase.

She opened her mouth wide and sucked the head of his cock in – her tongue swirled around the crown, lips welcoming him as she pushed him deeper. His moans of pleasure started faint and far away but got louder and closer the longer he was trapped in her mouth. His breathing became quick and raspy. His hips started shifting back and forth a little, trying to find her rhythm.

Coco's head bobbed and weaved for uncounted minutes, sucking, pushing and pulling, her tongue everywhere, sending Chase to some secret place in his head. When he recovered his senses, he pushed himself closer to the edge of the hot tub and grabbed her by the hair, taking over the push and pull at the pace he needed, while she sucked and licked at everything she could reach. Since Chase was now controlling the movement of Coco's head and mouth, she reached up and grasped the sides of his thighs – something to hang on to, to dig her nails into.

All the while Coco was showering Chase's cock with her attention, he was keeping up a rather one-sided conversation. "Oh, fuck, Coco, when you suck on my cock like that when you pull up, it just about blows the top of my head off!"

"Mmmmhmmmm."

"Fuck! When you hum like that I actually stop breathing for a few seconds. The sensation goes right up my spine! No one's ever done that to me before!"

"Hmmmmm."

"Oh, baby, I'm gonna come so hard, it might just blow you across the hot tub!"

Only the sound of the bubbling water of the hot tub was audible, along with the slurping sounds of Coco's mouth on Chase's cock, and every few seconds the sound of gasping breath. Coco's nails dug into Chase's thighs as she concentrated on her own breathing.

Chase's cock continued to engorge and Coco feared that he might have more cock than she had mouth to accommodate, but she kept breathing deliberately through her nose for as long as she could, opening her jaws as wide as she could, just enjoying being in the moment with him. The push and pull seemed to go on forever – it continued until Coco lost track of time and space – until there was only his cock and her mouth on the edge of a glorious orgasm.

She felt, more than heard, the low moan, felt him start to tremble all over as he neared his release – he started an unconscious stream of swearing as he inched closer and closer to his climax – "Fuck! Fuck!! Fucking FUCK! Baby, your fucking mouth is so fucking good! Oh, baby – fuck – I'm gonna come all over your tongue!!" And sure enough, he did.

Long hot spurts of semen shot so close to the back of her throat, she barely had to swallow at all. Even when he had no more to give her, Chase still shuddered for long seconds, rocking gently back and forth on Coco's lips until he had settled. She took the opportunity to lick his cock clean while he recovered, not wanting to lose the intimate connection between them, relishing the bond they had just forged.

Finally Chase released his grip on Coco's hair, removing his cock from her mouth, and coaxed her hands off his thighs. Coco slid down into the water a little, her cheek resting against Chase's thigh, her eyes closed. There was a little smile on her lips, her breathing slowly returning to normal, and he stared at the peaceful look on her face for several minutes. He finally slid off the edge of the hot tub into the swirling water, pushing Coco with him toward the center of the hot tub. Chase caught her in a tight hug and kissed her deep, tasting his essence still lingering on her lips and tongue.

When the kiss ended, Coco moved back to the side of the hot tub and grabbed for her wine glass on the bench, then realized the glass and the bottle were empty. Chase reached for his own glass and took a drink, then set the half full glass back on the bench. He looked deep into Coco's eyes and finally said "Fuck, woman, every time I think I have a handle on you, you do something that surprises the hell out of me! Where did you learn to do that?"

"I could ask you the same thing. But I'm not sure I really want to know. I'm just happy to be the beneficiary your in-depth education over the years."

"Well put, Ms. Brighton. That was really fucking good. You really are a sassy girl."

Still thirsty, Coco picked up Chase's wine glass and took a drink and then handed the glass to him. He looked a little indignant and said "Did you just drink out of my glass?"

"Yes, I did."

"That's a little gross!"

"I just had your cock in my mouth, gorgeous. You just shot your come down my throat and then you kissed me. What's the problem with me drinking out of your glass? I left a little for you."

"It just seems a little unsanitary, don't you think?"

"You're kidding, right? No, you're not kidding! Fine, I'll walk all the way to the kitchen and open another bottle and get my own damned glass of wine! How did you survive 20 years in the Rangers?"

"Nobody ever drank out of my glass!"

Coco laughed a little and said "It's good to know you're not completely perfect after all. Here, give me your glass. I'll bring you a refill."

"No, I'll come with you. You might spit in my glass!"

A sudden yawn overwhelmed Coco, and Chase followed suit. "Maybe we don't need that wine after all, baby. I think I'd like nothing better than getting back in your bed and cuddling you for a little while and maybe catching a few hours of sleep. God, when did I get to be so old??"

"I don't know about you being old, gorgeous, but I do like the sound of a little sleep."

Chase climbed out of the tub and helped Coco out as well. They wrapped up in their towels again and dried off, then turned off the hot tub for the night and put the cover over it. Then they gathered up the dessert glasses and the wine glasses, the empty wine bottle and the corkscrew, and headed inside.

The dirty dishes and glasses went in the sink, the towels went in the hamper in the bathroom, and the very tired lovers were back in bed together. They shared a few gentle, lazy kisses, the last one interrupted by another combined yawn. They ended up spooning comfortably, cooled by the ceiling fan turning lazily over the bed, covered with a soft angora throw in place of the wet bedspread. They were both asleep in 5 minutes and dead to the world for the next 5 hours.

11

Coco woke slowly, not sure what time it was, staring into the early morning Myrtle Beach sun. She had taken her watch off in the kitchen before their adventure in the hot tub, and the bedroom clock was behind her so she had no idea what time it was. She was wrapped in Chase's strong arms, and based on his easy, measured breathing, she assumed he was still asleep.

Coco had no desire to disturb him, but there were only two options – she either got up now, or peed in the bed. The choice was clear. She inched slowly away from Chase's warm body, hoping that her movement and the absence of her body heat didn't wake him. Coco finally moved far enough away that she could slide out the side of the bed and walked around it toward the bathroom. When she had reached the foot of the bed, she took just a moment to admire the man she had just spent the night with – the angora throw only covered him from his waist to his knees, and he had just rolled onto his back in his sleep as she exited the bed. She had a spectacular view of his chest, abs, biceps – and fuck, he was sporting morning wood, tenting the throw that covered him. Coco had already grown very fond of Chase's cock, and it was all she could do not to climb back into bed and wake him up in erotic fashion.

But her need had now reached emergency status and she padded into the bathroom, closing the door quietly behind her. After Coco had taken care of business, she washed her hands and face, fluffed her hair a little and

come hard – shooting his come all over Coco's hand, all over their bellies and chests, even hitting Coco's cheek as she bent down to catch him in her mouth. When it was over, Chase looked embarrassed and said "Fuck! What am I, 16?"

And he reached up and started to wipe Coco's cheek clean. But she caught his come-covered finger and pulled it to her mouth, licking it clean like it was some decadent treat. And she looked up at him and said "That was SO hot!! It almost made me feel young again!"

"You think that was hot?"

"Oh, fuck, yes! I haven't had a man come in my hand for years! I wouldn't mind doing that again some time."

"I guess I need to return the favor! How about you have a seat on this handy little built-in bench and I'll see if I can get you to come all over my tongue."

"You're on, Mr. Buckingham."

Coco sat on the little bench and Chase knelt down between her legs. He had her put her feet on his shoulders and lean back, exposing her pussy to his magic hands and tongue – and he went to work. She was already primed and ready to go, it wasn't going to take much, but he worked her like a master anyway. Chase ate Coco's pussy like it was the last meal of a starving man. He sucked and nibbled on her clit, flicking his tongue against the swelling little bud until she was a panting piece of womanhood. He licked into her folds and speared her cunt with his tongue until she was barely breathing, gasping for air with tiny screams he could hardly hear. He pushed those two fingers – Coco's favorite fingers – deep into her pussy, hitting that secret button with deadly aim.

Coco was only moments away from a crushing orgasm and Chase removed his fingers, leaving her feeling empty, a tiny cry of "No…" escaping from her lips. He laughed a little and replaced his fingers with his tongue again, delving into her body over and over again. Coco was so close again, she was almost pushing his shoulders away with her feet in an attempt to straighten her legs.

But Chase wasn't giving her the control she was trying to take. He maintained his position and hers, continued to lick at Coco like she was an ice cream treat.

Coco's tiny little voice begged, "Chase, please. I need to…"

He whispered against her pussy, "I know, baby, you want to come really badly, don't you?"

"Please, Chase…"

"Okay, baby, here we go."

And he speared his tongue into her one last time, pinching her clit hard between his thumb and forefinger at the same time. If Coco hadn't been pressed into the corner of the shower with her knees in her chest, the neighbors would surely have heard the scream as her orgasm swept through her. As it was, it echoed across the tiled walls of the bathroom even after she had stopped shaking, after Chase had released her and she had fallen forward into his arms.

"Holy fuck, gorgeous, how do you do these things to me?"

"I could ask you the same thing, baby, I haven't come in a woman's hands for so long I don't remember when." And they laughed a little, shared a quick kiss and an even quicker shower, actually washing each other this time, because the water was starting to get a little chilly. Just as they were finishing up and shutting off the shower, the oven timer went off, signaling that breakfast was almost ready.

They dried each other off and then wrapped in clean dry towels and headed for the kitchen. Coco removed the breakfast casserole from the oven and while it rested, she put the coffee on, and got juice and fruit out of the fridge. She sent Chase to the dining room with the juice and she followed him with the casserole and the bowl of delicious looking berries. She served him a large slice of casserole – hashbrown crust with eggs, pancetta, onions and green peppers baked to perfection – and spooned fruit into his bowl. The strawberries, raspberries and blueberries were fresh and ripe and looked mouth watering.

When Coco had gotten her own casserole and fruit, she raised her juice glass in Chase's direction and said "Cheers, Mr. Buckingham. I don't know what to say other than, thank you. It was quite a night."

"And morning. Thank you, Coco, you've been quite the hostess. I can't remember when I've had such a good time."

They stared at each other for a minute, both wondering what was left to say in that moment. And then they began to eat. "Coco, I know I keep saying this, but this is delicious. You are an outrageous cook and I consider myself very lucky to be sitting here right now."

"It's been my pleasure, Chase. I know that you will eventually want to leave here and I want to make sure you're well fed and satisfied when you go."

"I'm not sure I will ever 'want' to leave here, but you're right, eventually I will need to go. I promised to help my dad with some remodeling project he's working on in his basement. I told him I'd be over around 3:00."

"Can I get you anything else? Coffee? Tea? Milk?"

"I'd love some coffee. Can I help?"

"No, the coffee maker does most of the work. All I have to do is pour. I'll be right back." And she walked to the kitchen, feeling a growing emptiness at the thought of Chase leaving, then telling herself she was being really stupid. But the feeling didn't leave her.

She poured coffee for Chase, and a glass of milk for herself, forced a smile on her face and went back to the dining room. They finished their breakfast at a leisurely pace, enjoying some pleasant conversation, sharing childhood memories, funny stories from their professional careers. Chase wanted to know about Coco's family, and she was very curious about his as well. Chase talked about how his parents had met and married, how his dad had established his law practice, how Chase enjoyed being an only child growing up, but missed having a larger family as he got older.

Coco also shared how her parents met, how her dad and her uncle had started their pharmacy business, how she had worked in that store along with her cousins until she moved away from home. She talked about losing her older sister when Coco was only three, how the loss had changed her parents, how much closer Coco and her parents had become after that. The cloud of losing her mom and dad hung over the discussion for a minute, but it ended on a happy note with Coco talking about how her extended family had helped her celebrate her 50th birthday a few months before.

"Yes, they actually found two 25 year old male strippers and had them throw their junk in my face as they danced. It was all caught on video, including drunken me reaching for some of that junk. Luckily the video stops just before I completely embarrassed myself and those two unsuspecting dancers. I'm surprised my cousins didn't post it on YouTube!"

"I'm very sorry I missed that. Although, knowing what I know now, I would have been very jealous of you grabbing some young punk's junk instead of mine!"

"You never stop, do you?"

"I hope not. But unfortunately, I should go soon, so let me help you clean up before I leave."

They carried all the dishes to the kitchen, and once again, Coco busied herself with the leftovers while Chase loaded the dishwasher. They continued their light conversation while they worked, and almost before they were ready for it, the dining room was clean, the kitchen was tidied, and there was nothing left to do. They stared at each other for a minute, not saying anything, and then Chase made the first move. He stepped into Coco's space, barely an inch between them, and he reached up and gently took her face in his two hands. He leaned down, his mouth moving slowly toward her lips, stopping so close that they could feel each other's breath, but not their touch.

Chase whispered her name as Coco whispered his – a magnetic attraction pulled them together, closing that tiny bit of space between them. Lips touched lips and parted, mouths opened, tongues met and played against each other. At the same time, hands caressed arms, shoulders, everything that could be reached and touched softly. One second, fevered breath; the next, gentle easy purring. The kiss ended, they pulled apart a little from each other, and each took that deep breath they needed to bridle the building passion.

"Coco, I really don't want to, but I have to go. I think you're an amazing, beautiful woman, I had such an incredible time. And I don't just mean the sex, although it was AMAZING! I really liked talking to you and cuddling with you and listening to you breathe while you slept. And eating what you cooked! That was spectacular as well."

"Chase, I had a wonderful time too. You're smart, funny, interesting to talk to, god awful good looking – looking at you is no hardship either. Lord I suddenly sound so superficial! But you know what I mean. I enjoyed having you here. I'm so glad we ran into each other again. I hope you come back again some time."

"I'd like that very much. Maybe I could take you out for dinner next time. I'd offer to cook, but you'd probably get popcorn and beer. So dinner maybe?"

"I'd like that." And they kissed again, not wanting to lose the emotional bond.

"I have to go to Columbia for a few days, baby, but I should be back by Thursday. I'll give you a call one evening and we can set something up. Sound good?"

"Sounds great. Chase?"

"Yes, baby?"

"Should you maybe get dressed before you leave? I don't think I want anyone seeing how hot you look in that towel."

Twenty minutes later, they were dressed and standing in each other's arms next to Chase's car in Coco's driveway. "I'm sorry, Coco, I could stand here kissing you forever, but if I don't leave now, I'll never leave. I really am becoming addicted to you and detox is gonna be a bitch!"

"I know how you feel, gorgeous, I felt the same way last Sunday – standing in YOUR driveway. I don't know what it is about you, Mr. Buckingham, but I'm not looking forward to this week at all. Too much work and not enough you will equal a week that sucks royally. So – we're adults – we can do this."

"Right! Adults! One last kiss and then I'll go."

And he held her head in his hands and kissed her – gently at first, then gaining force as the passion grew. Lips crushed, tongues tangled, hands reached for all their favorite places. And then they seemed to know that it was now or never, and they pulled apart from each other, both panting just a little.

Chase took Coco's hand in his, lifted it to his lips and kissed it sweetly. "I'll call you this week and we'll make plans for dinner when I get back in town."

"I'll be here. Looking forward to it."

And Chase all but jumped into his Jeep, as if closing himself inside it would break the spell between them, and let him breathe just a little. He started the engine, backed out of the driveway and drove down the street, leaving her with a little wave. Which she returned. And stood in her driveway looking down the street, long after his car had turned the corner and was out of sight. The coming week was totally going to suck.

12

*C*oco spent Sunday tidying up the house, taking her still wet bedspread to the Laundromat, and missing Chase every time she looked at the damned thing. She soothed herself to sleep that night by reliving all of the sex and the tender moments they had shared the night before, and again that morning – she convinced herself that she could survive on those sweet memories alone, even if she never saw Chase again. Which she really hoped would not be the case.

Monday lulled Coco into a false sense of caught-up-ness on the work front, and then Tuesday hit like a hurricane of busy, keeping her at her computer from 5:30 AM to 10:30 PM with barely a break to chow down on leftovers from the weekend, even pre-empting her daily morning run. And no call from Chase.

But she did get a call from her legal colleague, Joshua Barkin, late Tuesday evening. "Coco, I don't know what you said or did, and I don't know who you said or did it to, but we got a call today from John Buckingham's office, inviting us to meet with him on Friday afternoon at 2:00 to discuss our issues with the proposed land grab bill. Obviously you have to be there."

"No, Josh, I don't have to be there. You and Geneva and Grace know what our issues are. You just have to remain calm and professional and you'll be fine. John Buckingham is a reasonable man, you will have to be a reasonable man as well."

"Coco, you were there, you know what a mess I caused at the last meeting, please don't leave us to flounder on our own."

"Josh, you made that mess intentionally, and don't bother trying to deny it. You forced me to do something I had intended not to do, and I won't let that happen again. You want a run at the State House in a few years? Now's the time to prove you have what it takes."

"Please, Coco, just babysit us one more time and I promise not to bother you again. This is too important to take a chance."

"No, I won't be at the meeting. You'll have to sink or swim on your own."

"This is about Chase, isn't it? Something's happening between the two of you and you're afraid to mess things up by being on the opposite side of this issue."

"That's none of your business, Josh. I won't be at the meeting. You can handle it on your own. I'm hanging up now, I still have a lot of work to do tonight. Good night and good luck."

Coco disconnected the call and went back to work. She hated to admit that Josh might be right. She could tell herself all she wanted that it had nothing to do with her relationship with Chase, but deep down, she knew that she was willing to give up all her hard work fighting this proposal rather than put that relationship in jeopardy. Coco worked until 10:30 PM and then decided she was too tired to finish her design work that night. She was also in a bit of a funk because Chase still hadn't called. Again she told herself she was being stupid, but the bad mood didn't go away.

Coco slept fitfully Tuesday night – she would sleep for an hour and be awake for an hour, then sleep for another hour. When her alarm went off Wednesday morning at 5:30 AM, she felt like she hadn't had any sleep at all. She started her day with a glass of milk and a 30 minute walk around the neighborhood to try to wake up, then forced herself back to her desk with toast, coffee, and the pile of work waiting there. She came up for air at 1:30 PM and had a quick lunch, then was hard at it again until 7:30 PM, when the ringing of her phone interrupted her thought process. She was happy when she saw it was Chase calling – until she heard the sound of his angry voice, not even giving her the chance to say hello.

"So my dad graciously sets up a meeting on Friday – at my request, mind you – so that we can all sit down and discuss our collective issues, and you aren't going to be there?"

"Chase, it's so nice to hear from you. Are you having a good week?"

"Well?"

"Is that a question or an answer?"

"Stop this. You know what I'm asking. Why aren't you going to be at the meeting?"

"How do you know I'm not going to be at the meeting?"

"Because your little bulldog, Barkin, called me this afternoon and accused me of seducing you so that you would give up your fight rather than risk losing a relationship with me. What the hell, Coco?"

"Chase, I don't know where Josh got that idea, and I certainly didn't think he'd ever make fools of all of us by calling you, but he's probably right, at least about me. I don't know what's going on between you and me, I just know I've been happy lately, and I don't think I want to lose that over this bill."

"Coco, do you think so little of me that you don't trust me to separate my work and my personal life?"

"Chase…"

"Coco, I don't know what's going on with us either, but I've also been happy lately and I'd hate to see it disappear. But you know that, even if you stepped away from this particular issue, something else would eventually come between us. We have to face this sooner or later and I'd rather do it now. So I expect to see you Friday afternoon at 2:00 PM at my dad's office, and I expect you to bring your A game. And if you can still stand the sight of me by the time the meeting is over, I'll take you to dinner. As a matter of fact, I'm taking you to dinner whether you can stand the sight of me or not! Now finish up a little more work and then get to bed. I can tell by the sound of your voice that you need more sleep than you apparently got last night."

"You're a bossy sonofabitch, aren't you!"

And a gentler voice answered, "You don't know the half of it. Sweet dreams, baby. I'll see you Friday afternoon." And he was gone.

Coco sat staring at her phone for a few minutes and was tempted to call Josh and blast him for interfering, but decided she wasn't going to give him the satisfaction. She spent two more hours tinkering with web site designs and then decided to call it a day. She took a bowl of cereal to her bedroom and watched a little TV while she ate "dinner" in bed, then turned out the light and tried to settle in. It took a little while to fall asleep, but when she finally did, she had those sweet dreams Chase had wished for her, and she slept all night.

Thursday found Coco refreshed from a good night's sleep, and very productive with her workload. She even got that 30 minute run and some breakfast in before she headed to her desk. She plowed through the backlog of maintenance changes for her existing clients, and finished up three design mock-ups for her newest clients. She even treated herself to a full hour for lunch – which she ate in her bedroom, while staring into her massive clothes closet, trying to find just the right outfit for the meeting with John and Chase Buckingham the next day. Coco was always well dressed in a business environment, but if Chase expected her A game, she needed to be dressed accordingly.

She waffled back and forth between a pant suit and a dress, and decided in the end on a black sleeveless ponte knit dress that was fitted at the top and flared in the skirt, just the right amount of short, topped with a red three quarter length sleeve bolero jacket, and matching red stiletto sandals. She had more professional looking shoes that would look good with the outfit but she thought she needed the extra boost the stilettos would give her. She was sure she could handle father and son Buckingham with no problem, but the added stress of having loose cannon Josh Barkin in the meeting required all the extra ammunition she could bring, even if he was on her side.

Coco was back at her desk in exactly one hour, satisfied that she was ready for Friday's meeting, and dove back into the work pile. By 7:30 PM, she had emailed off all of the maintenance changes and design presentations and had talked to five clients about face to face meetings scheduled for the next week.

At 8:00 PM, Coco was just finishing up a 30 minute yoga tape that stretched her enough to put her in a better mood, when her phone rang. She was disappointed that it wasn't Chase, but glad it wasn't Josh "Damn Him" Barkin again. The call was from her uncle, asking her about participating in the Independence Day parade that was scheduled for the next week. The local parade to honor the 4th of July and the military veterans of the

Myrtle Beach area was a tradition that was older than Coco. And her family's participation was part of the tradition.

Even when Coco was living outside the country, she always tried to get home for the parade and the holiday, but the last few years had been more of a challenge for her, missing her parents greatly at this time of year. But her aunt and uncle had convinced Coco that it was time to take her place in the parade, and she was looking forward to restarting the tradition, with the perfect way to honor her parents' memories at the same time.

Coco talked with her aunt and uncle for 20 minutes and then headed off to bed to watch a little TV and get prepped mentally for the big Friday meeting.

Friday morning, Coco concentrated on cleaning up the last of her maintenance work, then shut everything down at Noon to get ready for her meeting with the Buckinghams. Once she was dressed in her power outfit, she finished her makeup. She scarffed down a quick lunch, grabbed her tablet case and purse and was out the door. She walked through the door of Buckingham and Buckingham, Attorneys at Law, at 1:55 PM, finding Josh, Grace and Geneva already there.

Coco and her group were shown into a well appointed conference room and offered refreshments by Mr. Buckingham's receptionist, and then they were alone. The three young people seemed restless and nervous, but Coco had already put her disaster management attitude on and was ready for whatever happened. There was one last warning about "proper behavior" that she expected from these young people and then John and Chase walked through the conference room door and the game began.

John Buckingham was the consummate gentleman, greeting each member of Coco's team individually, commenting on the fact that they were each wearing a name badge, probably so that he wouldn't be confused when the conversation got lively again. There was nervous laughter around the room except for Coco – she looked the quintessential business woman – calm, cool and very collected. Chase also shook everyone's hand quickly, except for Coco – he looked tired to her, but he held her hand and her gaze just a few seconds longer than he would a normal legal adversary.

They all took their seats and John led them into the discussion by recounting what he recalled of the issues that had been brought up at the very uncomfortable meeting with the County. At the heart of their opposition to the legislation was the State-wide scope, Coco and her group feeling that the matter of land management was better handled at the County level.

Unfortunately, within 20 minutes, there was a room full of heated discourse, and everyone seemed to be yelling at the same time. And Coco was one of the loudest. John Buckingham was fending off arguments from Josh, Grace and Geneva, and Chase and Coco were having their own war of words.

"Chase, how can you be so stubborn about this? It's as plain as the nose on your gorgeous face that this is a bad bill!"

"No, Coco, you're the one being stubborn. How can you be so sweet in bed and so pig headed in a conference room??"

"Pig headed?!?! Did you just call me pig headed???"

"Coco, this bill will do more good in the long run, just the way it was originally written. We're looking out for the long term. How can you not see that?"

"Chase, this bill is bad for Myrtle Beach and Horry County, and I will fight it with everything I have!"

And they glared at each other for a full minute, saying nothing, until Coco couldn't take it anymore, and turned away from Chase, breathing hard and angry. And she began to listen to all the anger around her in the room. She looked at everyone yelling and no one listening. Chase had joined his dad against the three political rookies and it wasn't really a fair fight. Suddenly she saw Geneva begin to fight back tears, and then Grace started to cry openly.

And she knew that things couldn't go on this way. The young ladies on her team were too naïve and tender hearted for a bare knuckles brawl like this. They were getting nowhere fast and it was time to shut it all down.

Coco decided she needed to take control – immediately. And she reached into her well worn bag of management skills and pulled out the Queen Bitch technique she'd had to use in too many meetings over the years.

"Everybody stop talking!! Just shut up!!"

And everybody did – they all stopped talking and stared at Coco like she'd just slapped them. Only Chase had a little smirk on his face – John looked stunned, and the other three just looked scared.

"What the fuck is wrong with all of you?? With all of us?? Just settle down! Josh Barlow, I've never been more angry at you – or myself – than I am right now. And Mr. and Mr. Buckingham? Shame on you both! I hope you're really pleased with yourselves for making these young ladies cry. Grace and Geneva came here today in good faith, hoping to reach some kind of settlement on this. They're just trying to make their little corner of the world a bit better and we didn't help them at all! You say whatever you want to me, call me whatever you want, I'm battle-hardened after 30 years in business, but you don't EVER talk to these young ladies like that EVER again."

Chase took a step toward her and almost whispered "Coco…"

"No, Chase, just shut up. I'm choking on all the testosterone in the room, I'm calling bullshit on all of us. Grace, Geneva, Josh, pack up, we're out of here."

"Coco, maybe you're the one who needs to settle down a little." And Chase gave her an arrogant look that said she was as much to blame for the meltdown as anyone else in the room.

And Coco turned away from all of them, took several deep breaths to ward off her own impending tears, and forced herself to calm down. When she turned around again, she was ready to put a civil end to the nightmare.

Facing John, Coco said "I'm sorry, Mr. Buckingham, that was very rude of me. I apologize. I apologize to all of you. Why is it that every time we all gather in a room, we become 5 year old children? And why do I always have to be the voice of reason?? I'm not good at being the voice of reason! And I'm tired of always having to be that reasonable person. It's why I turned my back on Corporate America."

And John Buckingham turned to Coco with a slightly grumpy look on his face and said "Ms. Brighton, I appreciate the temporary diversion. Maybe we need to take 5 minutes and go to our neutral corners."

"No, Mr. Buckingham, I think today we'll just have to agree to disagree and call it a day. We're not getting anywhere here and I think we should just leave. I don't want to waste any more of your time. Maybe we can regroup and try again in a few weeks."

And then it was Chase's turn to step in. "Coco, I'd really like to make some kind of progress today. May I make a suggestion?"

Grudgingly, Coco said "Of course. What do you have in mind?"

And he stepped closer to her and whispered in her ear, "You take care of YOUR children, and I'll take care of MINE, and we'll try again in 10 minutes."

And she sighed – giving voice to her emotional fatigue. "Okay. One more try."

And Chase smiled at Coco and said to the group, "10 minutes, people, and we're coming back into this room. And we're not coming out again until we have a bill we can all live with. Pee now or forever hold your... Well, you know what I mean! Dad, a word with you in my office, please?" And the attorneys Buckingham left the room, leaving Coco to scold her team – gently – and then hustle everyone to the bathroom.

Once everyone was back in the room, Coco announced to her own team, "If I hear one more raised voice, one more rude comment, one more unproductive comment, I will drag your sorry asses out to the curb. And that includes myself! I got way out of control and did no one any good. Now we're going to crank up the 'civilized' meter a whole lot of notches and try again. Let's see if we can get something accomplished here people. Okay?"

And they all nodded. And Coco said sternly, "Voices, people, I want to hear you confirm your understanding."

And five subdued voices, two of which she had not expected, confirmed their understanding, making Coco shake her head, laugh a little, and say "Okay, then, let's get back to work."

After an hour of mostly civilized debate about the various merits of State vs County control of the land in question, John Buckingham was beginning to listen to their argument and Josh Barkin had become the eloquent – and controlled – voice of their issues. Another hour, and they had discussed alternative funding options, including several existing levies that had been in place for many years and were about to expire. Coco's group felt it would be an easy sell to the voters in the next election, to let the existing levies expire and replace them with a new levy of less total millage that would still allow for a small reduction in taxes, but fund the most needed land reclamation.

After another 30 minutes, points had been conceded on both sides, but there was proposed legislation on the table that everyone could live with. John Buckingham was agreeable to the changes, but he was looking somewhat defeated, and Coco was not comfortable with that. She thought she knew why he had pushed for sweeping changes, and why he now looked like he'd lost an opportunity – for a legacy.

She had been fairly silent throughout the final 30 minutes of the meeting but she felt it was now time for her to speak – to John Buckingham directly. "Mr. Buckingham – John – you seem very disappointed to be agreeing to these changes, and I believe I know why. Forgive me for being straightforward, but I think you were looking forward to one last piece of landmark legislation that you could consider your legacy to the county and the state when you retire.

"I understand why you would want to do that, but I think you're discounting 40 years of legislation that has stood your county and your state in good stead for years, and will continue for years to come. The name John Buckingham has been synonymous with well thought out, well written, practically unbreakable environmental law for almost as long as I've been alive. The beaches, the farmland, the marshland, the very essence of agricultural innovation, even the damned bees have been, and will continue to be, protected by your professional wisdom and foresight well into the future.

"Other counties have adopted similar legislation based on your blueprint, some of your legislation has even been so widely accepted that those laws are now considered state laws. And you never agreed to put your name on any of these laws, even unofficially, because you wanted the legislation to stand on its own merits. If you never passed another piece of legislation during the remainder of your career, that's a sweeping legacy that no one can dishonor."

"Thank you, Ms. Brighton, but you'll have to excuse an old man's desire to score that one last goal, hit that one last home run before the game ends."

"I guess we'll have to agree to disagree on that point, Mr. Buckingham, I think you've been hitting home runs for your entire career, and this bill, as it now stands, will be considered another huge win for the environment. And if you'll excuse me for saying so, I'd have to say that your biggest home run of all has been, and will continue to be, your son. You raised him to have a conscience, gave him a sense of responsibility for the world around him. He's been so inspired by your personal and professional life that he's following in your footsteps. Chase is a good man, John, and we will all be better for having him here, continuing your work whenever you decide to retire."

And she held out her hand to shake his, not only to say thank you for meeting with her team and agreeing to so many of their requested changes, but also to thank him for his life's work.

John shook Coco's hand, shook hands with all of her team, and then left the conference room. Josh, Geneva and Grace decided it was time for them to leave as well, Josh promising to call Coco some time during the next week to discuss next steps. And the three youngsters left the conference room. Leaving Coco and Chase in the room alone.

"Pig headed, Buckingham? Really?? Ugh!!"

"I'm sorry, Coco, I got carried away."

"No, you're right, sometimes I am pig headed. I'm sorry, too."

Without another word, Chase pulled Coco into his arms and held her like she was more necessary than his next breath, and Coco held on tight as well. They shared a minutes-long kiss that was slow, comforting – passionate without all the heat. Perfect.

Coco was concerned about John and asked "Is your dad okay? He seemed pretty subdued by the time he left the room."

"My dad will be fine. It just takes him awhile to process when things don't go exactly the way he wants them to. What you said was very nice, and very appropriate, he'll understand that in a few days. This legislation is still high impact, and I think when it passes and other counties see what we're doing, they'll get on board. This will be a statewide initiative in 10 years. I just hope Dad's around to see it."

"I know he's really disappointed right now and I'm sorry about that. How do YOU feel about all this right now?"

"I'm disappointed for him, but I think we stand a much better chance of passage this way. And I'm very sure that other counties will be sniffing around once it passes. Dad can help them move similar legislation forward, spend the next few years working on something he's very passionate about. It'll keep him in the game a little longer, give him one last issue to champion. It's all good."

Coco wrapped her arms tighter around Chase's waist, then looked up into his eyes and gently put a hand to the side of his face. "You look tired, gorgeous. Maybe we should skip dinner tonight."

"It was a long week, but no, we shouldn't skip dinner tonight, I've been looking forward to seeing you all week. The tension of this meeting today did nothing to lessen that desire. But maybe we should change the location and the menu a little. How about pizza and a nice bottle of wine at my place? We can watch a movie and decompress a little."

"Sounds perfect, gorgeous. What can I bring?"

"Just you, baby. What do you like on your pizza?"

"Anything but anchovies and jalapenos."

"7:00?"

"I'll be there."

13

*C*oco had gone home after the meeting, checked and handled a few emails, then changed into a pair of comfortable black leggings, a light pink floaty sleeveless tunic top and some black and pink flip flops. She had also changed to her black and pink purse, because in her heart, she was intuitively a matchy-matchy girly girl, and that made her laugh.

She had also made a few notes on her tablet about the afternoon's meeting, things she wanted to review with Josh the next time she talked to him. Then she had cleaned up her breakfast and lunch dishes and headed out to see Chase.

Coco pulled into Chase's driveway just before 7:00 PM and now, sitting in his driveway, she was edgy, having trouble getting a handle on her breathing. She was excited at the thought of getting her lips on him again, no doubt, but she was almost more excited by the thought of just talking to him, hearing about his week, dragging more childhood memories out of him. Chase was the first man she had met in years that stimulated her mind as well as her libido. The first one that she felt really at ease with – felt she could just be herself with, that she could skip the pretense with. It was a gift he gave her every time they were together and he didn't even know it.

A sudden movement by the front door caught Coco's eye, and she saw that Chase had come outside and was standing on the porch watching her. He was shirtless, wearing only a pair of sweatpants, his hair wet from a recent shower, or a swim in the ocean. His chest and abs were so well defined, and that tattoo was still so damned sexy, her breath caught in her lungs for just a few seconds, and her mouth began to water. She couldn't wait to run her fingers through that 'just right' amount of dark blond hair on his chest, and lick that tattoo just a little more. And then she noticed the outline of the erection that his sweat pants couldn't hide, and she just about drooled on herself.

Chase stepped off the porch and walked to Coco's car, opened the car door and offered her his hand to help her out. She grabbed her purse off the passenger seat as she climbed out, and was immediately wrapped in a tight embrace that made her drop her purse to the ground – so that she could get her hands on as much of Chase as possible. Their lips found each other, their tongues danced against each other, his notable erection pressed tight against her belly. Things were about to escalate.

"Coco, one of these days, I'm going to lay you out right here in the front yard and make you scream my name."

"But not today?"

"No, not today. Are you starving?"

"Not for food, gorgeous, but I'm very hungry for you. Let's go inside and see what we can find to eat."

He kind of growled at her, picked up her purse off the ground and pulled her into the house. They barely got the front door closed before Chase was pulling Coco's top off, unhooking her bra and dropping everything to the floor. He pushed her up against the wall and grabbed at her breasts, thumbing her nipples while his mouth attacked hers. And Coco was right there with him, her hands reaching for and finding his steel hard cock through his sweatpants. Their moans and shallow breaths combined into a duet of pleasure and increasing need.

As they continued to pant and rub against each other, Chase said "I had trouble paying attention during the meeting today. I kept imagining you naked, tied to the conference table, screaming my name as I ploughed into you over and over again."

"I saw you start to sweat, and for a few minutes, I actually thought you might be sick. And then you glared at me and I knew you were very healthy. I almost burned up from the heat of that stare."

"Future meetings could be difficult."

"Future anything could be difficult if I can't put my hands on you when I want to. I was eating a banana last night and I could see your face in my mind and feel your hands on me, feel you pinching my nipples and my clit. Half way through the banana, I realized my other hand was rubbing my clit. I kept eating at the banana and rubbing my clit and seeing you in my mind and feeling your hot breath on my body. Before I knew it, I was right on the edge – of the chair! And then I fell OFF the chair! And still I continued to rub and nibble and swallow until it was all too much. I screamed your name when I came and almost choked on the banana."

"No shit??"

"No shit, gorgeous. I used to hate bananas, but now I think I fucking love them!! But the banana was a sad substitute for your 2XL cock. So let me put my lips on the real thing and show you just how glad I am to see you."

Chase growled again and picked Coco up, carried her to his king size bed and laid her down in the center. She had kicked off her shoes in the hallway, and he climbed on the bed and started pulling off her leggings, thrilled to death that she had skipped the sexy panties for the evening.

Chase crawled onto the bed next to Coco and leered at her naked body. He said "I'm thinking of a number between 1 and 100. Can you guess what it is?"

"69?!?!?"

"You should really stop reading my mind, baby – it's a dirty, dangerous place! I know we haven't tried this before and our height differences might get in the way a little bit, but I'm dying to try. Are you up for it?"

"Bring it on, stud, bring it on!"

Chase pulled off his sweat pants and flung them across the bedroom, growling again as his eyes came back to Coco's naked body. Neither of them had attempted this position for years, and it took a few tries to get it right, but when they did, it was a money shot. Chase was lying in the middle of the bed on his right side. Coco had flipped herself around so that she was also lying on her right side with her feet at the top of the bed, and her head – specifically her mouth – directly opposite Chase's engorging cock.

She couldn't resist taking a little lick – since it was right there – and she could hear Chase moan a little. Memories of previous attempts at this position in years past were strong but the mechanics of their positions that evening almost needed a diagram. Coco had full use of her left arm and hand, but her right arm ended up under his thigh and all she could do was grab Chase's ass and hang on. He pulled Coco's left leg over his chest and pinned it with his left arm. He maneuvered her right leg under his right shoulder, giving him full use of both hands. Coco was wide open and looking like a tasty treat.

"You start, Coco, I'll catch up."

"Whatever you say, gorgeous. And if you get me all flustered with that sinful tongue of yours and I stop taking care of you, you just slap my ass a few times to get my attention, and I'll get right back to work."

"Like this, baby?" And a loud smack echoed off the bedroom walls, followed by a sting on her ass that went straight to her core.

"Oh, yeah! Just like that, gorgeous. I think I just came a little!"

"Oh baby, you're all juicy and ready for me. Whoever comes first, loses, okay?"

"Well, when I come all over your tongue and lose this race, you can just lay back and let me finish you off at a leisurely pace! Just like this." And she licked at the stream of come starting to run down Chase's cock, catching it all, not wanting to miss a drop.

Coco was in the moment immediately, taking the head of his cock inside her mouth, licking it, sucking it, humming against it, hearing Chase moaning loud, gifting her with another little stream of come.

"Oh, baby, I'm going to have to make you pay for that." And Chase started licking into Coco, flicking her clit with the tip of his tongue, adjusting her left leg across his chest to get the perfect access to Coco's goodies. Chase could feel Coco sucking at his dick, hear her moan against it, feel her reach up from behind and start palming his testicle. The intense pleasure she gave him only served to heighten his attention to her, and he was determined to make sure that she came first. He alternated between the lips of her pussy and her clit. His teeth edged her swollen clit, his demon tongue speared into her over and over, licking up the river of juice running out of her cunt. But neither of them could get just the right angle to finish the other one off.

It was finally all too obvious that their current position wasn't quite good enough for the best access. Chase rolled over onto his back, pulling Coco's legs with him as he moved. And she, not wanting to lose him for a second, rolled with him so that she ended up on her knees straddling him with her pussy in his face, and his cock still in her mouth. And the heat escalated. And the moans got louder. And the tongues and lips got more insistent. And the juices flowed faster. And Coco got caught up in her own orgasm closing in on her, and she stopped everything she was doing. And Chase slapped her ass twice, hard, and got her attention.

She had him back in her mouth with a loud moan in an instant, balancing herself on her left arm so that she could play with Chase's testicle with her right hand. Chase's assault on her pussy was relentless – licking, sucking, biting her clit, spearing deep into her cunt –and Coco could barely breathe from the pleasure she couldn't escape on one end and the huge cock she was trying to swallow on the other end.

Coco held out as long as she could but her orgasm finally hit her like a tidal wave, rolling out in all directions. Her scream passed through her lips, up and down the length of Chase's cock, and he came right after. In her compromised position, and still in the throes of her own orgasm, trying to swallow everything Chase had to give her was difficult, like trying to drink a glass of water upside down, but she managed to handle it all, and lick him clean as she finally let his cock slide out of her mouth.

Coco untangled her legs and fell to her left side, ending up next to Chase's hips, gasping for air, trying to breathe the last of her orgasm out of her body. Chase was sucking in so much air, he started to get a little dizzy. It was good that they were both lying down!

"Fuck, Coco, that was as good a hummer as I've had in years! You never disappoint, baby. But you came first so I win!!"

She laughed a little and asked "And what is the prize for winning this game tonight?"

"I get to feed you pizza and wine, and watch a bad movie with you, and then take you skinny dipping in the waves when it gets dark."

"Sounds like we both win, gorgeous."

Chase reached for the phone on the bedside table, called his favorite pizza place and ordered a large pizza that would go perfectly with the bottles of Moscato he already had chilling in the wine fridge. He pulled Coco off the bed and pulled his sweat pants back on. He tugged one of his tee shirts over Coco's head and dragged her to the kitchen, where they sat at the bar and ate a salad he'd made and drank most of their first bottle of wine.

They talked about all the things they'd accomplished during the week, bits of conversation separated by long silences when they let their fingertips touch each other, let their lips caress each other, and stared into each other's eyes. In those silent moments, they were in perfect harmony, like they were meant to be together.

They were just leaning into each other for another kiss when the doorbell rang, making them both jump. Chase grabbed his wallet and headed for the door – Coco stayed out of sight, not wanting to frighten the pizza delivery boy. When the front door closed again, Chase pointed at one of the cabinets over Coco's head and said "Plates up there. Napkins in the drawer next to you. Pizza Nirvana right here in my hands, baby. You will love this pizza."

"It smells incredible, and I'm going to eat so much, I'll have to run 10 miles a day for the next week to get the grease weight back off again. I have a feeling it's going to be worth every mile."

For the next hour, Chase and Coco sat at the bar and ate pizza, drank wine and nibbled on each other. Chase couldn't resist grabbing Coco's greasy, sauce covered fingers, sucking and licking them clean – a feeling that went straight to her pussy. And Chase couldn't seem to keep the sauce from his own pizza slices from covering his lips and chin. Coco felt compelled to pull him to her and lick his face clean, sneaking in a deep, tongue filled kiss each time – hitting right at her pussy and his cock. After the third time, she started to think he was doing it intentionally, but she didn't want him to stop so she didn't say anything.

They barely talked at all, too consumed with the delicious pizza and the silent, licking contact. But there was an impromptu giggle now and then from one or the other of them, thinking of something they had done, each wondering where the other had been all these years, amazed that they had found each other again. And that would lead to another kiss. This was the advantage of pizza at home – they certainly would not have been able to behave this way if they'd gone to the pizza parlor to eat. Which would have made the pizza so much less enjoyable.

Eventually they were both so painfully full that the previous, all-consuming passion had eased considerably, so they took their wine glasses and the last of the second bottle of wine to the family room, where they had a lively discussion about which really bad movie they were going to watch. Chase, considering himself a bad movie purist, held out for what he wanted and Coco finally agreed to the original 'Godzilla' movie, in Japanese, with English subtitles. Chase was expecting that Coco would understand at least some of the Japanese, since she had lived there for a year, but Coco assured him that unless someone in the movie asked where to find a bathroom, or used the few Japanese swear words she knew, she would be tied to the English subtext as much as he was.

Movie decision made, Chase invited Coco to have a seat and settle in – which was when she actually looked around in the family room and had a questioning moment. Directly opposite Chase's own 65 inch 3-D smart TV, surround sound speakers, cable tower and wireless hookup, along with the latest gaming system, Coco found the one piece of furniture on which to sit – a huge sectional sofa with a recliner on each end and about 7 miles of wheat colored fabric in between. At least the fabric color complemented the dusky rose colored walls that were almost a little too girly for a man like Chase. He caught Coco's expression and tried to head her off at the pass – "Before you say a word, I only bought the house about 4 months ago and I just moved in the end of May. It was a short sale and as soon as I had a contractor verify that it was structurally sound, I grabbed it. I've been too busy to worry about colors or furniture or anything else, other than the bed that you seemed to enjoy the hell out of just a little while ago."

"Yes, I did enjoy the bed. But this sofa looks like it has a few years on it. How many times has it been moved?"

"Only once – from my parents' house to here. I grew up with the damned thing and when they tried to get rid of it last month, I brought it here. Some girl lost her virginity on it – a long time ago – I don't recall her name – and yes, it's been cleaned many times since then!! I swear, you should never play poker, Coco – the question was right there on your lips!"

And Coco blushed a little and laughed. Then she settled herself in the recliner on the end with the best view of the TV. Within 2 minutes she had her feet up, her glass of wine on the end table next to her, and was looking very comfortable.

Chase put his wine glass and the bottle on the coffee table in front of them and seated himself next to Coco, stretching his long legs and propping his feet up on the coffee table. He took her hand in his, intertwining their fingers, and started the movie. The first 30 minutes, they drank wine and picked at each other about the movie choice, and laughed at the really bad acting and special effects. Thirty minutes after that, the wine bottle was empty, and their wine glasses were almost empty as well. And Chase began to yawn.

Coco suggested that she should leave so that he could go to bed, but he wanted no part of that. One more big yawn, and Coco offered another suggestion. "Chase, baby, you've had a really hard week, and you're not as young as you used to be. Put your head here in my lap and stretch out."

"No, I'll fall asleep."

"So fall asleep, gorgeous. I'm not going anywhere. Pull that throw over you and close your eyes. If you fall asleep for a little bit, you're not going to miss anything. I'm sure you've seen this movie a hundred times."

"Maybe two hundred times. Okay, I'll lie down but if I should happen to fall asleep, don't let me sleep long."

"I promise. I might even take a little nap myself. I'm not as young as I used to be either."

Chase smiled and placed a quick kiss on her lips, then stretched out on the sofa with his head in Coco's lap, covered with the soft cream colored throw. Two minutes later, he was snoring quietly. She ran her left hand gently through his hair a few times, and then placed that same hand on his shoulder, caressing his bare skin with her thumb. Satisfied that he was asleep, Coco reached up and turned off the table lamp next to her. She turned down the volume on the TV with the remote Chase had given her, turned off the movie and put on her favorite late night conservative talk show, then she stretched out in the recliner and closed her own eyes.

Coco stirred a little a few hours later when Chase slipped over onto his back in his sleep, his head still in her lap, but she rested her hand on his chest and went right back to sleep. A few hours after that, she woke again to something new. Chase had turned again, this time facing the back of the sofa. His head was still resting in her lap, his free right arm was over his head, and his hand was gently squeezing her breast in his sleep. Except that he wasn't completely asleep any more. As they both became more fully awake and Chase realized what his hand was doing, he started to laugh a little and so did Coco. But he didn't move his hand and he didn't stop squeezing.

"Even in your sleep, Mr. Buckingham?"

"Even in my sleep, Miss Brighton. I was dreaming about your breasts – touching them, tasting them, biting your nipples a little – and then I started to wake up and there they were. And my hand was right there. It was such a nice way to wake up."

"For both of us."

"How about a little skinny dipping in the ocean and then I'll feed you again."

"It's 3:30 in the morning, gorgeous."

"I know. That's the perfect time. The water is really warm right now, and it's dark enough that there won't be any prying eyes. Come on, it'll be fun."

"Okay, but I don't want to go out too deep. I can swim but not so well in the dark."

"Don't worry, baby, I'll protect you."

14

Chase pulled himself up off the sofa and then pulled Coco up with him. They both did a little stretching to ease the back pains people their age got after sleeping in the wrong place or in the wrong position. "Chase, baby, how in the world do you live with this sofa? Four hours on the damned thing and I'm in need of a really good physical therapist!"

"I think I can work out your muscle aches later, baby." And he laughed and did a few extra stretches of his own.

Once the worst of the stiffness was gone, Chase pulled Coco to him for a passionate, lip biting kiss, and then dragged her out the back door and down to the beach. Chase threw off his sweat pants on their way out the back door, but allowed Coco to keep her tee shirt on – temporarily. They didn't have far to walk to reach the waves rolling onto the shore because the tide was almost in. The water was indeed very warm, even at that hour of the morning, but Coco still squealed quietly when Chase pulled off her tee shirt, threw it in the sand, and pulled her naked into the shallows.

He pulled her in a little deeper, but when the water was up to her thighs, and she was obviously getting very nervous, he stopped and pulled her in for another kiss. Minutes later Chase picked Coco up in his arms and started walking deeper into the waves, and she clung so tightly to his neck that he didn't think he'd ever pry her loose, so he stopped where he was. He looked at her with an evil look in his eyes and said "Now what did you mean when you said I'm not as young as I used to be?"

"Chase…"

And he dropped to his knees, just as a new wave rolled in, crashing over them and drenching them.

Chase laughed but Coco was not amused – "You fucking, rat bastard son of a bitch…" And then she really got rocking with the curses, even the Japanese ones – which sounded so playful in her hushed, whispered voice.

In the interest of shutting her up, he descended on her with his magic lips and tongue, covering her mouth completely and making her moan into his mouth. When they finally came up for air, Coco was no longer cursing at Chase but she did speak very quietly to him – "Just wait, gorgeous, some day when you least expect it, I'm going to get my paybacks, and you'll remember this moment and take it like a man."

"The expression on your face just before we went under was worth a whole lot, baby. Whatever you come up with as punishment, I'll be a good sport about it." They stayed in the shallows for a few more minutes, just holding each other, but then all the naked touching, the kissing and the sudden drenching in the waves stirred their passion and they both decided it was time to go back inside.

They picked up Coco's tee shirt along the way and headed for the house, but before they went inside, Chase insisted that they needed to shower the sand off. "Coco, baby, you have a lot of sand on you and we need to get that off. I know the water is a little cold but you need to let me do this. Spread your ass cheeks and let me get that sand out of all your nooks and crannies before it starts to chafe."

"No, Chase, the water's too cold, I'll be fine."

"No, Coco, you won't be fine. Now get over here and let me clean all that sand off."

Just as he was pulling her under the outdoor shower, they heard the next door neighbor and his dog, heading for their very early morning walk down the beach. "Buckingham, I can hear you up there. Ma'am, I know we don't know each other, but he's right about the sand. You really need to get it all off, or you'll be really uncomfortable in a little while. You're a good for nothing pervert, Buckingham, but I'm glad you're having a good time tonight. I think this woman is good for you."

"Walk away, Johnson, walk away." And the neighbors laughed at each other.

"Chase, I grew up here, I know what to do with sand up my ass."

"Coco..."

Not wanting a repeat of her previous interaction with Chase's neighbor, she yelled "Thanks for your words of wisdom, Mr. Johnson." and dragged herself under the lukewarm water of the shower to let Chase remove the sand that was already starting to chafe.

Fifteen minutes later, they were back inside the house, dried off and sand free, sharing the bed that she liked so very much. The passion was on simmer, the kisses light and languid, the caresses gentle – there was no rush, there were no heights to scale, just a man and a woman enjoying each other's naked company.

"I don't know what it is about you, Coco, I don't know how you do the things you do to me. The other night on the phone, you said you were happy lately. Because of me?"

"Yes. Because of you. I can't really explain it, but I feel like I can be myself around you. After 30 years of clawing my way up the corporate ladder, of having to be 'on' all the time, you make me feel like I can relax. That's a gift I'll always treasure, gorgeous. I would miss you very much if you weren't around anymore."

"You make me happy, too, baby. If you were to ask Gigi and Robert, they would tell you I haven't been happy for a long time, I was just going through the motions, because there was something missing from my life, and I couldn't put a name on that thing that was missing. But I guess they both knew what I needed, maybe what you needed as well. I almost didn't go to Gigi and Robert's wedding. I'd had a shitty day and the last thing in the world I wanted to do that night was get dressed up and pretend to enjoy myself for their benefit. I was going to stay for 1 hour, say goodbye, and come back here with a six-pack and a bottle of Jack Daniels and get drunk. And then I found my table, and I found you there, and the hour came and went and I couldn't drag myself away. I had to keep you talking, keep you touching me, keep you looking at me like I was someone important, someone you wanted to know. I know it's only been a few weeks, but I'd be completely miserable if you weren't around anymore."

"Don't ever let anyone make you feel like you're not important, Chase, because you ARE important – to me. You're a very special person, don't ever forget that."

"You make me feel important, Coco – only you."

"We sound like we were sad, pathetic creatures before Mr. and Mrs. Matchmaker got their hooks into us."

"I was sad and pathetic, Coco."

"I was too, Chase. I don't want to be sad and pathetic anymore."

They spent a few minutes gazing into each other's eyes in the low light of the bedroom, and then Coco leaned up and kissed Chase – sweetly at first and then more insistently. And Chase responded to that kiss, and the passion torch blazed again. Their breathing became ragged, tongues tangled with each other for ultimate domination of the one mouth that had formed from their two mouths. Their hands reached for and stroked their favorite parts of each other's bodies, and the world around them fell away, leaving only the two of them, moaning with desire, clutching each other, hanging on for dear life.

Chase broke the kiss, rolled to his back, and pulled Coco with him. When they settled, she was straddling him, his cock straining to get where it wanted to be most. She was staring down at him with such suffocating desire in her eyes, he struggled to breathe.

In a whispered voice, Chase said "Take me, Coco. I want to watch my cock disappear into your juicy pussy. I want to watch the wonder in your eyes as you push me deeper and deeper into your cunt, feel your heat the entire length of my cock. Ride me, baby, I need to feel you and see you and be consumed by you."

"You really are good at the dirty talk, gorgeous, and you're good at so many other things as well. But this is one thing I'm really good at. I'm going to ride your cock like you've never been ridden before, until there's nothing left of either of us except a big puddle of goo and gasping breath."

One last kiss and then Coco balanced herself with a hand on Chase's chest and reached for his cock with the other hand. That cock was like a thick steel rod in her hand as she guided him to her pussy. She coated him with the juice that was almost streaming out of her, rubbing the head around her clit, her body responding with shivers up and down her spine. She moved up enough on her knees to get the head of Chase's cock started tunneling in, and then she sat up straight and let gravity do its work. Chase reached up with his big man hands and cupped her breasts. His thumbs and forefingers toyed with her nipples, getting that tightening, budding reaction he'd come to expect from his touch, hearing Coco moan from the pleasure he gave her.

Before Coco could force herself all the way down on Chase's cock, he got a little impatient, grabbed her hips and pulled her the rest of the way down. At least he was able to get her most of the way down, but there was still a little of his cock waiting outside her pussy and feeling a little unloved. But Coco was determined to make room for Chase's whole cock, and she'd done this a time or two in the past also, although never with anyone as big as Chase. She shifted her hips to change up the angle, put her hands around Chase's waist, and pulled hard. At the same time, Chase reached up and thumbed her clit, making her shudder, making more juice.

Their combined efforts made enough room for the rest of Chase's cock to slide deep inside Coco's pussy, dragging a loud moan from the back of her throat, and the extra come was what she would need for the ride. Neither one moved for a minute, enjoying the feel of each other, gathering themselves for the sensations that were about to overwhelm them. And then she moved.

Coco's hands were back on Chase's chest, his hands stayed on her hips. "Here we go, gorgeous, let's ride!"

"You drive, baby, I'll try not to help unless you need me." She nodded and pulled up a few inches, paused and then slammed back down again. Another pause, then she pulled up a little farther and then slammed back down again. The third time, she pulled all the way up, so that only the head of Chase's so hard cock was still inside, and with a mighty push, she took him completely again. Coco now had a feel for the distance she could move up and down and her pace quickened, surprising Chase with her speed, her agility and the tightness of her vaginal muscles.

Coco was close now, Chase was close as well. He couldn't help himself now, and he started pounding up into her every time she slammed down against him. The only sounds were the constant slap of Coco's ass against Chase's hips, and the groaning, panting breaths they gulped in when they could. Coco's fingers dug into his pecs as she struggled to balance herself against their strokes. And then they paused for a quiet conversation.

"Coco, baby, you're killing me. You are so tight and every move you make squeezes my cock tighter. I can't hold on much longer."

"Oh gorgeous, your cock fills me so full, I can barely think. You must have the longest, thickest cock in the world! This angle is hitting a sweet spot in my pussy I didn't know I had. Every stroke makes me feel like the top of my head is going to blow right off. I can't hold off any longer, I have to come but I just can't get there. Please help me!" She started to move again, setting a punishing pace, creating the friction she needed, however she could. And as he pummeled into her, matching her strokes, he reached up again and attacked her clit with both thumbs as he helped pull her down on top of him. She threw her head back and a strangled scream escaped her throat as she came. He barely recognized her screaming his name, and he screamed hers as he came moments later. They continued to pump at each other for another minute, slowing gradually, until the after-effects of their simultaneous orgasms began to subside. She finally fell on Chase's chest with a moan and a quiet "Oh, fuck!"

And Chase responded "Yeah, baby, that may have been the best yet."

They finally separated and Coco settled next to Chase, her head in the hollow of his shoulder, her left hand on his chest, her left leg slung across his. And without another word, they were both asleep, recovering from lovemaking that was more than just two bodies coming together but two minds, and maybe two hearts as well.

15

*C*oco woke up and found herself alone in Chase's bed. A quick look at the clock said she'd slept way longer than usual, even for a Saturday morning. Chase also had the bad sense to buy a house with a master bedroom facing east – into the morning Myrtle Beach sun – but he'd made a much better choice of window coverings than she had. The sunlight was filtering through the edges of the curtains at the window but it wasn't the blinding light she was now used to getting in her own bedroom.

As she became more awake, she heard sounds from outside the bedroom, from the direction of the kitchen, and was suddenly very hungry. She heard sudden footsteps coming closer, then Chase popped his head into the bedroom. "Good morning, sleepy head. I made breakfast, come get it while it's hot."

"You made breakfast? You cook?"

"Only breakfast, baby, it's the only thing I'm good at, but I really rock at breakfast. So hurry up. You have three minutes to get to the kitchen, and then I eat it all."

"You can cook?"

"Now, baby!"

She grabbed one of Chase's tee shirts off the bedroom floor and headed for the bathroom. Three minutes later she was in the kitchen, sitting in front of the best looking omelet she'd ever seen. There was little conversation at the kitchen table, they were both starved and Chase really did rock at breakfast. But eventually they were both full, awake and ready to chat.

"So, Coco, what do you have going on this weekend? Any big plans?"

"Only one, but I'm saving that for tomorrow. So today, I should be at home cleaning, maybe doing some batch cooking, getting the fridge and freezer stocked for the next few weeks."

"That doesn't sound like any fun. I have a support group meeting down on Pawley's tonight that will probably go pretty late, so I thought maybe we could go for a ride this morning."

"A ride??" And she wiggled her eyebrows at him.

"Not that kind of ride! Good lord, woman, you're sex crazed! Although I would love to do that again sometime – soon. But no, I meant on my bike. I have a Harley Electra Glide and an extra helmet you can wear. And I'll give you a sweatshirt to put on so that you don't get too cold while we're riding."

"You can cook – AND you ride a Harley!?!? I've fallen into a little bit of heaven!"

"Does that mean you like bikers, baby?"

"I AM a biker, gorgeous. At least I used to be."

"You? On a bike? We ARE talking motorcycle here, yes?"

"Why is that such an unbelievable idea? Yes, I had a bike when I lived in Phoenix. A 2005 Honda Shadow Spirit. A friend found it and fixed it up for me. I had it for two years, but I decided to sell it back to my friend when I moved back here. I haven't decided if I want another one."

"I think I need proof on this one, baby, I just can't see you riding down the highway with the wind blowing through your hair and bugs in your teeth!!" And he came to stand next to her with his arms around her, and gave her a sexy, nibbly little kiss.

"First, gorgeous, I can't believe you think I'd lie about this. Second, I have a full screen helmet so no bugs in my teeth. And third, I have a picture at home of me in my leathers standing next to my bike outside a bar in San Diego. That was a wild trip."

"You? In leathers? Oh, fuck, I gotta see this picture."

"Come over tomorrow and maybe I'll let you see it. I still have my leathers, maybe I'll let you see those too."

"I'm about to have a heart attack just thinking about this. My tomorrow just got a lot more interesting! But in the meantime, go put some clothes on and we'll take a little ride."

"I need a shower!"

"Later! Ride now, shower after! Go!"

"Bossy SOB!" And a smack on her ass got her moving toward the bedroom to get dressed.

Two hours later, they were back from their ride up Hwy 17 to Little River and back, with a stop at one of Chase's favorite bars to see friends and have a quick beer. Coco decided against taking a shower at Chase's house, because her clothes, which she had put on the day before, were starting to feel a little over-worn. And GROSS!

Chase tried to talk her into staying a little longer, but she decided if she didn't leave right then, she'd never leave, and Chase wouldn't get to his group session that night.

"Come on, baby, stay a little while. I promise I'll make it worth your while."

And he started kissing his way from her lips, down her throat, back up her neck to her ear, licking and nipping along the way. And she was getting all tingly – and wet! And stubborn! She was getting very stubborn.

"Chase, as much as I'd like to stay, one of us has to be responsible and I guess that's going to be me. I don't want you going all the way down to Pawley's tonight as tired as you look right now. So I'm going to leave and I want you to take a nap so that you don't fall asleep on your support group mates, or worse, get into an accident coming home. Now give me one more kiss, and a little pussy grope, maybe a boob squeeze, just so I know you care, and then I'm out of here."

"Oh, baby, who's being bossy now?"

And he pushed her up against the wall by the front door, and started to inhale her lips and tongue, while one hand reached for a breast, and the other hand slid down for a little pussy love. When Coco's eyes started to cross, and she was panting like a marathon runner, she pushed Chase away and said "I gotta go, gorgeous. Give me a call tomorrow when you wake up, I'll make you lunch and show you another surprise."

"What? What surprise?"

"I gotta go!!" And she was out the door with him running after her.

Coco climbed into her car and headed down the street while Chase stood in the driveway yelling "What surprise?!?"

After the shower she'd been looking forward to for hours, Coco spent the afternoon and early evening batch cooking mass quantities of food – a large pan of turkey lasagna, two dozen chicken breasts, and a sinfully low-fat meatloaf that didn't taste low-fat. While the lasagna and the meatloaf were in the oven, she cleaned up that mess, and then started prepping the chicken breasts to go in the oven next.

With every dish she cooked, she thought of Chase, what meals she would feed him from the dishes she was making, how his lips felt against her skin, how his hands felt caressing her breasts and her pussy and her ass. She was grateful that by the end of the evening, she hadn't burned anything she was cooking!

But she was so hot by the time she was done cooking and the kitchen was cleaned up, that she took a cold shower – and pulled one of her "special" books off the bedroom bookshelf and read for awhile – and then took another cold shower.

At midnight, she realized she was picturing Chase and herself as the hero and heroine of her erotic romance novel, and probably wouldn't get much sleep that night. At 12:30, she got a text from Chase that he was back home from his group meeting – safe and sound. She texted a quick message back to him – "Glad you're home safe, gorgeous. Get some sleep and call me when you get up in the morning. SWAK."

And he texted back "SWAK??"

"Sealed with a kiss, lovey. Get some sleep."

"SWAK right back at you, baby. Sleep well." And she did.

Coco was up at 8:30 Sunday morning, feeling refreshed, looking forward to the day. She took a quick run around the neighborhood and then came home and did 30 minutes of yoga to stretch herself out, which she desperately needed. Another 30 minutes and she had showered and eaten breakfast. She was just putting her breakfast dishes in the dishwasher when her aunt called.

"Coco, honey, are you ready for Thursday? Do you need any help? I could send a few of the grandkids over to do the hard work."

"No, Aunt Monica, I got this covered. I washed that car so many times growing up, it's a wonder there's still paint left on it. I think I can handle one more time."

"Well, your Uncle Bob had it clear coated again right before you came home so it should be just fine. I swear, that man and his cars – and he protected your dad's car – your car – just like he does all of his own. You know it means so much to us that you came back home, it makes losing your mom and dad a tiny bit easier to take."

"I know, Aunt Monica, I feel the same way about having all of you around me. And yes, I'm ready for Thursday. I might actually have someone riding in the car with me. I just haven't asked him yet."

"Him? So the rumors are true!"

"What rumors?"

"That you've been seen around town the last few weeks with a very good looking man. Are you bringing him to the picnic after the parade on Thursday?"

"Someone must be stalking me, Aunt Mon, because we haven't really been around town. Hmmm? And I don't know if he's going to be there, I haven't asked him yet!"

And she laughed at her aunt's intrusive, but loving, nature. They talked for a few more minutes, making plans for their Independence Day celebration, and then Coco hung up the phone and headed out to the garage – she had a chore to do that would spark many happy memories.

Coco's parents had gotten married in 1955, just as Coco's dad was starting what would become the family business with his fellow pharmacist and new brother-in-law, Bob. Sugar Grove Drugs was an instant success because it filled a need in their little neighborhood. There wasn't another pharmacy for miles around, and the new owners were hometown boys recently back from the Korean war. One of the first things Coco's dad bought after the business got going was a 1957 Chevy Bel Air convertible, mint green with cream colored upholstery. Her dad had treated that car like a priceless gem for the rest of his life, and his daughter had learned to love it as well. That same '57 Chevy was sitting in Coco's garage, and her big chore for the day was to pull it into the driveway, wash and wax it, prepping and priming until it sparkled like it was brand new. It would take several hours, but when she was done, it would be a spectacular sight for anyone with an appreciation for classic cars. Maybe even Chase would be impressed.

Coco had just pulled the car out of the garage into the driveway, and she was imagining herself and Chase riding down the road with the top down, enjoying a beautiful summer day in the country. Her cell phone ringing brought her back to reality. And then she realized it was Chase calling, and she smiled. When she answered the phone, she gave Chase a breathy "Hi, gorgeous."

And he responded with a low, lusty "Good morning, baby, how are you today? Did you sleep well last night?"

"I slept very well last night, and I dreamed of you."

"More Jell-O?"

"No Jell-O. But lots of hot, sweaty, kinky sex. Mmmm. You were spectacular, gorgeous."

"So now I'm getting competition from myself?? Will it be hard to live up to?"

"No, gorgeous, you always bring your A game."

And he laughed – and then growled again. "Maybe we should take this conversation in another direction for a little while, baby, or I won't be able to get behind the wheel to get to you!"

"Okay, so I have a different kind of proposition for you."

"And what's that, baby."

"You come here and help me with something, and I'll provide lunch and maybe a shower after."

"You've piqued my curiosity. What's the 'something'?"

"You have to come here to find out. I don't want to ruin the surprise. And bring an extra pair of shorts and a tee shirt that you don't mind getting wet."

"Lunch and a wet surprise? And a picture of you in leathers with a motorcycle. And maybe the actual leathers as well. This all sounds like something I can't afford to miss. I'm on my way, baby!" And he was off the phone. And Coco started prepping to wash and wax her pride and joy, thinking about hot, sweaty, kinky sex with Chase.

Coco had just started washing the car, starting with the convertible top and some special cleaner her dad had always used, when Chase pulled up at the curb in front of her house. He got out of his Jeep and whistled long and loud, staring at the car. "Holy shit, Coco, you have a '57?!?!? How long have you had this? Where did you get it? It's in incredible shape."

"Take a deep breath there, counselor. Yes, I have a '57. My dad bought it new in the Spring of 1958, and it's never left the family. Mom always said dad took better care of this car than he did her. And then he'd grab her ass and she'd laugh. He did take really good care of the car, though. After they were gone, I didn't think I could handle having it, so my Uncle Bob agreed to watch over it until I was ready. He's got a ton of classic cars but he always looked at this one like it was special."

And she paused for a minute while a sad memory quickly passed by. And then she smiled again. "Anyway, when I moved home, he convinced me that I needed to take the car back. He brought it over two months ago and parked it in the garage for me. He's been coming over every week and starting it up, driving it around the block a few times, making sure it would be ready when I was. And I am."

"Oh, Coco, I'm glad you're ready. This car is beautiful, it needs a beautiful woman driving it now and then. So I take it you're going to wash and wax it, and maybe take it for a spin around the block?"

"Yes, I'm washing and waxing it today, but the spin around the block doesn't come until Thursday."

"And what's so special about Thursday?"

"It's Independence Day, Chase. You know, the 4th of July?"

"Oh, right, I forgot!"

"Really?"

"Oh hell no, that's one holiday that I hold very dear."

"So I'm guessing you and your parents have big plans that day. Some family celebration or something?"

"No, this year we don't. My parents are going to Savannah on Wednesday to visit friends for the holiday, and I'm staying home. I thought a long, quiet weekend would be just what I need. What kind of plans do you have for the holiday?"

"Funny you should ask. The old neighborhood has always celebrated Independence Day with a parade, a tribute to our active duty and retired military, and all the other veterans in the area. Then my extended family always has a picnic at my Uncle Bob and Aunt Monica's house. Then of course, there will be fireworks at the Cherry Grove Pier after dark. I was wondering if you might be available and maybe interested in riding in this car in the parade with me and then spending a little time at the picnic. Maybe watch a few fireworks that night? We don't have to stay long, and we can skip the fireworks, but my aunt and uncle are interested in meeting you. It seems we're the subject of family gossip lately and they require an audience with you – just to check you out a little."

"So, a ride in the parade in this incredible car, and then some family picnic time so your family can grill me a little about my intentions. And fireworks? Hmmm. I think I could get into that. After putting in our appearance at the picnic, then what did you have in mind?"

"I thought maybe we could take the car out on the highway, head south on 17 and see where we end up. This car has a really big back seat. I caught my mom and dad back there one night in the garage when I was little. They were naked and loud, and the unlit cigarette in my hand was suddenly much less interesting than hiding and watching them. That was the first time I ever saw a penis – and in retrospect, a pretty spectacular one at that! Not to mention, a little scary!"

"Oh my god!! How old were you??"

"I was probably 12 or 13 at the time. I don't think they knew I was there, but if they did, they never said anything. And it certainly didn't stop them from doing what they were doing. I had the sex talk with my mom not long after that, and it was very enlightening. She didn't just talk about the mechanics of sex, although we did discuss that at length, with diagrams and pictures and everything."

"Holy Fuck!! Are you kidding?"

"No, I am not kidding. But like I said, she didn't just explain the body parts and how they fit together. She talked about the emotional and psychological aspects. She made it sound like so much fun – but such a big responsibility – that I really thought long and hard before I had sex for the first time. And when I finally did, I couldn't wait to run home and tell her all about it. She was very cool."

Seeing Chase's shocked look, Coco was quick to apologize – "Oh, crap, that was too much information, wasn't it? I'm sorry Chase, you're just so easy to talk to, things sort of fall out of my mouth."

"No problem, baby, I'm just remembering my sex talk with my dad. I thought he was making things up. And then we finally had 'the class' at the academy in Columbia and I found out he hadn't been lying at all. And then Debbie McIntyre showed me how it all really worked."

"What class? Oh, the sex education class? That was not fun at all, our phys ed teacher taught our class and we ALL thought she was lying about some things. Now who's Debbie McIntyre?"

Chase laughed and avoided the whole conversation about his first sexual conquest by grabbing a bucket and a big sponge, and heading to the back of the car to start washing. Ninety minutes later, the car was washed, waxed, and put back in the garage, and Chase and Coco were soaked – too many hose fights and "sponge baths" along the way.

16

"So are you ready for lunch, gorgeous?" Chase and Coco were standing on the front porch, wrapped in each other's wet arms, getting a little more handsy with each other than she thought the neighborhood would tolerate.

"You now, lunch later, baby. Let's take this inside so I can really get my hands on you." And he bit her lip just a little and squeezed her ass cheeks playfully as he opened the front door and pushed her inside, away from prying eyes.

Coco found herself pushed up against the living room wall just inside the front door, hands held in place above her head, smothered by Chase's kiss. His passion was so sudden and so intense, she was swept away by it. Chase finally broke the kiss, and stared into Coco's eyes for timeless minutes, then started pulling on her tee shirt – he needed contact, skin to skin. They struggled with each other's wet clothes, and the struggle, the delay in continuing the kiss, only intensified the passion.

They managed to get each other's tee shirts off, and Coco's bra flew across the room in Chase's haste to get her shorts off. It seemed this driving need had been anticipated by both of them because there was no underwear beneath either pair of shorts. The kiss continued as they both kicked at the shorts trapping their ankles, the desire to be finally free of the wet material reaching epic proportions. Panting breath made them both dizzy and they knew that they needed to slow things down just a little.

Getting the last of their clothes off – the skin to skin contact – surprisingly calmed them, reduced the tension enough to let them both catch a breath.

Chase went back to nibbling on her neck, and Coco whispered "Good god, Chase, why is it always so intense with the two of us? All I have to do is see you coming toward me and I can't breathe. I can't think of anything but tearing your clothes off and putting my hands on every inch of your body. This isn't normal for me – I can't decide if it's a really good thing or a really bad thing. Do you wear one of those pheromone colognes? What is it about you that makes me so crazy?"

The nibbling stopped and they looked at each other again, eye contact so deep it seemed they were looking inside each other. "I don't know, Coco, but I feel the same way. When I see you, look into your eyes, my brain shuts off and I'm left with nothing but instinct. I get all caveman-y and I'm still not able to control it very well. If my pheromones are reacting to your pheromones, it's not anything I'm doing on purpose – I'm pretty sure that Polo isn't putting secret ingredients in my cologne."

"Damn, gorgeous, I need you to fuck me – right now. Fuck me hard and maybe we can actually have a normal conversation after!"

"Your wish is my command, baby. Do you trust me?"

Her whispered "Yes" almost set Chase on fire.

"Make me stop if it gets to be too much, Coco. Just say NO – really loud – and I'll stop." And she nodded as they blew the top off the passion scale.

Chase pulled Coco away from the wall and laughed at the wet impression of her body on the wall. He clutched her hands behind her with one of his big hands, and reached between her legs with the other hand. "You're so wet, so ready, and I'm feeling so evil. I'm going to do something I've been wanting to do with you – to you – since that first night – but I've been afraid you're too delicate."

"Chase, baby, when it comes to you and sex, I don't want to be delicate. I want everything you want to give me."

"Remember what I said – stop me if it gets too intense."

"Don't worry about me, gorgeous." And she reached over with her mouth and settled over one of his nipples. She swirled the tip of her tongue around it and then as he moaned from the pleasure, she bit down, just a little, just to see if he could handle it.

"Oh, fuck! Harder, baby, bite me again." He still had her hands behind her back and he pulled her even closer, putting his incredibly large cock against her belly so she could feel it growing even larger with every second. And she gave him that harder bite he was looking for, thinking they'd be able to see the teeth marks for a few hours. And Chase lost his control completely.

He had to practically pry Coco's mouth off his chest, and in the throes of his pleasure/pain, Chase spun Coco around, facing away from him. He still had her hands behind her back and he pushed her toward the end of the sofa. He forced her to kneel on the cushion at the end and bent her at her waist over the arm so that her head was hanging down, half way to the floor, and her curvy ass was in the air. He knelt behind her on the sofa, between her legs, still holding her hands tightly, and lined up his cock at the opening of her pussy – he could feel her body tense beneath him.

He leaned down, his chest pressed against her back, his cock sliding between her legs and nudging her clit. As Coco shivered from the nudge, Chase whispered in her ear, "I promise I won't let you fall, baby." And she took a deep breath against him and nodded her head to let him know she was okay. Chase could feel another stream of Coco's juice dribble out and coat his waiting cock.

Knowing Coco was ready for him set him off. He pulled back and slammed into her, sinking balls deep on the first thrust, making Coco cry out. He stopped moving, fearing she was frightened or in pain, but she turned her head and yelled "Don't stop! Please don't stop! Keep moving!!"

With Coco's permission to do his worst – or his best – Chase started thrusting again, using his grip on her hands to steady him and keep them connected. He slammed into her fast and hard for almost a minute, and then his pace was slow and measured for a few seconds as he leaned down and licked the line of her spine up her back, causing goose bumps to cover her body. Then he pounded into her again fast, over and over. He knew he wouldn't last and he wanted to feel Coco's orgasm squeeze his cock so he pushed his free hand between Coco and the sofa cushion and started swirling his fingers around her clit while he continued to thrust into her.

He could tell he was driving her crazy – she was making mumbling sounds that weren't words, and she started to tremble beneath his body. Coco's choked scream as she came was music to his ears, and the tight grasping sensation of her cunt around his cock took his breath away. Chase could see spots before his eyes when he came and he was unable to stop himself from falling on Coco's back, finally releasing her hands, gasping for air.

As soon as Chase could move, he sat up, and slowly pulled Coco up over the end of the sofa, fearing that a fast maneuver might make her light-headed or dizzy. He held her close in his lap, stroking her hair, massaging and caressing her shoulders and her arms and her breasts. Coco's arms hung limp at her sides, and they both continued gasping for air for several minutes, but eventually breathing returned to normal, heart rates calmed, and they felt satisfied and content. When Chase looked around Coco to see her face, he could see tears running down her cheeks, and his heart lurched.

"Coco, baby, you're crying. Please tell me you're okay, at least nod or something!"

"Oh, Chase, that was… Fuck, that was intense! That was… I don't know, it just WAS!"

"Does that mean you're okay? I'm still not sure!"

"Yes, gorgeous, I'm good – no, I'm great. Or maybe I should say I'm in the presence of greatness! You're a big ball of stud, and that was way better than the sex I dreamed about the other night. Although I'm afraid a repeat of this any time soon might just drive me back to my Celebrex, but I think it would be worth it."

"Remind me what Celebrex is for?"

"It's my arthritis miracle drug. I was able to stop taking it when I started doing yoga, but I think I might have to start again if you and I don't stop attacking each other like this. But I'm willing to risk it. I don't know what books you've been reading, gorgeous, but I'd be happy to get you some more if you're short on dirty ideas."

"That reminds me. I borrowed a book off your bedroom bookshelf the last time I was here. I read it while I was in Columbia. Baby, that's some dirty stuff you read, and I loved every word of it."

"What book did you borrow? I didn't notice any books missing."

"It was one of those 50 books, a pretty interesting concept if I do say so myself."

"You could learn a few things from that guy."

"Hell, that guy could learn a few things from me!"

"I wouldn't disagree with that, gorgeous." And they laughed quietly, but they didn't move. They were enjoying the peace and quiet of the moment.

Sometime later, neither of them sure how long they'd been together on the sofa, there was a sound Coco had heard before, that made Chase hang his head and laugh. His stomach was growling again, and he was finally ready for lunch. Coco finally got off Chase's lap and helped him up off the sofa. They shared a quiet kiss and a little laugh about what they'd just done, thinking that the 20- and 30-somethings in Coco's erotic romance novels had nothing on the two of them. It would just take Chase and Coco a little longer to recover before round 2.

There was a short bathroom break, during which Coco grabbed a pair of sweat shorts she had bought for Chase to wear around the house, and she pulled a long tee shirt over herself. When she got back to the living room, Chase was picking up all the wet clothes off the floor and she threw the shorts at him.

"Here, gorgeous, I need you to cover yourself up a little so that I can make lunch without being distracted. If you'd like to be even more helpful, you can take those wet clothes and put them in the dryer. Put the setting on permanent press and set it for 30 minutes. Then you can keep me company in the kitchen while I make lunch."

"Your wish is my command, mistress!" They both laughed and headed for the kitchen and the laundry.

Shortly after, they sat down at the dining room table and enjoyed grilled chicken Caesar salad and cheesy biscuits with a glass of wine. Their conversation had nothing to do with the landmark sex they'd just had, just casual talk about Chase's support group meeting the night before, their plans for the parade coming up on Thursday, a few more memories of holiday celebrations and family get-togethers. They took their grilled peaches and ice cream out on the deck and sat on the swing in the shade and talked about work, hobbies, life – enjoying the peaceful contentment that came after the breath stealing insanity.

When the dryer was finished and their clothes were dry again, they got dressed and took a walk around the neighborhood, past the high school where Coco had spent four formative years, stopping to chat with a few neighbors who were out working in the yard. Chase talked about leaving the Myrtle Beach school system to attend a private military academy high school in Columbia, how it took him awhile to make new friends. It wasn't until he joined the school debate team that he started getting to know himself as well as the other students, started making friends – friends who went on to military and political careers, and one crazy dude who ended up a hippie in California.

When they got back to Coco's house, Chase said "I think there's something you still owe me, Ms. Brighton."

She smiled and said "And what is that, Mr. Buckingham?"

"It seems to me there's a photo you promised to show me, and maybe something else as well."

"Oh, yes, I forgot. I'm not sure you can handle this, but follow me."

And she led him into her bedroom. She sat him on the bed and pulled a photo album off the bottom shelf of the small book case, now noticing the spot where the missing book had been. At least he had started with book 1. She hoped he'd be interested in reading book 2 and book 3 as well. It would be fun to see what moves they could copy from all of her erotic romance novels, and she was lost in thought for a moment. She finally shook her head to clear her thoughts and bring herself back to the present. She brought the photo album back to the bed, and started flipping through the pages, looking for the one photo she had promised to show Chase, but he decided he wanted to see all the pictures, from beginning to end.

As they started to review the different photos and she named other people in the pictures, and where they had been taken, she shared some very happy memories, some not quite so happy, and one that she had thought she was over. Coco tensed a little when she saw the photo, and Chase picked up on it immediately. "Who's this, Coco? Where was it taken?"

"It was taken in Phoenix, he was a friend."

"Was?"

"Yes. He died. He'd been sick and he decided he had nothing left to live for."

"I'm sorry, I didn't mean to bring back ugly memories."

"It's okay, it was quite a long time ago."

She turned the page and found the photo she'd been hunting for – her, in her leathers, on her motorcycle, outside the Coronado Hotel in San Diego.

"Fuck, Coco, when was this taken? You were HOT!!"

"Are you telling me I'm not HOT now??"

"On, no, baby, you're like a fine wine, you have improved with time – aged to perfection."

"Good save, Buckingham!" And they both laughed.

Coco told Chase to stay where he was and she disappeared into the back of her too large clothes closet. As he continued to look at random photos in the album, Chase could hear her sliding hangers on the racks, muttering to herself, until she finally exclaimed "There you are!"

Five minutes later, she walked out of her closet, wrapped in black leather – almost too tight leather pants, a snug leather vest with a plunging V neckline, and a fitted black jacket. Chase had been looking at the album, and he was still talking, without noticing that she had come out of the closet.

"Coco, you really rode that bike, didn't you? This picture of you riding down the road is... Uh... I... I... Fuuuuck..."

Mid-sentence, he had finally looked up, saw her, and lost the power of speech – and breath. It took him more than a minute to recover and Coco just stood there waiting for him to say something. Finally she broke the silence between them.

"I may have put on a few pounds since I wore this outfit last. The pants are just a little tight."

"Oh, no, baby, those pants are a perfect fit, just the way you are. Turn around for me, baby – slowly – I want to get the full view." And she did.

Breathing heavily, Chase stood up and absentmindedly dropped the photo album on the floor. His look of wonder changed in an instant to a look of such lust, it was Coco's turn to stop breathing. And they just stared at each other for several minutes – Chase in his tenting sweat pants, and Coco in her tight leathers, and they were both hopping on the passion train again.

Chase closed the distance between them, needing to touch Coco anywhere and everywhere she was encased in the sexiest black leather he'd ever seen. His fingertips went first to the edges of the V neckline of her vest – whisper soft touch from her collarbone down to the point of the V between her breasts, then back up the other side – making Coco shiver at his touch. She tried to put her hands on his chest, but he gently grasped her hands and put them back at her sides.

"Sorry, Coco, this is all for me right now. You're a Ranger's wet dream in this outfit and I need to savor this first experience – kind of desensitize myself – so that when we're riding down the road with you dressed in this again, we don't have to stop every 15 minutes so I can fuck you on the side of the road."

"You're such a sweet talker, Buckingham, you take my breath away." And she laughed – but she didn't move and she didn't try to touch him again.

Chase spent several minutes caressing Coco's arms, wrapped in the leather jacket, squeezing the soft material and her arms beneath. His devilish eyes darted from one shiny buckle to another, fingers skimmed over the metal studs of the jacket until his breathing was raspy with desire, his sweat pants tenting further with every touch.

He finally took Coco's leather jacket by the lapels and slowly slid it off her shoulders, down her arms, and then tossed it to a chair a few feet from the bed. Minus the jacket, Chase was able to see more of Coco's outrageously sexy leather vest – and the breasts that were trying to escape through that V neckline. His hands went directly to her breasts, cupping and squeezing them beneath the leather, finding her nipples hard and distended through the surprisingly soft, thin material. Every flick of his thumbs over her nipples was rewarded with a little gasp or moan from Coco, putting them on a collision course, no way to turn back even if they had wanted to.

Chase reached up to the zipper on the vest and with devastatingly slow motion, pulled it down, every inch allowing more of her breasts to escape. He took the last three inches of the zipper with lightning speed, unable to hold off any longer. The sides of the vest separated, freeing Coco's breasts completely, and she took her first deep breath. As she inhaled fully, her breasts moved forward into Chase's waiting hands, and they both started breathing deeply – more like gasping and gulping for air to slow them down. But there was no slowing down the passion train, they would clutch each other tight and enjoy the ride all the way.

In less than two seconds, the vest joined the jacket on the chair, and

Chase's mouth and fingers were on her nipples, sucking and biting like she was the last meal he would ever have. Then he was kneeling in front of Coco, undoing the snap on her leather pants, pulling down the zipper, his tongue and lips licking and nipping every inch of Coco's skin as it was freed from the tight pants.

When the zipper was as low as it was going to go, and Chase still couldn't reach Coco's promised land with his tongue, he reached around behind her and slipped his thumbs inside the waistband of her pants. She tried to reach down and help remove the pants but Chase didn't need or want any help – he was enjoying himself too much – and he moved her hands away. He continued pushing on the waistband, and slowly the leather began to slide down across Coco's curvy hips, to the tops of her thighs, where Chase could finally put his lips and tongue on her exposed magic button. He took one introductory lick and then pulled her swollen clit into his mouth to suck and nibble, making her scream and start to shake all over. "Chase, we've talked about this before. You keep doing that while I'm standing up and I'm just not strong enough. When I fall on you in the throes of my orgasm, you'll be sorry."

He replaced his mouth with his thumbs, continuing to torment her clit, looked up at her and said "Who says I'm ready to let you have an orgasm, baby? I could do this all day – sweep forward, pull back, forward, back. Knowing you're so responsive makes me want to play all day."

"Chase!!"

"I know, baby, you have needs and so do I. Let's get you on the bed and out of these pants. Then I can play as long as I like. Yes?"

"Yes!!"

Chase continued pulling on Coco's leather pants until they were down around her ankles, and then he stood and pushed her back toward the bed. When she couldn't back up any farther, she fell back, with her body and thighs on the bed and her lower legs hanging down toward the floor. Chase knelt down again and pulled the leather off, throwing it onto the chair with her jacket and vest. He picked up Coco's feet as he stood again, bending her knees up into her chest, and took a long taste of her pussy, which made Coco moan again. He stepped back from the bed and pulled off his sweat pants, showing off his long, thick, erect cock, getting another moan from Coco.

He climbed onto the bed beside Coco, gathered her under one arm and pulled her toward the head of the bed. When he stopped, she was resting against all the pillows, her knees bent and spread, giving Chase an erotic view and full access to everything he wanted to touch.

"You just lie back and enjoy the show, baby, I need to play some more."

He knelt down between her legs and dropped his lips and tongue to her clit. She made a gurgling sound in her throat, he laughed, and the play continued until Coco could no longer form words and was no longer in touch with reality.

Sometime later, Coco woke, spooning against Chase's warm body, covered with her soft angora throw. She could see through the curtains on the window that evening was approaching, and wondered what time it was. She stretched out one leg and felt Chase move behind her, pulling her close again with the arm he had around her waist. She leaned back into him again, and felt the kiss he placed gently on her exposed shoulder.

"Wow, gorgeous, you never fail to amaze. I recall three screeching orgasms, and I think there may have been a fourth right at the end. You are the 'O' Master, and apparently I'm your willing slave."

"Yes, I was trying for five but when you passed out on number four, I figured you had reached your limit, at least until you were able to sleep a little bit."

There was a quiet moment between them, suddenly interrupted by the growling of Chase's stomach and he whispered in her ear "I guess that chicken Caesar salad wasn't quite enough, baby. What would you like for dinner?"

"How about a shower, then some wings and beer? I have the beer in the fridge and my favorite wing joint is five minutes away – and they deliver. My treat."

"Sounds great. Can you walk or do I need to carry you to the shower?" They both laughed, but Coco did wonder if her legs were steady enough to carry her all the way to the bathroom.

Shower finished and wings ordered, Chase and Coco took their beer down to the entertainment room, turned on the big screen TV and surfed for something sports-ish to watch. They settled in the theater style recliner seats and found some sumo wrestling, pretending to be live from Tokyo. Not really watching the TV, but wanting the low noise in the background, they began talking about the next three days, full of work that would need to get done before the Independence Day holiday. Chase told Coco about the friends his parents were going to visit for the long weekend, and Coco talked about the cousins, aunts and uncles he would meet at the family picnic after Thursday's parade.

Coco had been keeping an eye on the clock and went upstairs just in time to meet the delivery boy at the door with their dinner. When she went back downstairs, she carried a huge tray full of wings in three different heat levels, plus celery and carrot sticks, blue cheese dressing, and an order of French fries with tartar sauce to dip them in.

Chase looked up at her and said "Coralee, I don't think you've ever looked sexier than you do right now. So hand me a wing before I attack you and eat everything on the tray." They sat on the floor with the tray between them and started shoveling in the food, talking with their mouths full, and laughing as they continued to talk about everything and nothing in particular.

Before they realized it, it was 10:00 PM and Chase was yawning. Coco tried to talk him into spending the night, but he decided that his early morning meeting was too early to sleep at Coco's house, go home and change and get his briefcase and get to the meeting on time. So she walked him to his car and gave him one last good night kiss, with instructions to call or text when he got home. She waved after him as he drove away, with a smile on her face that wouldn't go away. She was already tucked into bed with a book when she got the text from Chase – "Home safe and sound. Have a good day tomorrow. SWAK."

And she smiled bigger and texted back "SWAK to you too. Sweet dreams, gorgeous." Then she put the book on the night stand, turned off the light and fell asleep, having some sweet dreams of her own.

July 2013, Myrtle Beach, SC

*M*onday turned out to be a busy day for Coco. She went out at 6:00 AM to get her run out of the way, smiling at the stiffness she was feeling after the athletic sex of the prior day, and then sat down at her desk with a large glass of juice and got to work. It was July 1st and she was on a deadline. She wanted to have all her work caught up by midday Wednesday so that she could enjoy a long holiday weekend for the 4th.

Her workload included lots of emails with maintenance requests from clients with existing websites, plus a few calls from new clients with questions about what should be included in their sites. She had barely enough time for a quick breakfast break at 9:00 AM and a quicker lunch break at 2:00 PM.

Coco's last call of the day was from Josh Barlow, asking questions about processes for some work he'd not done before. He was excited about working with John Buckingham, getting the marshland bill ready for the rollup to the November election – almost a changed man compared to his performance at the disastrous first meeting with the Buckingham's and the County board. She was happy to see the changes in Josh but was glad to get him off the phone when they were done.

Coco had dinner in bed – a bowl of cereal while watching a review of the day's events on her favorite Conservative talk show. She was just about to turn off the light and get some sleep when she got a text from Chase.

It was 11:30 PM and he was just finishing up for the day. But at least he was home safe and had grabbed a carry-out salad for "dinner" from the all-night diner down the street on his way home. They texted back and forth for a few minutes while Chase ate his salad, then they SWAK'd each other goodnight and hit their separate sheets, each dreaming of the other during the night.

Tuesday was drizzly but not busy, so Coco was able to take care of some errands during the day, getting ready for the parade on Thursday. Her most important errand was at a local sign shop, where she picked up something she had ordered several weeks before, to be attached to the back of her '57 Chevy for the parade. She got a text from Chase around Noon, letting her know that he had gone to Columbia and would be there overnight, but he would definitely be back by Wednesday night, and that he was very much looking forward to the parade and meeting her family after. He promised to call her when he got home so they could discuss plans for Thursday.

She was a little sad that he'd had to go out of town, but was very happy that he was looking forward to meeting everyone. She was concerned about Chase meeting her aunt and uncle, they were both known as loose cannons in the family, and they expected a private conversation with him – without her! But she figured if Chase could argue before the South Carolina Supreme Court and win, he could probably handle Uncle Bob and Aunt Monica.

Wednesday started out cloudy but was all sun and breeze by afternoon. The forecast for Thursday was spectacular – sunny, warm and breezy enough to keep the day comfortable. Coco finished up the last of the work she still needed to do, and let all of her clients know that she would be offline from 3 PM Wednesday through 7 AM Monday, for the Independence Day holiday. She got one last business call at 2:55 PM from a new client, panicked about something she decided needed to be included on her web site. Coco was able to talk her down from her anxiety ledge – they discussed the pros and cons of the addition, and everything was settled to the client's satisfaction by 3:05 PM. Coco promised to call her Monday morning with updates and she was off the phone, done with work for the extra long weekend.

Coco spent the rest of the afternoon at the grocery store, then was back home putting together her special Four Bean Salad, the one she would take to the family picnic the next day. She packed the completed salad in three large plastic containers and stashed them in the fridge, then she went to the garage to check on the large cooler she would put in the trunk of the '57 before the parade so that everything would stay nice and cold until lunch was ready. She checked the ice stash in the chest freezer in the garage, then completed the last prep step for the parade – attaching the sign she'd had made to the frame and brackets on the back of the Chevy. The sign would be a tribute to her parents, and looking at it mounted to the back of her dad's car made her smile and nod – they would be there in spirit and Coco knew they would be very proud.

Coco made herself a grilled chicken salad for dinner around 7:00 PM, watching some trash TV while she ate, yelling at the TV several times when something she saw or heard got her riled up. Her cell phone rang right after 8:00 PM and when she saw who was calling, she smiled. "Hey, gorgeous, are you home?"

"I just walked in the door, sassy girl, and you were the first call I made."

"I'm honored, Mr. Buckingham. I hope you had a productive trip."

"It was very productive. I met with all the people I needed to see, spent an hour in court, arguing my opponent into the dust, wined and dined a new associate into accepting a job with the law firm, in the Columbia office. She's got a lot of experience with environmental law in Florida and she just passed her bar exam here so she's free to practice in South Carolina immediately."

"She??"

"Yes, she! Isn't it so very liberal that we finally have a woman lawyer in the firm?"

"How old is she?"

"She's 45."

"Is she attractive?"

"Some men might think so, but she does nothing for me. She's not a sassy girl like you!"

"Good save, counselor."

"How was your day, baby?"

"It was productive, and then it was over for the next four days."

"I'm glad you were productive, baby. Maybe you can stop thinking about business for a few days."

"I missed you, Chase."

"I missed you too, Coco. So, what's the plan for tomorrow?"

"We have to be at the start of the parade route by 9:45, so we should probably be there by 9:30."

"Okay, I'll be at your house at 9:00 so we don't have to rush."

"Sounds good, gorgeous. Wear comfortable clothes, you'll be in them for a while."

"Will I be out of them at any point during the day?"

"If you're very lucky."

"Well then, here's to a lot of luck tomorrow."

"My aunt and uncle have a really nice pool, so bring some trunks with you if you want. I'll have my bathing suit with me."

"I'll bring something just in case. And before I forget, I may have left my onyx ring at your house last weekend. Did you find it?"

"No, I haven't seen it, but I'll look around a little before I go to bed."

"Thanks, I appreciate it. It was a graduation present from my aunt and I'd hate to lose it. But don't stay up too late looking for it. You need to be rested for tomorrow. Sweet dreams, baby."

"Sweet dreams to you too, gorgeous."

"I'll be dreaming of you in a bathing suit, baby."

"I'll be dreaming of you wearing nothing, gorgeous." And the call ended. And Coco did indeed dream of naked Chase, splashing in her aunt's pool, fucking her on the very bouncy diving board.

Independence Day dawned bright, warm, cloudless – it would be a beautiful day. Coco was up at 7:00 AM, ate breakfast and packed up the cooler with her salad and six bottles of water, then covered everything in ice from the freezer. She was just pulling the Chevy out of the garage into the driveway when Chase pulled up at the curb. He was dressed in navy shorts, a red, white and blue short-sleeved button down shirt and sandals – when he jumped out of his jeep and walked toward her, Coco thought of one word – YUMMY! He had managed to dress in something that was a perfect complement to her navy knit dress, sprinkled with tiny red and white stars. Her red sun hat and matching red sandals would make them look the perfect pair.

"Hey, gorgeous, how are you? You look very patriotic today!"

Chase wrapped Coco in a big hug and kissed her deep, then said "You just look good enough to eat, baby. Did you sleep well last night?"

"I dreamed about you naked in my aunt's pool. We fucked on the diving board! It was rockin'!"

"My dirty, sassy little girl! Are we ready to head out?"

"I just need you to help me put the cooler in the trunk and then we'll be ready to roll."

"Lead the way, Ms. Brighton."

When they walked to the back of the car and Chase got a good look at the sign on the back, he stopped short. The background was a picture of the Chevy with the top down. There were a man and woman in the front seat, and two little girls kneeling on the back seat, everyone dressed in their Sunday finest. They were all waving to the crowd as the car drove down the parade route, huge smiles on everyone's faces. Printed across the top of the sign was 'SUGAR GROVE – Yesterday, Today, and Tomorrow'.

Chase knelt down to get a better look at the photo in the background and smiled. He pointed to the younger of the two little girls and said "That's you!! I can see your face in this little girl."

"Yes, that's me – and that's my sister Virginia. And my mom and dad, of course. This was in 1965 – it was Gin's last parade, she died in the fall of that year. There weren't any more parade pictures for a few years – not until I started gymnastics and dance classes and we somersaulted and tapped our way down the parade route. Those were some tough parades – Betsy Rolley vomited somewhere on the parade route every year for five years straight!" And Coco laughed at the picture and the memories. And Chase stood and held her close while she took a little trip down memory lane in her head.

"Let's hit it, Buckingham! There's a spot in a parade with our name on it and we don't want to be late!"

Chase loaded the cooler into the trunk, then they got into the car, buckled up, and headed out, waving at some of the neighbors who were also heading out to the parade. The usual 5 minute drive took 15 minutes because of traffic and pedestrians, all jockeying for position on the route. Coco's cousin, Glenn, was in charge of getting the parade participants into the correct order in line, and they stopped to chat for a minute so she could introduce Chase. The two men shook hands and Glenn gave Coco some grief about taking so long to get her car back into the parade, and then they were lined up and ready to go. Coco and Chase ended up in line right behind her Uncle Bob and Aunt Monica, and they yelled a few greetings back and forth, waiting for the parade to start.

Coco turned the car radio on and dialed in the local AM station that was broadcasting the parade, so that they would know when everything started. Within just a few minutes, the parade started and they both got caught up in the fun. The broadcaster announced every band, float and car in the parade, starting with the marching band from Coco's high school.

The band was followed by members of the dance/gymnastics school Coco had attended – now owned and run by Betsy Rolley's daughter. She and Chase laughed again about her former dance mate's bad luck with parades, and they started keeping an eye on the road ahead of them, looking for evidence that a current generation Betsy was in the parade.

The dance/gymnastics team was followed by the Grand Marshall's car. And the Grand Marshall for 2013 happened to be their State Representative – a Republican Chase had run into a few times and didn't have much good to say about. Coco tried to keep her opinions to herself, but Chase just couldn't shut up about how much he didn't like the guy.

"I can't believe anyone would ask that inept bastard to be in this parade. They're just celebrating his inability to do his job!"

"Chase, stop."

"No, Coco, this guy is the worst State Rep in Columbia and everyone knows it. He's a complete embarrassment to the whole region."

"Chase, I may not have mentioned this before but I committed to working Banner's re-election campaign this fall. I think he's done a very good job for us in the past two years and, frankly, the alternative is an abomination against all registered voters."

"That abomination happens to be a good friend of mine."

"Then maybe you need to re-examine your friendships."

"Maybe I need to re-examine my romantic interests!!"

"Maybe you do! As a matter of fact, feel free to get out of the car any time. I wouldn't want you to be uncomfortable, associating with the enemy."

"Don't tempt me. Honestly, Coco, how can you work his re-election campaign? I assumed you would be helping with the campaign for the marshland bill. You pushed hard enough to get the changes you wanted, I figured you would be there to help with the campaign. Apparently I figured wrong if you're going to work for Banner and not with us."

"Chase, you know what happens when you assume! And what makes you think I can't do both? I'm just as committed to the marshland bill as you are, but it's not going to be a full time commitment. And neither is the work I'll be doing for Representative Banner. I'm already planning on cutting back my work hours – you know, the business I'm trying to keep going – so that I'll have time for all my political activities. I had no idea how stubborn and selfish you can be! God!"

"Coco, I thought I knew you, but I guess there's a big part of you that I haven't got a clue about. Maybe we don't know each other well enough."

Coco pinned Chase with a glare and asked "Well enough for what?" But he didn't respond.

They had stopped paying attention to the radio in the heat of their argument, and in the silence after, but when they were about to turn the corner by the reviewing stand, they started listening again, just as the announcer introduced Uncle Bob, Aunt Monica and their three little great-grandchildren, riding in the gold 1966 Lincoln Continental convertible Coco had loved riding in as a child. The three little girls waved from the back seat of the Lincoln, reminding Coco that her own happy childhood times were being repeated again by a much younger generation. She smiled at the continuity of that thought – that the same events which had made her happy as a kid were making the latest generation of kids happy as well, handed down from generation to generation. And then it was Coco and Chase making the turn in front of the reviewing stand.

A deep male voice came across the radio speakers – "Yes, Ladies and Gentlemen, we haven't seen this classic car for a few years, but here it is, finally back again. This classic 1957 Chevy Bel Air convertible, which we've always associated with David and Mary Lynn Brighton of Sugar Grove Drugs, is now being driven by their daughter, Coralee, who's back home again, living and working in the Myrtle Beach area. Welcome home, Coco! And she's being escorted today by well known local attorney Chase Buckingham. Don't they make a great looking couple? We hope to see Coralee and her classic '57 in our parade for many more years."

"Chase! Smile and wave or so help me, I'll..."

"You'll what?"

"You're embarrassing both of us." And they both pasted smiles on their faces that they didn't mean, long enough to get past the reviewing stand.

They rode the remaining distance to the end of the parade route in silence, not even looking at each other.

When Coco and Chase reached the end of the parade route, they stopped in a large parking lot and exited the car, slamming doors as they went. Neither one went far from the car, but they both paced back and forth, huffing and puffing loudly. Coco's friends and relatives who saw them decided maybe this wasn't the best time to stop by and chat, which made Coco feel a little juvenile. She finally stopped pacing and stared at Chase until she got his attention.

"So, are you coming with me to my aunt's house or not?"

"Well, I have nothing else to do today. I can be miserable with you or be miserable at home. I might as well be miserable with you!"

"Thanks a lot! Get in the car."

"Bossy bitch!"

"You have no idea, gorgeous." And she shook her head and finally laughed – just a little.

They both got back in the car and headed out to her aunt and uncle's house for the family picnic but there was no conversation on the way. The house turned out to be just this side of a mansion – large, rambling and very welcoming – just like the people who lived there. Coco parked the '57 in the yard between two trees, but they didn't get out of the car right away.

"Chase, we have to talk about this."

"I'm not ready."

"Chase, you're the one who said you could separate your work and your personal life."

"Coco, we'll talk later. We'll figure it out. I promise. But not right now."

"Fine. Come on. People are starting to wonder why we haven't gotten out of the car yet."

They both got out of the car, and after Chase had removed the cooler from the trunk, Coco covered the car with a large tarp to keep the birds and the sap off the upholstery and the shiny finish.

They were immediately surrounded by happy relatives and Coco started introducing Chase to everyone, not expecting him to really remember everyone's name. Two of Coco's teenage cousins took the cooler off Chase's hands and carried it away, and the mass of relatives finally thinned enough that Coco and Chase could catch a breath. When they started walking toward the house, it looked like they weren't even together, but eventually, Chase took Coco's hand in his and she let him – at least it looked like they were there as a couple, although they still weren't talking. When they got to the house, Coco led Chase to the refreshment table to get a drink and some snacks to tide them over until lunch was ready.

They had just grabbed some wine and some snacks and were walking toward the pool where the little kids were having a water fight, when Uncle Bob and Aunt Monica caught up to them. "There you two are. We thought you'd be here sooner."

"We took the scenic route." And she held up her hand as if to say, don't ask. Then Coco continued the introduction. "Anyway, Aunt Monica, Uncle Bob, I'd like to introduce you to my friend, Chase Buckingham. Chase, this is my Uncle Bob Wyeth and his wife, my Aunt Monica."

Chase reached out to shake Bob's hand and allowed Monica to give him her standard "pleased to meet you" hug. When the hug was over, Monica gave Coco a curious look and whispered in her ear "Trouble in paradise?"

"Leave it alone, please."

But then Coco noticed that her aunt wasn't quite herself either. "Aunt Monica, why so flustered? That's not like you. Is everything okay?"

"Yes, everything's fine, luckily. I just got a call from Bob, Jr. He's at the Emergency Room with the family moron again."

Chase looked at Coco and she said "My aunt is referring to her youngest grandson, Chad. He seems to be a little accident prone." Then she turned back to her aunt and asked, "So what happened this time, Aunt Mon?"

"Chad decided to hit the surf early this morning on his new board and got caught in that damned rip current. By the time he finally dragged himself up onto the beach, the board was gone and he was pretty wiped out. Some other surfers found him in the shallows and called the paramedics. By the time he got to the ER, he was alert enough to give someone his dad's cell number and Bob, Jr. went flying out the door to the hospital. Chad will be fine, but he's been given orders to stay out of the water for a week. And he has to buy his next board himself."

"Well, I'm glad he'll be okay. Hopefully we'll still get to see Bob, Jr. before we leave."

"Speaking of leaving, Coco, I think you need to go chat with your cousins for a while so your uncle and I can spend a little time with your 'friend' here. Go on, Coco, scoot. And Chase, why don't you come with my husband and me, and we'll show you around the house, get to know each other a little better."

Coco gave Chase an "I'm really sorry" look, and Chase gave her a look that said 'If I'm not back in 30 minutes, save yourself!'

As Chase walked into the house, arm in arm with Aunt Monica, followed closely by Uncle Bob, there was a friendly, albeit short, discussion about the fabulous weather, marred by the rip current that had been eating up swimmers and surfers for the past few days. Then Chase found himself in a large office, alone with Bob and Monica, surrounded by an uncomfortable silence. Monica finally ended the silence.

"Chase, honey, we don't mean to make you uncomfortable. A man your age shouldn't have to explain his intentions toward anyone, to anyone. That being said, Bob and I are very fond of Coco, and we don't want to see her get hurt by a relationship that she might be taking more seriously than you do. Coco always thinks she's fooling us when she says she's doing well, but in the past, we've known that she wasn't. And then all of a sudden, in the past few weeks, she really has seemed happier, and I'm sure it's because she's been seeing you. But I sensed a little strain between the two of you in the yard, and frankly, Chase, I don't want to be the one to have to pick up all the little pieces if you break up with her now. I know this isn't fair to you, honey, but I don't think I can do it again."

And Chase saw tears in Monica's eyes that broke his heart. Before he could say anything, Uncle Bob had a few things he wanted to add, just to make sure Chase felt appropriately bad. He picked up a framed photo off a bookshelf and handed it to Chase.

"Chase, take a look at this picture. This couple is Coco's parents. Her mother, Mary Lynn, was my little sister – my only sister – and I loved her very much. Coco's father, David, was my best friend and my business partner for 40 years. Coco looks so much like her mother, seeing her makes me happy and sad all at the same time – happy because I still have a little piece of two of the people I loved most in the world, and sad because there's been such sadness in Coco's eyes since her parents died. The last few weeks, she's had a light in her eyes again that I haven't seen in way too long, almost like the old free-spirited Coco. I don't want to put any pressure on you, but I do need you to know that if you hurt that girl, you won't be able to run far enough to get away from the ass kicking I will rain down on you."

Chase met Bob's intense gaze and held it, saying "So, no pressure, right?"

And Bob's gaze lost a little intensity – "Right, no pressure."

And Monica came up with one last thing she wanted to ask – "Chase, even though there was some tension between the two of you earlier, I saw the way you and Coco looked at each other. I think she might be falling in love with you, and I can see why she might. You seem like a good man. Chase, could you be falling in love with my Coco?"

More uncomfortable silence filled the room, and then Chase finally spoke. "Mr. and Mrs. Wyeth, I understand why you're so protective of Coco. I think there hasn't been much joy in her life – for far too long – and you and your family have been the ones to support her through everything she's been through. I can't imagine how devastating the loss of her parents has been for all of you, you seem to be such a close-knit family. I know we're only having this conversation out of your concern for her.

"I don't know if you realize Coco and I met for the first time more than 30 years ago. It was a brief encounter – a week when she tried to teach me how to dance so that I could propose to the love of my life. And it worked, she taught me how to dance really well. Unfortunately, three months after we got engaged, my fiancé gave back my ring and married someone else. And I was so heartbroken, I quit college and joined the Army. And I stayed in the Army for 20 years, hiding from my old life while I looked in vain for a new one. And during that whole 20 years, and the years that followed after the Army, it wasn't my ex fiancé that filled my thoughts and my dreams, it was that little ball of fluff dance instructor from freaking Arthur Murray." And Monica tried unsuccessfully to hide her tears.

And Chase continued – "Imagine my wonder and surprise when I went to my very good friend's wedding a few weeks ago, prepared to spend a miserable hour and then go home and get drunk, and realized I was dancing with the little ball of fluff whose scent and touch and essence had kept me going through my own dark times. You say that Coco has been happy since we met again, my friends would tell you the same thing about me. There's been a piece missing inside me for so many years, and now all of a sudden, that hole is filling in, thanks to my sassy Coco.

"Bob, Monica, you were right to sense some tension between Coco and me today. We're on opposite sides of town politically and we got into a big fight in the middle of the parade. I'm surprised you didn't hear us yelling at each driving down the street behind you. My biggest concern is that our fundamental opinions about how to fix what's wrong with this world are so far apart. I'm not sure how we're going to make a relationship work like that, but I'm sure not going to walk away from her.

"I wish I could tell you where my relationship with Coco is headed, but I can't, I just don't know. I wish I could put a name on what I feel for her. I wish I could tell you that I'll never make her sad or angry, but obviously I can't. She's probably out there right now bitching up a storm about what a damned tree hugger I am. What I CAN tell you is that I'm going to do everything I can to make her happy, keep that light in her eyes, and maybe have a little happiness for myself at the same time. I hope that's enough to reassure you, at least for now, because Coco really loves the two of you and she values your opinion. I wouldn't want to come between her and her family. Monica, you're crying again. That can't be good."

"Oh, Chase, it's good! It's all good! The only thing I ask is that when you figure out how you feel about Coco, you let her know – don't keep her guessing."

"Monica, you can count on that."

And they all stood and she hugged him so tight, he thought she was never going to let him go – kind of like the hugs he got from Coco – he figured it must run in the family. When Monica finally let Chase loose, Bob held out his hand and Chase shook it, and they shared a little man hug. Then they headed back outside to see if Coco was speaking to him again and maybe have some lunch.

Coco had been talking with her cousins, but not necessarily hearing what anyone was saying. Her focus was directed at the back door of the house – the one Chase had disappeared through with her aunt and uncle 15 long minutes before. Fifteen minutes when she didn't realize she wasn't really breathing. She had immediately regretted turning Chase over to her aunt and uncle right after their big fight and she was concerned about what they could be talking about for so long.

Coco didn't start breathing again until the back door opened and Chase stepped out onto the patio, followed closely by Bob and Monica. The three of them were smiling, almost laughing, and Coco took one deep breath before she looked at her smirking cousins and said "Excuse me, girls."

She all but leapt out of her lawn chair and walked very quickly to where Chase was standing, watching her. When she reached Chase, she wrapped her arms around him, looked up into his face and whispered "I'm sorry about the fight."

And Chase leaned down and whispered in her ear "So am I, baby. We'll talk later and work it out."

As Bob and Monica looked on, still smiling, Chase gave Coco a quick kiss on the lips.

Loud enough for Bob and Monica to hear him, Chase said "Coco, your aunt and uncle are lovely people, and we had a very nice conversation. They seem to care about you very much. As a matter of fact, I think your whole family loves you more than you might know. Speaking of family, there are a WHOLE lot of people here I've not been introduced to, so why don't we mingle a little and you can acquaint me with the whole lot."

And leaning down again, whispering so that only she could hear, "Arguing with you made my cock really hard. You have one hour to get lunch and let me meet a few more people, and then we're out of here. Unless you'd like for me to strip you naked and ravage you right here on the patio, in front of the crowd."

And she whispered back "Lunch would be good, but I have alternate plans for the ravaging, gorgeous."

"Lead the way, baby."

An hour later, Chase and Coco had eaten lunch and drank another glass of wine. Chase had also been introduced to the rest of Coco's aunts and uncles, and many of her cousins, most of whom he would not remember the next day. "Coco, are there any more aunts and uncles that I haven't met yet?"

"No, that's all of them. My dad was an only child but my mom had six brothers, and you met them all – plus five wives and one gay significant other. Let me just grab a bottle of wine and we'll be on our way."

Coco went to the outdoor bar, selected a bottle of Moscato and had her bartender cousin open it, then put the cork part way back into the bottle. Then they said their quick goodbyes and they were off.

Coco put the bottle and two baggies of food she'd snagged along the way into the ice in her cooler, and had two of her teenage cousins haul it back to the car. They placed the cooler in the trunk along with the tarp and the sign that she took off the back of the car, and she threw Chase the keys to the '57. He caught them but didn't make a move to get into the car.

He just kept staring at her – "You want me to drive your car? This car?"

"Yes, gorgeous, I trust you with my life AND my car."

"Fuck, Coco, are you sure? What if I'm a really bad driver and I wreck it? I'm not sure this is a good idea."

"It's a great idea, Chase. I've never gotten to ride in the front seat as a passenger and this is my chance. Come on, get in, we're burning daylight!"

So he opened the passenger door and helped Coco into the car, and then he walked around and got in behind the wheel. His hands were just the slightest bit shaky when he put the key in the ignition and turned the engine over. The motor purred to life, and the smile on Chase's face was huge. They both buckled up, Chase put the car in gear and off they went. He drove "old lady" slow at first, trying to get a feel for the power steering, but after a few minutes, he thought he had a feel for the way the car handled and accelerated to normal speed.

As a matter of fact, the car handled like a damned dream, and he was enjoying himself so much, he wanted to shout. They found Highway 17 South and picked up speed. Chase looked at Coco and asked "Do we know where we're going, baby?"

"Nope, we're just going to drive and see where we end up. If we drive long enough, I know the perfect spot for a little wine and a romp in the back seat."

Chase's breathing accelerated like the speed they were moving, and he said "Just tell me when you want me to turn, baby."

An hour later, Chase was pulling into a small meadow and Coco had him park under a stand of young birch trees. They had driven south on Hwy 17 for about 45 minutes, and then turned east onto a county road that took them toward the shore. With the ocean visible about 5 minutes ahead, Coco directed Chase through a fence gate and down a lane that led into the meadow. Once they had parked, Chase leaned back against the seat and looked up.

Through the dappled shade of the young trees, the blue sky and fluffy white clouds looked like his vision of heaven. When he turned his head and looked at Coco, and the gentle smile on her face, he was SURE he was in heaven. "Where are we, Coco? This place is beautiful but I would hate to think we're trespassing."

"We're not trespassing. This land has belonged to my Uncle Will for 45 years. You met him today."

"Is he the one with the wife Maggie, or the one with the significant other Freddie?"

"Will and Freddie. Will inherited a lot of money through some crazy circumstances last year and Freddie is helping him spend it on a new farm house at the end of the road. It sits on the bluff above the shore. It's going to be beautiful when it's done. Seriously, they've been together for 25 years. They're both retired now and enjoying it to the hilt. Will's nieces and nephews have been using this meadow for as long as he's owned it – a little mini destination vacation. When we were little, we used to come here and camp overnight with Will, and over the years, he had us plant all the trees you see here. These young trees right here must have been planted by my younger cousins."

"It's a beautiful place, Coco. The more I hear you talk about your family, and meet the people who are close to you, the more jealous I am of your big family. I really did love being an only child growing up but by the time I got out of high school, I realized I missed having a bigger family. I only had one aunt, the one I lived with while I was in Columbia for high school, and she was widowed before she had any kids. She never remarried and I think when she died a few years ago, she was glad to be at the end of a very lonely life."

"Sometimes I don't appreciate my family. Sometimes I think they're a huge invasion of my privacy, like my aunt and uncle insisting on meeting with you privately today. But when I look back over my life so far, all I see is face after face after face of the people who loved me, who still love me, and who have supported me through some ugly times. And I realize just how blessed I've been. I'd like to count you among those people, Chase. I'm really glad we ran into each other again."

"Me too, baby, more than you could ever know." And he leaned in and kissed her – gently, almost lovingly. And Coco put her hand over Chase's heart and let her mind slip away.

Uncounted minutes later, the kiss broke and they stared at each other, then they both nodded and started to smile, started to chuckle a little. But Coco was a little pre-occupied and had to get that conversation – the one that was prompted by their argument – under way.

"Chase, we really need to talk. We have to find a way to…"

"Coco, it can wait."

"Chase…"

"No, Coco, not now. I have other things on my mind. But I promise, before we go to bed tonight, we'll talk about things. Just not now. Okay?"

"You promise?"

"Yes, I promise. Now I think we have a date in the back seat! Let's get this party started!"

Chase and Coco each exited the car on their own side and met at the trunk. Coco opened the cooler and took out the bottle of wine and two baggies filled with cheese, salami and crackers, and told Chase to grab the blanket.

"Coco, why do we need a blanket? It's not cold out at all."

"No, it's not cold, but I'm hoping you make me all juicy in that back seat and my dad would come up out of his grave and beat me if I got anything on his upholstery!"

"Right, protect the upholstery! What was I thinking??"

"I'm sure you were just distracted with thoughts of me riding your cock in the back of my '57 Chevy. But the huge question before us is – do we know each other well enough now to drink out of the same wine bottle? Because I brought everything else and forgot to bring wine glasses."

"Oh, Coco, say it isn't so!! Oh well, I guess I'll just have to suffer through it."

"Good answer, Mr. Buckingham."

*C*hase threw the blanket down on the back seat and climbed in, unbuttoning his shorts and lowering the zipper as he sat down. Coco pulled the front seatback forward and put the wine bottle and baggies on the floor of the back seat. Then she stood in the open space in front of Chase, wiggled her hips a little and winked at him. She needed to reconnect with him on an emotional level as much as a physical one after their argument, and this was what she needed to ensure that they were okay.

Chase reached up under her patriotic little knit dress until he reached her red lace panties. His face pressed against her dress with his nose in her crotch; his hands slid behind her and caressed her ass cheeks for several minutes, moaning at the scent and the feel, causing a shiver and a smile on Coco's face. Then his hands slid back around to the front of her panties, between her legs, gently massaging her pussy, thumbing her clit lightly over the soft material, eliciting moans from deep in her throat.

When Coco started panting at his touch, Chase tucked his thumbs inside the waistband of her panties and slowly pulled them over her ass, down her thighs and let them drop to the floor at her feet. She stepped out of the panties so that Chase could pick them up and lift them to his nose to take a deep breath. Coco shuddered watching him sniff her wet underwear, not understanding why he liked to do it, but knowing that the sight of it made her clench tight, deep inside.

Chase lifted his ass a little off the seat and Coco pulled his shorts and tighty-whiteys down his hips, freeing his swelling cock for her to see and to touch. He just barely managed to grab his cell phone out of his pocket as she pulled him free of his shorts and underwear, and he threw the phone carelessly on the seat beside him. Coco knelt down on the floor of the back seat and crawled between Chase's naked thighs, bringing the wine bottle close. She took a swig from the open bottle, then spit on her hands for some lubricant, reached up and grabbed his cock, pumping up and down for several strokes, almost drooling as his length and girth grew in her hands. As Coco leaned forward and took him in her mouth, licking playfully around the head, sucking gently, Chase gasped and began his own panting breathing.

She smiled as her mouth watered, and she began to slide her lips up and down the length of Chase's cock, taking him in a little farther with each slide. After a few minutes, she pulled up again so that only the head of his cock remained in her mouth, teasing the little slit with her tongue. She kept one hand on the shaft and lowered her other hand to her pussy, playing in the juice she found there, thumbing her clit with slippery fingers. In seconds, Coco was moaning along with Chase. Her moans started deep in her chest and the vibrations played through her lips onto the head of Chase's cock, making him groan.

When he thought he couldn't take any more without blowing his load into her mouth, he pushed her away, and pulled her slippery fingers up and into his mouth. His eyes turned dark and lusty with the taste of her and he whispered "Oh fuck, baby, what you do to me!! But I want you riding me when I come so grab that wine bottle and climb on up here into my lap. Take me deep, baby, I need you really bad."

Coco handed Chase the bottle, then hiked up her dress as she got up from the floor and straddled him – her own eyes turned dark as she slid onto his waiting cock, sinking to his lap in one slow, sweet slide. Chase held her in place when all she really wanted was to start moving – he needed a few minutes to savor the feel of her wrapped around his aching cock before they did anything more.

They stared into each other's eyes for uncounted minutes, passing the bottle back and forth a few times, catching the start of a steamy buzz. As Coco sat in his lap with his cock buried deep inside her, Chase reached up behind her and lowered the zipper of her dress, pulling it off her shoulders, letting it pool at her waist. He reached up and cupped her breasts in his hands, enjoying the look and feel of the red lace balconette bra she was wearing, teasing her nipples beneath the soft material that matched her lace panties.

They both finally needed skin to skin contact so he put his hands on the straps of her bra on her shoulders while she reached behind and unhooked the clasp. With no effort at all, the straps slipped down Coco's arms and Chase pulled her bra away from her, tossing it in the front seat. A sudden breeze across Coco's naked breasts made her shiver and made her nipples bead tighter than Chase's touch had already made them. As an afterthought, he reached down and gathered her dress in his hands and pulled it over her head, tossing it into the front seat with the rest of her clothes.

Coco's nakedness put a wanton, lusty look in her eyes, and she decided that Chase's shirt needed to go as well. His palms moved up and down her arms with light feathery strokes as she reached up and started unbuttoning his shirt – slowly freeing one button at a time. As she unbuttoned each button, she placed a kiss and a lick on the newly exposed skin. She clenched and released her tiny little cunt muscles around Chase's cock, getting a look and a moan from him each time. When all the buttons were undone, she slipped the shirt off his shoulders. He had to slide forward an inch or so with Coco on his lap to get it off, but it finally ended up in the front seat with her panties, her bra and her dress.

Chase stared at Coco's breasts like they were the sweetest candy, and he could no longer resist the urge to lick her tasty treats while he kept her still in his lap. He licked first one nipple and then the other, lavishing his affection on them by sucking the little nubs, teasing them with just the tip of his tongue, biting down a little, enough to make Coco do some groaning of her own. When one nipple was in his mouth, he would grasp the other between his thumb and forefinger, pinch, tug, twist a little, just enough to keep the torment going. And then he would switch to the other side, giving both buds equal attention.

Chase reached down and picked up the bottle off the seat, took a swig, and leered at Coco with an evil smile. With his mouth full of cold wine, he went back to her nipple and sucked, swishing the chilly liquid across her sensitive bud, making her gasp. He opened his mouth just the slightest, and let the chilly wine dribble across her breast, down her belly, past her already wet pussy, and onto the blanket beneath him. Coco stared a hole in Chase's forehead as the sensation made her moan and clench everything south of her waist. Then he put the bottle back down on the blanket next to him and with his cold hand, covered her other breast and pinched her nipple hard, eliciting a groan from Coco that sounded like it started at her toes and swept through her whole body.

Finally Coco couldn't take anymore and she started giving some attention to Chase's nipples as well. "Two can play at that game, Buckingham."

She knew from recent experience that his nipples were as sensitive as her own, and it wasn't long before Chase was moaning and panting as loudly as she was. She grabbed the wine bottle and got her hands and finger tips really cold, then went to work, thumbing and scratching and tugging at his tiny little buds, making them bigger than she'd seen before. As they continued tormenting each other, the panting and groaning got louder. Chase's cock started pulsing inside Coco, and her cunt started dripping juice into his lap.

As her eyes were starting to roll back in her head, Coco moaned to Chase, "Please, Chase, you're killing me. I need to move, gorgeous, I can't just sit with your 2XL cock in my pussy and do nothing. Pinch my nipples all you want, but please let me move."

"Oh, baby, I love how you beg. That breathy sound goes right to my dick."

"Chase!! Please!! I'm going to explode if I don't do something soon."

He chilled his fingers on the wine bottle again and reached down to swish around her overly warm clit.

"Chase!!!"

"Okay, baby, let's ride this motherfucker!"

"Oh, thank god!"

Coco leaned in and took possession of Chase's mouth, almost smothering him with the urgency of her kiss. He continued pinching and pulling at her nipples as she steadied herself with her hands on his shoulders and began sliding up and down on his cock. Clenching the tiny but oh so strong muscles of her cunt, she was giving them both a tight ride. Coco's orgasm started in her belly, clawed its way out from behind her clit and shot through her system in all directions. It hit her so fast, she didn't have time to scream – the only sound she made was a now familiar strangled gurgling noise at the back of her throat that evened out into a low, desperate moan.

Her pussy clamped down on Chase's cock so tight he couldn't breathe – by the time her muscles let him loose, his eyes were bugging out of his head. He helped her stroke him a few more times and then he struggled through his own freight train orgasm, his come filling Coco and oozing back down his cock, between his thighs and onto the blanket covering the seat. Breathless, Coco whispered in Chase's ear – "And that, gorgeous, is why we put a blanket down on the upholstery!"

They would have laughed if they could, but the only thing they could manage was a smile, as Coco fell against Chase and laid her head on his chest while they tried to breathe. Chase's hands running gently up and down Coco's spine had a soothing touch, and Coco's soft, even strokes across Chase's shoulders put him at ease more than anything anyone had ever done for him in the past.

Neither of them knew how long they sat together, lost in the sun, the breeze through the trees, and the perfectly timed beats of their hearts. But the spell was suddenly broken by a chirping sound that didn't come from nature. It was coming from Chase's cell phone! He picked it up to click ignore on the call and noticed who the caller was. "Shit, it's my mom!! I'll let it go to voice mail."

"No, you won't, Chase, you don't ever not take your mother's call."

They fussed about it long enough that the call did go to voice mail, so Coco took the phone from him, clicked redial to call her back, and handed the phone back to Chase. She started to extricate herself from him and the back seat, but he held her tight on his lap, still stuffing her pussy with his cock. She was just about to shout at him when his mom picked up the call.

"Hey, mom, sorry I didn't pick up just now, I couldn't get to the phone."

And Coco glared at him as he continued to hold her in his lap with a strong arm around her waist. And his mother started a very casual conversation with her son, having no idea that he was naked in a meadow with a lovely woman she'd never met, who was sitting naked across her son's lap, impaled on his cock.

"Chase, darling, how was your day? Did you have a good time at the parade? And did you say something about going to a picnic after? Are you still there? Am I interrupting something?"

"Of course you're not interrupting anything, mom." And all Coco could do was laugh quietly and shake her head. "Mom, you and dad should come to the parade next year, I had a great time. I got to ride in a mint condition '57 Chevy. Dad would be so jealous if he could see it. And the picnic was excellent – great food, good company, Coco has a big family full of wonderful people."

Coco tried again to get away from Chase without making too much noise, but he still wasn't letting go.

"Chase, sweetheart, we're coming back from Savannah a day early. Come to dinner on Saturday and bring your lady friend with you."

"Dinner at your house Saturday night? And I should bring Coco with me?"

"Of course you should bring her with you. You've been spending quite a bit of time with her from what I hear, and I haven't met her yet." And Coco gave Chase a questioning glance but didn't make a sound.

"Mom, we'd love to come. Coco's a great cook, can she make something to bring along?" And Coco's questioning look continued.

"I don't think so, son, but I should call her to invite her myself, don't you think?"

"Well, mom, she's sitting right here with me. Let me put her on the phone." And Coco's eyes got huge as Chase tried to hand her his cell phone. He was laughing and she could feel his cock growing again inside her. She took the phone but was about to panic, thinking about talking to his mom while she straddled Chase, feeling every inch of his cock inside her.

And Chase said, loud enough for his mom to hear, "Here, Coco, my mom wants to talk to you. Just say hello and mom will do the rest!"

And Coco put the phone to her ear and said "Mrs. Buckingham, it's lovely to talk to you. Thank you very much for the dinner invitation, I'm looking forward to it." And Coco gasped at the feel of Chase sucking on her nipple, biting down just a little while she talked to his mother on the phone. And she slapped him on the arm, but he didn't stop.

And Mrs. Buckingham said "What's that, dear? Are you okay?"

"Yes, I'm fine, Mrs. Buckingham, we're outside and something's biting me. I was trying to swat it away, but it keeps buzzing around."

"Oh, well, I know how those pesky flying insects can be this time of year. Anyway, if you could bring something for dessert Saturday night, that would be excellent. Chase's father is something of a choc-a-holic so feel free to bring something that will make him happy."

"I'm sure I can come up with something you and Mr. Buckingham will enjoy. Thank you again for inviting me, I'll see you Saturday. Here, I'll put Chase back on the phone."

Coco listened to the last of the conversation, but could only hear half - "Mom, yeah, I'm back… Yes, she's very nice… And very smart… Yes, and very pretty… What time Saturday night? 7:00? Yes, we'll be there. We'll even dress up a little. I know how you hate when I wear jeans to dinner on Saturday night. Yes, I love you too. Tell dad hello for me. Yes, I love him too! Goodbye mother!"

Chase disconnected the call, threw the phone on the seat beside him and pulled Coco close so that he could wrap his arms around her. She laid her head on his shoulder and they sat in silence for a few minutes.

"Chase, you're twitching inside me. It kind of tickles but it's making me crazy horny. We need to do something about that before I bite your neck!"

"Baby, you are just so perfect for me. Just listening to you breathe, having your nipples coming to life against my chest, watching those goose bumps on your arms when I'm inside you. You make my head spin. You make my dick really hard!"

"Well let's do something about that, gorgeous! You've lit another fire in me and you're just going to have to put it out."

She squeezed his cock inside her one more time and it felt like he doubled in size from one second to the next. Chase grabbed Coco's hips, she dug her fingernails into his shoulders, and they were off, stroking fast and furious, headed for the Promised Land they had come to know so well.

The rest of the Independence Day holiday was a blur, punctuated by more wine and snacks, a leisurely naked conversation in the back of the '57, about everything BUT what Coco wanted to talk about, and a slow drive back to Coco's house. It was dusk when they got back and the neighbors were lighting sparklers and shooting off small firecrackers in the street. As much as Chase didn't want to seem like a wuss about the sounds, Coco could tell that he was bothered by the fireworks and she didn't want him to be uncomfortable.

"Chase, sweetie, if the noise makes you uncomfortable, we don't have to go to the pier."

"It's okay, Coco. I guess I've been avoiding fireworks the last few years."

"Then I think we should just stay here and entertain ourselves in the basement, doing other things that might take our minds off the noise. Maybe make a little noise of our own?" And she gave Chase a sidelong glance that held lusty promises he couldn't resist.

"Okay, Coco, let's just stay here and see what you have in mind."

They spent that night dancing to tunes they played on her old turntable, watching terrible foreign TV and enjoying each other's company. A quick romp on the sofa and a shower, and they were in bed, exhausted, and content to be in each other's arms.

Needless to say, the 'conversation' Chase had promised earlier never occurred.

On Friday, Chase and Coco slept in, then went for a run around the track at the high school down the street. This wasn't the usual measured pace run Coco had been taking on a regular basis lately, they actually ran – almost raced around the track, neither one wanting to lose to the other in their impromptu track meet. When they got back to Coco's house, they ate breakfast, took a shower and then went to Chase's house, taking along a small bag Coco packed for her planned overnighter. Friday at Chase's house was spent walking on the beach, watching TV, and enjoying each other in slow, unhurried passion in every room.

They were settling in as a comfortable couple, each one completing the other, adding something special that had been missing from both their lives for too long. Friday evening, they went for a ride around town on Chase's motorcycle, stopping at their favorite local ice cream parlor because Chase recognized some of his friends' bikes in the parking lot. He introduced Coco to his friends as his 'girl', and they all chatted freely about their jobs and hobbies, easy conversation between good people.

That night Chase and Coco sat together on the swing on his back porch, watching the moon and the waves as the tide rolled in, his arm around her shoulders, her hand on his thigh. There was a long satisfying silent stretch and then Chase broached a subject they hadn't discussed before. "Coco, do you ever wish you'd gotten married, had kids? Had a 'normal' life?"

"I guess if I was brutally honest, I'd have to say yes, sometimes I wish that had been my path. I know I have a very large family that provides a good role model. But I have as many divorced aunts, uncles and cousins as ones who have stayed together. And I have as many family members who are shit parents as I do family members who are really good parents. Even my closest friends haven't had perfect lives when it comes to their relationships.

"Maggs and Russ are dedicated to each other and their kids now, but it hasn't been easy over the years. And I'm sure you know that Gigi had a hellacious first husband that Maggs and I wanted to kill – right up until he killed himself and took one of their kids with him. We've always been there for each other, but some of those times were really hard on all of us. In my dark hours, when I wished my life had been different, those were the times when I regretted not having someone beside me who loved me, kids who loved and respected me. But most of the time, I'm pretty sure I would not have been a good parent, and I was probably too selfish to have been a good wife. I was too consumed with chasing my career for all those years to devote any serious time to someone else.

"What about you? Do you miss the 8 to 5 grind? The crazy sex with your perfect wife? 2.3 kids lined up to tell you what they did all day while you were at work?"

Chase was thoughtful for a few minutes and then pulled Coco a little closer and almost whispered a reply. "When I proposed to Gail, and she accepted, I didn't think my life could get any better. My future was all mapped out – perfect career ahead of me, perfect wife beside me, a few kids on the horizon – the American Dream. And then she broke off our engagement and married someone else. And I wasn't sure how I was going to take my next breath, much less continue with my life plan.

"So I chucked that plan and that life, and jumped into a new one. I had no idea how things were going to turn out, I just knew I needed to shake things up – a lot. The next 20 years were glorious, and horrible, and fulfilling and soul stealing. And I don't regret a minute of it. Because ultimately it led me back around to this minute, right here, right now, with you. Monica told me yesterday she thinks you're falling in love with me, and she wanted to know how I feel about you."

Coco was glad she wasn't facing Chase when he said that. All she could manage in response was "God, I'm so embarrassed. I can't believe she did that."

"Don't be embarrassed, Coco. She loves you and she just wants you to be happy. She doesn't want some throwback neanderthal breaking your heart and walking away. I don't want that either. Coco, I don't think I've ever really been in love before so I don't know how it feels. But I think it might feel something like I feel now. I catch myself thinking about you when I'm in meetings, when I'm supposed to be concentrating on work. I stumbled over my summation in court on Wednesday because a memory of you naked in my bed, beautiful, coming like a rocket, suddenly flashed through my mind. I had to stop and restart my thought, and I finished a little faster than I might have, so that I could sit down and hide my sudden hard-on."

"Oh, Chase..."

"I know, it was stupendous. Coco, when I think of my life going forward, you're there. When I see myself in 20 years, you're there beside me. Do you ever see me in your future?"

And there was no delay in Coco's response. "Chase, I've been seeing you in my future since that first dance lesson. That's probably why I never successfully settled down – no one was ever going to measure up to my fantasy of you. I don't know that you and I all those years ago would have survived, we still had a lot of growing up to do. But you and I now seem to have clicked in some elemental way, like I never dreamed would happen for me. I don't know if this is love either, but what I feel for you is so much more than I've ever felt for anyone. I think maybe we should give this a chance and see where it goes."

"Oh baby, I think so too." And he picked up the hand she had rested on his thigh, and he kissed it gently. Then he turned and lifted her face to his until his lips were just millimeters from hers, and he whispered "Stay with me."

And she put her hand on his and whispered "Always." They closed the tiny gap between them, let their lips touch, and the world fell away, so that there was only Chase and Coco, the moon and the waves, and gentle passion on the swing.

And that conversation that they needed to have about their political discord didn't happen – again.

20

Saturday morning, they got up early so that Chase could take Coco back to her house, and then go on to work for a few hours. As she was getting ready to take a shower, she sat on the bed for a moment and her eyes landed on her photo album on the bookshelf. She thought of the man in the picture Chase had asked about that day she had modeled her leathers for him. She looked from the photo album to her jewelry box, and a nagging memory, filled with regret, tugged at her heart. She was crazy about Chase, and she thought he was crazy about her as well. She just hoped that once she found the right time to tell him about the 'someone' from her past, he'd still feel the same way. But for the time being, she shoved the memory away and forced herself to get started on her day.

Coco grabbed a quick shower when she got home and then headed to the grocery store to get what she needed for the dessert she planned to make. When she got back home, she put her dessert together and stashed the individual serving glasses in a carrier and put them in the fridge to chill. She made herself some lunch and then texted Chase to see how he was doing with his workload. He texted back that he was making good progress and would be headed home within the hour. He told her to be ready at 6:15 and he would pick her up. He also suggested that she pack another overnight bag so that they could spend the night at his house again. She started thinking about keeping some things at his house permanently so that she wouldn't have to keep doing that. She made a quick trip to the store to pick up some things and was back home in time for another shower, with plenty of time to get ready to meet Chase's mother and see his father again. She was shocked at how nervous she was, and she wondered if Chase had been this nervous before meeting her family.

Coco was standing in the living room when Chase drove up. He was wearing the black chinos she'd seen before along with a white button down shirt and a dark grey jacket. Seeing him walk up onto the porch and come through the front door, giving her that 'I want to rip your clothes off' look, she knew she'd maybe gone a bit overboard with her dress choice to meet his mother. "I should change my dress, shouldn't I? This dress is a little too much to meet your mother, don't you think?"

"Coco, I think you look spectacular, and my father will love this dress on you! My mother will think you're very appropriately dressed. Don't worry."

She looked down at her red dress with the little black knit jacket, set off with her black patent leather stilettos, and wasn't convinced. Her platinum jewelry suddenly looked a little gaudy. The concerned look on her face drew Chase to her for a hug and a kiss hello.

"Coco, please, my mother will love you, and your outfit is perfect. The only thing she'll notice tonight is me looking at you with stars in my eyes, and my tongue hanging out. She'll be happy to see that. My parents have tried to set me up with every unmarried woman they know and I've never taken the bait. So they haven't seen me with a woman for a very long time. I did run into them coming out of a restaurant down on Pawley's a few years ago. I was on my way in with a lovely young lady – young enough to be my daughter. My mother didn't know what to say and my dad just gave me that look fathers give their sons when they do stupid things. Trust me, my dad already thinks you're great and my mom will too."

"Okay, I'll trust your judgment. Let me get dessert out of the fridge and I'll be ready to go. Don't let me forget my backpack and my purse, please."

Thirty minutes later they were sitting in John and Claudia Buckingham's driveway, and Coco was having another panic attack. "Coco, baby, just breathe, honey. This is silly. My mother has been looking forward to meeting you and she'll love you, I know it."

"Okay, I'll just have to fake it for a while. Once I get through the initial introduction, I'm sure I'll be fine."

"Come on, the sooner we get into the house and get that introduction over with, the sooner you'll see that she isn't some demon out to steal your soul."

"Chase, you're not making this any easier!"

"Come on!"

As they headed up the walk to the front door, it opened, and John Buckingham stepped out, looking genuinely happy to see both of them. But he did have something to say about them not coming into the house for so long.

"Chase, Coco, it's so good to see you tonight. Coco, you look beautiful, as I expected you would. And Chase, you cleaned up very nicely. Your mother will be very pleased. But what in the world were you doing sitting in the car for so long? I've been standing at the door waiting for 5 minutes! I was beginning to think you were never coming in!"

"Mr. Buckingham, it's lovely to see you again. I understand from Josh Barlow that things are coming along nicely getting the marshland bill on the November ballot. He's very impressed with your knowledge and your experience. He hopes to learn a lot from you in the next few months."

"Yes, young Mr. Barlow is all enthusiasm and no tact sometimes, but we seem to work pretty well together. He's no Chase Buckingham, by any means, but what he lacks in experience right now, he makes up for with bravado. He'll be a fine attorney some day."

"Yes, well, there is only one Chase Buckingham, and the world is probably better off with just the one." And Coco looked at Chase and smiled, and the look she gave him made him absolutely melt.

"Chase, Coco, come inside. Claudia is in the kitchen fussing over dinner. Can I get you both something to drink?"

"Yes, dad, let me help you. Coco, the usual?"

"Yes, please, that would be great."

Chase was just handing Coco a glass of white wine when his mother came into the room. She smiled at her son, gave him a big, motherly hug, and then turned her attention to Coco. Coco had taken just a minute to admire the woman who had given birth to and raised Chase – she was sure he'd been a handful. Coco had seen pictures of Claudia at Chase's house, and wondered if she would be anything like she originally imagined.

Claudia approached and put a hand on Coco's arm and said "Coco, it's so nice to finally meet you. You're every bit as pretty as Chase said, and I understand you have your own business. I admire anyone who can start a business and keep it going. You must be very smart as well."

"Thank you, Mrs. Buckingham. I've actually been trying to talk Chase into letting me update the law firm's web site, but I'm not sure he trusts me quite enough yet."

They all laughed at Coco's comment and then Claudia noticed the small package that Coco was carrying. "Please, Coco, call me Claudia. Is that dessert?"

"Yes, it is, I hope you both enjoy it."

Chase looked curious and quietly asked, "That's not the strawberry Jell-O thing, is it?"

"No, gorgeous, that strawberry Jell-O thing is only for you. Tonight I brought something chocolate for your dad."

"Coco, why don't you bring your dessert along and come help me in the kitchen. You boys, don't get too settled on anything on that TV, we'll be ready to eat in 10 minutes."

Knowing that 10 minutes would likely turn into 20, Chase said "Yes, mother, we'll be ready when you are."

Chase and his father headed for the family room and Coco followed Claudia into the kitchen. "You have a beautiful home, Mrs. Buckingham. You have excellent taste in decorating. And this kitchen must have been custom made for someone with chef skills."

"Yes, we just remodeled the kitchen a few years ago. It was quite fun to do, although I'm afraid it's a little beyond my skills as a cook. I'm sure I don't really do it justice."

"Well it certainly does seem to suit you."

"Thank you, Coco."

Claudia motioned for Coco to put dessert in the massive fridge, then she opened the oven door and checked the roast, declaring that it was done and just needed to rest a few minutes. She pulled out the pan and set it on the counter with some foil over it, and said "Let's have a seat while we wait for this. We can have a chat." Coco was a little wary but kept a smile on her face and pulled out a chair. She was suddenly glad she'd brought her large glass of wine with her to the kitchen.

Claudia had sat down at the table as well, and just as Coco was about to take a sip from her glass, Claudia asked "So, Coco, are you sleeping with my son?" And wine sprayed from Coco's mouth, all over the small table, narrowly missing Claudia and her lovely blouse and pants.

Coco coughed for a few minutes, Claudia attempting to help by patting her a little too forcefully on the back. "Goodness, Coco, are you all right? Did the wine go down wrong?"

"Yes, I believe it did. I'm afraid you surprised me a little with your question."

With a little chuckle that reminded Coco of Chase, Claudia said "I'm so sorry, Coco, I just couldn't resist."

Claudia got up and grabbed a towel, and started drying off the table, and continued talking as she cleaned up the mess. "You see, I stopped by Chase's house the other day while he was in Columbia, and I thought I'd tidy up a little for him, he's been working so hard lately. Anyway, I did some laundry and when I was folding what came out of the dryer, I found the loveliest pair of lace panties among his tee shirts and shorts. They look to be about your size so I assumed..."

"Well I suppose there are any number of reasons why there would be lace panties in Chase's laundry, like..."

"Please, Coco, don't be embarrassed. I'm thrilled to think that Chase has finally found someone he wants to charm out of her underwear."

"Yes, well..."

"Coco, please. I'm his mother. I've been in tune with that man's moods since before he was born. Ever since he got out of the Army, he's just seemed so lost, I didn't think he was ever going to be happy again and it hurt my heart to watch him search and not find what he was looking for. And then a few weeks ago, he stopped by the house, completely unannounced, said he just wanted to say hello, and he couldn't stop smiling. I thought maybe he was on drugs or something, but I decided if there was a drug that made him happy, maybe it wasn't so bad. Now I'm pretty sure you're the drug that's made him so happy. And I could just hug you. I understand you never got married either. Maybe you were out there searching as well?"

"Maybe..."

"You know, Coco, you remind me a lot of your mother. Yes, I knew Mary Lynn, we served on quite a few committees together over the years. She was so active in the community, always so full of great ideas. And she was so proud of you. She always spent a few minutes talking about your latest accomplishment, your most recent visit home. You seem to have her sweet personality and good nature. And her good looks."

"I'm not sure I'd go that far, but thank you very much for saying that."

Coco smiled a little but Claudia could see a few tears in her eyes. Chase was just coming into the kitchen to check on Coco and his mother when the kitchen timer went off. He saw the look on Coco's face and was just about to scold his mother for whatever she had done to make Coco sad. But Coco just smiled and squeezed his hand as if to say everything was just fine. And Claudia took command of dinner.

"Chase, darling, take this bowl to the table and get your father into the dining room. It's time to eat. Coco, why don't you take that bowl and the water pitcher and I'll bring the roast. Let's go, I'm starving!!"

An hour later, the foursome at the dining room table were enjoying the last of their dessert, and John Buckingham couldn't say enough good about it. "Coco, this dessert is incredible. What all do you have in here?"

"Well, John, I was told that you love chocolate so I put little chunks of brownies in the bottom of the glass and drizzled caramel sauce and toffee bits over it, then added a layer of whipped cream. Then I made a second layer just like the first. I drizzled more caramel sauce and toffee bits on top and there it is. It couldn't be any easier or more delicious."

"Well, Coco, you can make this for me any time. I love my wife's cooking, but I'm afraid she's not so much of a baker or dessert maker. Or maybe she just thinks I shouldn't eat so many sweets."

Coco started to think that maybe she had a magic touch when it came to concocting wonderful treats that everyone loved – seeing John and Chase finishing their second helpings made her smile. "I'm glad you liked it, John. And Claudia, if I haven't said so before now, dinner was outstanding. The roast was perfect and you'll have to tell me how you made the broccoli and carrots so delicious."

"Mom, Coco, you both did an excellent job getting dinner on the table. Now I think it's up to dad and me to clean up. Mom, why don't you show Coco around the house while we make this mess disappear?"

"Chase, that sounds wonderful. Coco, how about another glass of wine and a tour of the house?"

"Lead the way, Claudia." Chase poured them both a glass of wine and they were off on their tour.

When Claudia and Coco got back to the kitchen 30 minutes later, the dishwasher was running and everything was spic and span. When Claudia inspected the fridge, she found the leftovers perfectly packaged, and in the correct drawers.

"Coco, don't I have those two men trained really well?"

"I'm impressed, Claudia. You've done a fine job."

The dining room was clean as well, so the ladies headed to the family room, sure that their men would be watching some sports thing on John's new huge screen TV. By the time the baseball game was over, Chase was ready to move Coco toward the door and head home. His eyes were a combination of tired and lusty, and Coco wasn't exactly which one she wanted to win out, but she was in agreement that it was time to go.

Coco thanked Claudia and John for their hospitality. When Claudia hugged her goodbye, she whispered in Coco's ear – "I left your panties in Chase's underwear drawer. It never hurts to have a spare pair around, just in case."

"Thank you, Claudia, that was very considerate. Embarrassing, but considerate!" And they were out the door, in the car and headed down the road.

The drive back to Chase's house was shorter and faster than their original drive to his parents' house, and Coco was in a much calmer state of mind heading home. "Chase, I had a lovely evening. Your parents are wonderful people. But I think your mother can be a little feisty when she wants to be. She asked me if I was sleeping with you and my surprised reaction was to spit wine all over the kitchen table."

"She asked you what??"

"Yes, she found a pair of lace panties in your laundry on Wednesday and wanted to know if they belonged to me."

"Oh my god!! What did you say?"

"I didn't say anything – I spit wine at her across the kitchen table!! I never actually admitted that they were mine, but I didn't see any point in denying it either. She seemed fairly happy that you're actually getting into some woman's dainties. I'm just wondering how the hell I managed to leave your house at some point in the past three weeks, minus the underwear I showed up in. I don't remember doing that at all. They are mine, right? Those lace panties don't belong to you, do they? Or some other woman you're boinking when I'm not around?"

"Boinking? Did you really say that? Of course, they're yours, I just don't remember exactly when I acquired them. Now, my mom! Did she actually say she was happy about finding panties in my laundry?"

"Yes, she did."

"Holy crap, my mother knows I'm having sex!! I feel like I'm 16 again."

"16? I don't think I even want to know!!"

They were quiet for the rest of the drive, but every now and then, one of them would laugh a little and they would smile at each other, very pleased with how the evening had turned out. As tired as they both were, Chase couldn't resist getting inside Coco before they fell asleep. When she came out of the bathroom after a quick shower, he grabbed her around the waist, threw her on the bed, and had his way with her. It was a quick tryst, but they were both completely satisfied when they were done. Coco snuggled under the covers while Chase showered and checked a few emails, and by the time he came to bed, she was almost asleep, a little smile on her face. He settled into bed and cuddled up against her, kissed her cheek, and whispered "Sweet dreams, baby."

Chase fell off to sleep immediately, but Coco had trouble getting settled. She drifted off several times, only to wake up again, thinking about her parents. Around 2:00 AM, she got up and went into the bathroom, neglecting to turn on the light. She thought she'd spent enough time in Chase's bathroom that she didn't need to actually see what she was doing. Sadly, she was wrong. She didn't look closely enough and when she sat down on the toilet, there was a loud splash and then cursing loud enough to wake the dead. "God damn motherfucking son of a bitch!! Buckingham, get in here!!"

Chase sat bolt upright in bed, thinking for a minute that he had dreamed the loud noise. Then he heard splashing and screaming coming from the bathroom and raced to the door to see what was going on. He flipped on the bathroom light – and laughed – hard. Which didn't really help. Coco was naked, sitting in the toilet, arms and legs flailing around trying to get herself out. She almost had herself removed from her little porcelain prison when Chase came flying into the bathroom, slid on the water on the floor, and knocked her back in. Which just started him laughing again, and her cursing again.

"Oh my god, Coco, are you alright?"

"Do I look like I'm alright? Get me out of this damned thing!"

Chase finally managed to get Coco out of the toilet and on her feet, and she headed immediately for the shower, yelling at him over her shoulder all the way. "Chase, I've reminded you multiple times about putting the seat back down on the toilet when you're done."

"I know, Coco, I'm so sorry, I'm just not used to having a woman in the house. I promise, it won't happen again." And he snickered as she ducked under the shower and started scrubbing herself like she would never get clean.

"Coco, honey, can I help?"

"Don't touch me. I don't need any help. Just clean up the water on the floor – use some bleach – and go back to bed!"

Ten minutes later, she was out of the shower, dried off and glaring at Chase from the foot of the bed.

"I'm really tempted to go sleep on the sofa, Buckingham, but I'm really tired and that damned thing is a death trap for my back. So I'm getting back into bed, and I'd better not hear one more chuckle from you – ever! As a matter of fact, I'd better never hear you speak about this ever again – to anyone!"

"Maybe we could speak about it one time? In thirty years? Just to reminisce?"

"Chase…"

"Agreed. Never again. Just let me get one last laugh out of the way and then never again." And he laughed one time, so hard he cried. And then he was done.

Coco got back into bed but she seemed determined to stay on her own side of the bed, nowhere near Chase. He scooted to the center of the bed, and pulled a resisting Coco into his arms, hugging her close until she stopped struggling and started to fall back to sleep. She giggled a little to herself one time and whispered "Never again, Buckingham." And then she was out.

Chase laughed to himself a little, kissing Coco's head, stroking her exposed shoulder gently, feeling a sense of peace he'd never felt before. Coco leaned back into him a little closer in her sleep, and Chase fell off to sleep himself, knowing that this was exactly what love felt like.

21

*C*oco woke up Sunday morning with Chase's arms holding her legs open and his face attached to her pussy. She had been dreaming that she was spread wide and that a long, disembodied tongue had settled between her legs. The tongue was taking leisurely licks at her pussy, spearing into her cunt, flicking against her clit like it knew exactly what she wanted. And she was rolling closer and closer to a larger than life orgasm.

Just about the time the tongue grew teeth and started nibbling on her clit, she woke up with a jolt and a scream, hands flying to her crotch to brush away whatever was there, slapping the face she found there. And then she recognized the face that looked up at her, huge smile beaming at her, and the now familiar evil chuckle rolling out of Chase's throat. "What the hell? What are you doing, Buckingham?"

"Making up for last night?"

"Fuck you, Chase, you scared me to death!"

"Isn't this the way every woman dreams of waking up?"

"The dream part is the problem – until five seconds ago, I was dreaming there was a disembodied tongue with teeth, trying to eat me up!"

"Well, it's not disembodied, baby, but it is trying to eat you up. Now just lay back and let me finish. I'll have my fill of you and then I'll make you breakfast. And then we're going to take a little ride."

"Chase, I think you should just… OH!! FUCK!!! Oh, holy fuck!" And she fell back on the pillows breathless, gurgling noises coming from her throat. Her eyes crossed, and she came like a freight train all over her lover's tongue.

As much as Chase had planned to just give Coco a little "good morning" orgasm to make up for her fall into the toilet, the look on her face as she drowned in her pleasure was more than he could withstand. Her body was still shuddering and her pussy was still quivering when he slid his painfully hard cock inside her, cloaked in the heat of her. Chase took Coco's mouth in a burning kiss that almost devoured them both. She wrapped her trembling legs around his waist, clutched his head to hers, lips crushing lips, exchanging breath until they were both dizzy.

As Chase plunged into Coco's tunnel of love over and over again, hitting that magic spot inside her, another orgasm shot through her. The tremors that fired in her pussy threatened to strangle Chase as he came. He thrust into her three more times before he was paralyzed by the force of his own orgasm. The full weight of him dropped on top of her and she hugged him like she was never going to let him go. They lay together for long minutes, gasping for breath, Chase's head resting on the pillow he was sharing with Coco.

She finally turned her head toward him and whispered "Fuck, gorgeous, you know that just never gets old. How many years do you think we have before we don't want to do this anymore?"

And he whispered back "Forty, maybe fifty, baby. For as long as I can still breathe, I'll always want to be right here with you."

"Forty or fifty years? I think I could handle that. Even if we split the difference, I'll only be 95 when we finally quit. Sounds about right." And they laughed for a few minutes – until Chase's growling stomach got them out of bed and headed to the kitchen for breakfast.

Two hours later, breakfast was a delicious memory, the kitchen was cleaned up and they had showered and dressed. Looking at herself dressed in yoga pants, a tank top and a light jacket, Coco decided she needed to bring more clothes to Chase's house. And he needed to bring more clothes to her house for the mornings after he spent the night there with her. They picked at each other about it for a few minutes, and then Chase finally gave up and said "Okay, baby, whatever you say." And she smiled at him like he had just declared her empress of the world.

But Coco was determined that they weren't going anywhere until they had the discussion Chase has been putting off – the one about their vast political differences.

"Chase, we're not moving out of this house until we talk about what happens every time we discuss anything remotely political."

"Coco, not now, we're both in too good a mood."

"Yes, Chase. Now. While we're both in a good mood!"

"Okay, what do you want to say? What do you want ME to say?"

"Right now, gorgeous, I just want you to listen. Because I've made a list of the major points of pain between us. It's a long list." And she walked to her purse and pulled out an actual list. She was right, it was a pretty long list.

"Is there anything we actually agree on?"

"Yes, there are a few things. That's a significantly shorter list."

"So where do we start?" He was getting grumpier by the second and his mood probably wasn't going to improve any time soon.

"Okay, let's just discuss the major obstacles for now. If we can come to some kind of agreement on these few biggies, quite of few of the others should fall into place."

"Like?"

"Like every time the subject of Representative Banner comes up, your fuse lights and I fear spontaneous combustion is close at hand. I know you disagree with me about his voting record the past two years. Tell me why you're so against him."

"He teases the voters with a promise of tax cuts, but doesn't tell everyone the opportunity costs of those cuts – like no funding for marshland reclamation, which is vital to the local ecology. He's always somewhere other than Columbia and he's missed four votes in the past two months. I hate that he votes against bills I think would be good for the state, but I hate even more that he doesn't respect his position or his constituents enough to show up and do his fucking job. His biggest donors are major polluters in the state and frankly, I think he's got his hands in the pockets of a growing organized crime base."

"Okay, fine. I can see I'll have to do some additional research before I do any actual work on his campaign. Fair enough?"

"Yes, fair enough."

"And you won't try to run him over with your car the next time you see him? Just in case maybe you're a little bit wrong about him?"

"Fine. What's next on your list."

"I know it's part of your basic personality, gorgeous, but you have to stop being so fucking arrogant all the time."

"I'm not arrogant. I'm just always right."

"And there you go. I'm sure you said that just to get me all pissed off, and I'm not taking the bait – this time. I hate to admit it, but you are right, quite often. But not all the time. Not about all things. You don't know everything there is to know in the world and you refuse to acknowledge that anyone else has half a brain if they dare to have a different opinion about something. Or heaven forbid, contradict something you spout as gospel!"

"Coco, I can't help how I am. Blame it on the Army. They took my natural tendency to be a controlling know-it-all and molded it into something that can be pretty daunting for the enemy – I mean the opposition. It made me a damn good soldier. It makes me a damn good attorney. And you have to admit, it makes me an ass kicking lover."

"Chase…"

"Coco, I don't know if I can change such a basic part of myself, and I'm not sure I want to try. Even for you."

"Chase, I'm not asking you to completely change your personality. I care about you because of it, in spite of it. But I am asking you to stop before you call someone a mindless dumb ass – or pig headed – and just listen to what they have to say. You did it grudgingly during our meeting about the marshland bill and it worked out okay. Maybe you could do it again now and then. Maybe just once a day you could focus on what someone with a different point of view has to say. Maybe listen to FOX News now and then. You don't have to change your opinion every time but you do need to listen to other people more often. Please? For me?"

"Oh, Coco, you don't know what you're asking."

"Chase…"

"But I'll try. You actually say really smart things now and then. Like 'Oh, Chase, you're the greatest lover I've ever had! You rock my world just by touching me! You give me orgasms like no one ever has!' You know, stuff like that!"

"Chase! Be serious!"

"I am, Coco, I'm being very serious. I promise. I'll try. Don't expect miracles. But I'll try. Now can we go?"

"I guess I'll just have to take what I can get in the short term and work on you over time. Yes, we can go now. Where are we going?"

"It's a surprise. You'll just have to wait and see. Be patient – something YOU'RE not very good at, if I may say so."

"You may NOT say so. But I'll try. We need to stop by my house first so let's hit it!"

They climbed into Chase's jeep and headed out, Coco trying to get their final destination out of him, and Chase refusing to tell her. They stopped by Coco's house so she could change clothes quick and while she was in the kitchen cleaning a few things up, she remembered she had found Chase's missing ring in the basement bathroom, and she yelled to him over her shoulder, "Chase, I found your onyx ring on Thursday. It almost went down the bathroom sink drain, I only caught it just at the last second."

"Where did you put it?"

"It's in my jewelry box. I'll get it for you."

"I'm already in the bedroom, I'll get it."

And a flood of panic hit her, knowing that when he opened her jewelry box to get his ring, he would see something else that she wasn't ready for him to see yet. "Chase, wait!" She headed toward the bedroom but it was too late – she ran into Chase in the living room. She could see that he had his ring on, but he was holding up a woman's engagement ring, a combination of shock and accusation on his face.

"Coco, tell me this is your mother's engagement ring."

"Chase, I... It's mine."

"Coco, that night at Robert and Gigi's wedding, I asked you if anyone had ever captured your heart and you said no. This tells me something different. And it tells me you lied to me. How many other lies have you told me?"

"Chase, I can explain. It's not what you think."

"Really? Were you engaged to someone, Coco?"

"Yes, but it wasn't... I wasn't in love with him. I only..."

"You accepted an engagement ring from a man you didn't love? Just like Gail accepted my ring and agreed to marry me when she knew she didn't love me? At least when she broke up with me, she gave my ring back. What kind of woman are you? I'm beginning to think I don't know you at all. Like this is all just a big mistake." And he dropped the ring on the floor like it was burning him.

As tears streamed down her face, Coco whispered "Chase, please, let me explain."

And Chase just shook his head, his own tears starting to fall. When Coco reached for him, he backed away from her and said "No, don't touch me. I can't be here right now, I can't look at you right now. I have to go."

And he turned and went out the front door, never looking back.

Coco ran to the door, crying so hard she couldn't breathe. As he drove away from the house, she whispered "Chase, I can explain." But he was gone, and she knew in her heart he wouldn't be back.

22

*C*oco sat in her bed all night, crying, clutching the engagement ring she had picked up off the floor, thinking about the man she had promised to marry, even though they both knew she didn't love him. He was sick, and he wasn't going to get better, but that hadn't mattered to Coco. He was her friend and she wanted to stand by him. But he didn't want her pity and he left. After he was gone, Coco had taken off her engagement ring, and shortly after that, she had taken her first assignment in Japan, hoping that the distance would help to ease the sense of loss she didn't think she had the right to feel.

She had failed Martin all those years ago, and now she had failed Chase. And she didn't think her heart would ever be the same, weighed down by more guilt.

Every day that week became harder to handle, rather than easier. Her mind was on Chase constantly, to the point where she couldn't concentrate on work at all. She had texted Chase too many times, had left too many messages on his cell phone, left him too many emails. And got zero response from any of them. And instead of relying on her best friends to help her get over her heartbreak, she couldn't bring herself to reach out to them at all. On Friday morning, when she started getting emails and text messages from both Gigi and Maggs, messages she couldn't return, she started thinking about going away for a few days. Friday at the end of the day, she put an out of office message on her email and her phone, and started packing a bag. She wasn't sure where she was going but she knew she needed to get away for just a little while.

Unfortunately, she wasn't fast enough getting out of the house. She wasn't even finished packing yet when her phone started ringing, showing UNKNOWN as the phone number. Every time she declined the call, the phone would ring again. Then someone started pounding on her front door, scaring the shit out of her. Then she heard the voices she had been trying to get away from, yelling through the door.

"Damn it, Coco, open the fucking door, or we'll break it down! And you know we can!!" She did know they could, they had done it before. Gigi and Maggs. Even when she didn't want to see them, they intended to be there for her. And the tears started to fall again. And she opened the front door, only to be surrounded by the arms of her oldest, dearest friends, the ones who were always there for her. And she sobbed and couldn't speak.

Minutes later, Coco finally started to settle, and she was led to the sofa, with Gigi on one side and Maggs on the other, neither one letting her go. They sat with her for a little longer, holding her hands until she stopped crying. Then Gigi took control of the conversation.

"Maggs, why don't you go open that bottle of wine. We don't need glasses, we can just drink from the bottle." And Maggs was off to the kitchen to open the wine. She was always handy with a corkscrew and was back with the opened bottle in no time. Maggs took a big swig from the bottle and handed it to Gigi, who also took a big swig. By the time the bottle came to Coco, she was crying again, remembering the day in the '57 when she and Chase had drunk out of the wine bottle while they made love.

After a few more minutes and a few more swigs of wine all around, Coco asked "Why are you two here? How did you know something was wrong?"

And Gigi answered "Coco, honey, Chase stopped by the house last night after his group session. He wouldn't talk to me, he insisted on taking Robert out in the backyard to talk. I could hear raised voices but no words. They were out there a long time. I finally couldn't stand it any longer. I went out in the yard and asked Chase if he had killed you or something, but he looked like the one who'd been killed."

"Is he okay?"

"No, he's really not okay. He doesn't understand and he feels like you lied to him. Honey, why didn't you ever tell him about Martin? He would have understood if you had just told him. After he told you what had happened with Gail, you should have told him about Martin right away."

Coco looked at Gigi like she was taking Chase's side and Gigi said to Maggs, "I think we're gonna need more wine. It's gonna be a long night." And Maggs was off to the kitchen to fetch another bottle of wine.

For the next hour, the three best friends argued and yelled and talked and cried. Coco finally said "I don't know why I didn't tell him about Martin. I should have told him when he saw the picture, but I just couldn't do it. And things just happened between Chase and me so fast. I guess I hoped I'd never have to tell him. And I've been trying to contact him all week. I've left phone messages and texts and emails. It's a wonder he hasn't had me arrested for stalking him. I did everything but drive to his house and sit in my car in the driveway. What did Mr. Righteous Indignation have to say about that!?"

"He admitted that he's been ignoring your calls. And he looks like hell. I don't think he's gotten any more sleep this week than you have. You look like hell too."

"Thanks, Gigi, I can always count on you to have my back!"

"Yes, you can, Coco. You know that. So why didn't you call Maggs or me Sunday night? We're both really pissed that you've been miserable all week and never reached out to either of us. What kind of friend suffers alone like that when she could be getting drunk with her best friends??"

"I guess I should have known better than to think I could outrun the two of you. I'm sorry, I should have shared my personal disaster with the two of you right away. So, brainiacs, can this be fixed? Is there some way I can get Chase to listen to me, to understand what I did? Or do I just apologize and walk away, let him get on with his life? Of course, I'll never love another man, so I'll just go to the animal shelter and adopt a bunch of cats – become the crazy cat lady of the neighborhood, with 17 litter boxes in the basement."

"No, Coco, no cats! And I don't know if you can fix this or not. But you do owe Chase an apology in person. I happen to know that he's going to be home tomorrow afternoon because Robert made plans to pick him up and take him fishing in the morning. They'll be home by 1:00 because

Robert is going to come down with a stomach bug around Noon. This may be your one shot to talk to him for a while. He says he's going back to Columbia for a while to check on the new woman lawyer in the office. He may not be back before the fall election."

Gigi and Maggs spent the next hour with Coco, plotting and scheming as much as they could, to get Coco at least a few minutes of face time with Chase. She would have to be quick and she would have to be sincere. After that, she would just have to hope for the best. They finished off the second bottle of wine and then a third bottle before they all passed out in Coco's big bed.

Gigi and Maggs left early Saturday morning so that Coco could have some alone time to collect her thoughts before seeing Chase. She ended up writing him a letter, fully expecting that he wouldn't speak to her or let her talk. She only hoped that he would take the letter and read it later, and would maybe agree to talk with her in a few days. She ran a few laps on the track at the high school down the street, but no matter how fast she ran, she couldn't outrun her past. She just hoped it wouldn't break her when it finally caught up with her.

Coco pulled into Chase's driveway, thunder rumbling and lightning visible in the approaching storm coming in off the ocean. She hoped that Chase and Robert hadn't been on the water as the storm approached. Almost answering her prayers, Robert's car pulled into the driveway 5 minutes after she arrived. Chase got out of Robert's car, and Robert backed out of the driveway, but he didn't leave, fearing an ugly confrontation that might need witnesses, or a referee. Coco got out of her car, clutching the letter in her hands, and attempted to talk to Chase as he stormed past her toward the house. She reached out to grab his arm, but he sidestepped her, eluding her grasp. But he didn't move any further away from her.

"Chase, I'm sorry, I never meant to hurt you. I didn't lie to you."

"I'm not interested in anything you have to say to me, Coralee. I can't trust anything that comes out of your mouth."

"Chase, please. I can explain."

"No, Coco, just go home." And he turned and started walking toward the house.

And Coco lost herself, and screamed at him as tears streamed down her cheeks, stopping him again in his tracks. "You arrogant son of a bitch! Do you really think you're the only one with demons in your past? I expected you would be too stubborn to listen to me, but by God, you will hear my story one way or another." And she took the envelope in her hand and crumpled it up in a ball. And she marched up to him and stuffed it in his jacket pocket. "There, asshole, forgive me or don't, but at least hear me out before you judge me." And the rain started to fall.

Chase stared at Coco for a minute, and then pulled the crumpled letter out of his pocket. He looked at it for a few seconds and then let it fall from his hand to the ground. And he turned and walked up the steps and into the house, slamming the front door behind him.

Coco looked at the wadded up paper on the ground, knowing Chase would never read it. But he'd broken her, and she didn't care anymore. She left it on the ground and got into her car, out of the rain. Robert was still sitting in his car at the curb, and as Coco backed out of the driveway, she nearly hit him. But she didn't care about that either, she just knew that she had to get away, far away, so that she could wallow in her sorrow alone for a while.

Robert was just about to pull back into the driveway and retrieve the wet letter, fully intending to beat Chase to a pulp and then stuff the letter up his ass. But he decided he needed to stay out of it for the time being. Coco needed to calm down, and Chase needed to grow up, and they both needed to talk to each other, or nothing would ever be resolved. So Robert drove away, rain pouring down, wind raging, Chase staring out the kitchen window at the bit of wet, crumpled paper blowing around in the yard.

When Coco got home, she raced into the house, finished packing her bag and left. She had turned off her cell phone and left it on her desk, but grabbed a prepaid phone she's acquired a few months before when her previous cell phone had died. She wanted some kind of phone, just in case, but she didn't want to be tracked by anyone who knew her and wanted to keep tabs on her. When she left the house, she had planned on driving down to Marco Island, but the rain was so intense that by the time she got to Savannah 5 hours later, she was too tired to continue. She headed downtown and found a hotel with a vacancy, checked in and ordered room service. A lot of room service, including two bottles of wine. She settled in with the Do Not Disturb sign on the door, planning on a three or four day pity party before she headed back home to rebuild her life, minus Chase Buckingham.

Just about the time Coco was checking into her hotel in Savannah, Chase was finally ready to read the letter she'd written him. But when he looked out in the yard, he couldn't see the crumpled paper anywhere. It was still raining and windy, and he was afraid it had blown away – the thought that he had lost the letter before he could read it stabbed at his heart. The pain of that thought was almost as bad as the memory of the look on Coco's face as she got back into her car and drove away. He had been a major prick, and the guilt he piled on himself almost crushed him.

Muttering to himself, he ran out the front door into the rain, racing around the yard, searching for the letter. "No, no, no, no. Please be here. Please be here. You have to be here." He got all the way to the street and still hadn't found it – the letter wasn't there anymore. Tears mixed with the rain falling down his face as he trudged back to the house and sat down on the front step. He pulled his cell phone out of his pocket and called Coco, but the call went to voice mail so he left a message. "Coco, I'm sorry. Please call me back. We need to talk. Please, baby, call me back."

Chase sat on the step in the rain for ten minutes, trying to figure out what to do next. He finally decided he just needed to go to Coco's house. As he was getting up off the step, he happened to turn toward the corner of the flower bed and something up against the garage wall caught his eye. Something white and crumpled. Something that looked like Coco's letter. He jumped down and grabbed the paper and ran into the house out of the rain. With cold, shaking hands, Chase carefully opened the envelope and found a letter and a photo inside. The photo was soaked but he recognized it as the one he had asked about that day at Coco's house, the one that had made her look so sad. And he remembered her words when he asked who it was. *"He was a friend… He died. He'd been sick and he decided he had nothing left to live for."*

His tears added to the dampness of the photo as he asked himself angrily "Why didn't she just tell me then? Why couldn't she tell me then?" As he pulled the letter out of the envelope, he realized that the photo had protected it from most of the rain. It was wet but still readable. He held the folded papers in his hands for a few minutes, afraid to read what she'd written, afraid he might have to admit what a giant bastard he'd been.

Finally his curiosity got the best of him – he unfolded the papers and read what she'd written.

Dearest Chase,

If you're reading this letter, we haven't spoken yet. I'm trying to understand your reaction on Sunday, I'm trying to put myself in your shoes and imagine how I would feel if you had told me similar news.

I know you think I lied to you when I said no one had ever captured my heart, but that was a true statement. If my not telling you about being engaged was a lie, it was a lie of omission. If that's even possible. I doubt that I can change your mind at this point, but I can at least explain.

You see, Chase, I'm not as brave as you. I'm not as strong. You face your past and your demons every day, and I admire you so much for your courage. But that's not me. I ignore my past at all cost, only acknowledging my demons when I have to. I guess I have to now.

The man in the photo is Martin Rice. He was a co-worker many times over the years, and we ended up in Phoenix together. Martin was considerably older than me but he had a young heart and we were good friends. We were comfortable together and it seemed natural to him for us to get married. I held him off for quite a while, but he finally wore me down and I accepted his proposal. We both knew that I wasn't in love with him, but when he was diagnosed with MS, I knew I was meant to marry him and take care of him.

We hadn't set a date yet, he wouldn't let me pin him down. Unfortunately, his disease progressed much faster than the doctors had anticipated, and Martin was quickly becoming dependent on me for just about everything, something he couldn't tolerate. I came home from work one day and found Martin nearly dead. He was participating in a drug trial and he took a full bottle of pills that were supposed to prolong his life and ended up killing him instead.

I failed Martin, I wasn't able to make him see that no matter how incapacitated he might become, he would always be a valuable human being and his friends needed his wit and his charm and his sharp mind. Sometimes the guilt I feel weighs on me so heavily, I can barely breathe. So I hide it away and ignore that whole chapter of my life.

After Martin's funeral, I stopped wearing his ring but I couldn't bring myself to get rid of it. Maybe that was a subconscious attempt on my part to continue punishing myself, I guess we'll never know.

A few months after Martin died, I took my first assignment in Japan. Yes, I was absolutely running away from the pain, running is what I do, but the distance did help me in the end.

Chase, I wish you could understand that what I did wasn't like what Gail did. I would never have turned my back on Martin, no matter how bad things got. He was my friend. He was a good man. He just wasn't a strong man.

I've missed you this past week, Chase. I hope we can be friends again someday.

SWAK.

Coco

Chase re-read the letter twice, and by the time he was done, he realized he was sitting on the kitchen floor sobbing. All he could do was whisper to himself, "Coco, I'm so sorry." Knowing that she couldn't hear him. Knowing that he had to find her. Try to make things right between them again.

During the next two hours, Chase called Coco's cell phone and left 15 messages. He decided it was time to go to her house and make his own apologies, make her talk to him, make her listen, make her work things out between them.

When Chase got to Coco's house, her car wasn't in the driveway and the house was dark. He saw Coco's next door neighbor out in the yard so he approached him and asked if he had seen Coco at all that day. Coco had introduced Chase to Corey Bingham a few weeks before and Corey was feeling chatty.

"Chase, good to see you again! I did see Coco earlier this afternoon. She flew into the driveway and ran into the house. A few minutes later she came out again with her suitcase, asked me to keep an eye on things for a few days, and she was gone. She seemed in a real hurry. Is everything okay?"

"Yeah, everything's fine. We just keep missing each other today. I'm going to go in and check on a few things and then I'll take off. When Coco gets back, tell her to call me."

"Will do, buddy."

Chase let himself into the house with his key to the front door and turned on a small lamp in the living room. He started looking around and ended up in Coco's office, where he found her cell phone, turned off, sitting on her desk. He started rifling through the notes on her desk but couldn't find anything that might indicate where she could have gone. She was out there somewhere alone, with no phone, thinking he hated her, and he was terrified what she might do. He needed to talk to the only person who might know where she would go. He locked up Coco's house and waved to the neighbor, and headed at a high rate of speed to Robert and Gigi's house.

When he got there, he was disappointed that Coco's car wasn't there, but he hoped against hope that Gigi knew where she was. Chase ran up the sidewalk onto the porch and started pounding on the door, almost hitting Robert in the face when the door opened.

"Dude, you just about clobbered me!"

"Is Coco here?"

"No, she's not. We don't know where she is. And after this afternoon, I'm not sure I'd tell you if I did know. Dude, you were a Class A asshat today. We've known each other for a lot of years, man, and I've never been more ashamed of your behavior than I was today."

"I know. Can I come in?"

"Of course. Even a major asshat deserves to come in out of the rain."

Gigi came into the living room as Robert was closing the front door. She looked at Chase and all she could do was shake her head and sigh.

"Gigi, where is she? I'm so worried about her. I found her cell phone turned off on her desk, and her neighbor said she took off this afternoon and asked him to keep an eye on things for a few days. Where would she go?"

"Chase, I've known Coco most of my life. If she took off, she's just being Coco. When she gets overwhelmed like she has been the past week, she runs. She needs to be alone for a few days to process what's going on. When she runs, she's never gone more than a few days. She just needs time to map out how she's going to go on without you in her life."

"Gigi, do you think she would do something – something like Martin did? She hurt me pretty bad last Sunday, and I lashed out pretty hard this afternoon. If anything happens to her, I'll never forgive myself. And I know her Uncle Bob will come after me with a fucking gun and a pack of relatives ready to tar and feather me."

Gigi chuckled a little at the thought of Uncle Bob going after Chase with a gun. "No, Chase, I don't think she'll do anything like Martin did. Coco's too chicken to actually go through with something like suicide. She'll come home eventually and make us all wish we were somewhere else for a while. So what's your plan when she does come home? Do you just want to ease your guilty conscience and move on without her? Or do you plan to fix things between the two of you and move forward together? Assuming, of course, that she's willing to do that."

"Gigi, I have no idea what I'm going to do. The one thing I do know is that I'm not letting her get away from me. She promised me the next 45 years and I intend to collect on that promise."

"Okay, sweetie, just be prepared to grovel."

23

M onday morning, Coco woke up in her hotel room with a really bad hangover. She'd drank more wine and eaten more junk food since Saturday evening than she had in the past six months. And she hadn't showered, had only gotten out of bed long enough to let the steady stream of room service waiters in to bring more food and wine. She was sure they would have to fumigate her room when she left. But it was time to go home and face her friends, maybe even face Chase one last time, and then get on with her life without him.

After her shower and a reasonable breakfast, Coco was feeling up to the drive home. She checked out of the hotel, cringing at the long list of room service charges on her bill, dragged her suitcase to the car and stowed it in the trunk. Just before she pulled out of the hotel parking lot, she texted Gigi.

"On my way home. I'll call you later. C."

Then she turned off the phone so she wouldn't be tempted to text and drive, and headed north. The weather was beautiful after the rainy weekend, and the drive was easy, but she wasn't really looking forward to going into her empty house yet, so she took her time. Four hours later, Coco pulled into her driveway, not noticing a familiar Jeep parked on the street. She texted Gigi again that she was home and would call her later. Then she got her suitcase out of the trunk and headed for the house.

She went in through the back door so that she could dump everything out of her suitcase directly into the washer, then realized she hadn't stopped for lunch and she was hungry. Not knowing exactly what was in the fridge that might still be edible, she bent over and leaned way in to see what had gotten pushed to the back. In the quiet of the house, she clearly heard a deep voice say her name. She was startled by the sound and smacked her head on the top of the fridge compartment, practically crawling the rest of the way in. And then she was instantly terrified of the unidentified intruder. Her scream echoed around inside the fridge but it didn't stop her from grabbing every condiment and leftover she could get her hands on, throwing bottles and jars and containers over her shoulder in the direction of the intruder.

"Jesus, Coco, stop throwing shit at me! I don't want my friends to know I was killed by a jar of pickles!"

And then she recognized the voice. But she continued to throw things at Chase when she turned around and saw him deflecting glass and plastic projectiles with her pillow.

"What the fuck are you doing in my house?! I distinctly remember you saying you never wanted to see me again! And what the fuck are you doing with my pillow??"

In a quiet voice, Chase said "I've been so worried about you. I've been waiting for you to come home. Your pillow smells like you so I've been holding it. Since yesterday. I was afraid if I didn't camp out here, you'd refuse to see me."

"Pardon my lack of empathy. I learned from the master. On Saturday! And where the fuck did this sudden concern for my welfare come from, anyway?? I've sent you about a hundred texts and voice mails and emails in the last week and what did I get from the concerned Mr. Buckingham?? Not a fucking thing. Not one fucking word, you asshole! So just take your concern and get the fuck out of my house!"

"For the record, Coco, I never said I never wanted to see you again. I just needed a little time to cool off. It's already been pointed out that I was a giant asshat about this whole thing, I admit that. I guess it took seeing you on Saturday to make me realize what I was throwing away. Coco, please, can we just talk?"

Coco's face lost some of its anger and took on a sad, almost dejected look. "It sure felt like you never wanted to see me again, having all of my calls and emails and texts ignored all week. And then having you turn your back on me on Saturday? What was that supposed to tell me?"

"Coco, I've been a total prick. I was hurt and confused and I don't handle those emotions well, especially when they aren't logical or justified."

"What's changed in the past week, Chase? You still think I lied to you, I still have an engagement ring in my jewelry box from a man I didn't love. You and I said terrible things to each other, things we meant. I don't think there's anything left to salvage."

"Coco, do you not have any feelings left for me? Is it all gone between us? I've read your letter about a hundred times since Saturday. It starts '*Dearest Chase.*' Just reading it, I can hear your voice speak the words. It soothes my heart a little. That can't be all gone. Coco, we were both wrong, you and I. I was so hurt by what Gail did that I changed my whole life trying to get rid of the feeling that I wasn't good enough for anyone. And all of a sudden, you were there, and I thought maybe I was getting a second chance. And then I thought you had done the same thing to some other man and I reacted to it. It took me right back to that apartment, that feeling of being insignificant, and Gail standing in the doorway telling me she didn't love me.

"Coco, I know I reacted badly, I should have stayed and let you explain. But why didn't you tell me about it right away? The opportunity was right there the first time I saw the picture. We could have had a five minute discussion about it and it would have been behind us. Why did it have to come to this?"

"Chase, I told you, I'm not brave like you are. I hide from my ugly memories. I don't drag them out and dust them off and show them to everyone. I don't share them easily, especially that one. It's juvenile and I'm not proud of it, but it works for me. Most days. That day that Martin killed himself, I had just talked to him at lunch. We joked about something that had happened that morning. He seemed fine, in really good spirits. And then a few hours later I came home and found him, barely alive, on the bathroom floor. He had a faint pulse and I called 9-1-1. I kept shaking him, trying to wake him up, but he never regained consciousness. He died in the Emergency Room.

"All the time I waited for the rescue squad to get to the house, I kept yelling at him, asking him why. Why would he do that? How could he do it? Is it some macho guy thing that he couldn't face being less than perfect? I didn't understand it then, and I don't understand it now. And I blame myself for not finding a way to show him how many people cared about him, wanted to keep him around for as long as we could." And she turned away from Chase and sobbed into the still open refrigerator.

"So maybe you cared about him just a little more than you let on? Coco, I know it means nothing coming from me, I didn't know him, but maybe he just didn't want to be a burden to anyone, especially you. And maybe he was just tired of the daily grind, getting his hopes up about a cure or remission and then having those hopes crushed every time. I can understand a little about how he might have felt. Maybe he had to do what was best for him, and hope that you and all your friends would understand. If he loved you, he wouldn't want you to feel guilty about something you couldn't prevent, something you couldn't fix."

Chase had been creeping closer and closer to Coco, not wanting to invade her space but wanting desperately to hold her, to comfort her, to regain the connection they'd had before. He finally couldn't stop himself — his hand reached out and touched her shoulder. And he whispered "Coco." And she turned into his arms and let him hold her while she cried. Finally holding her again was the best feeling he'd had in days.

Neither one knew how long they stood like that, but they were both calmed by the peace of their embrace. But eventually Chase grew bolder, his hands starting to skim over Coco's back, down to her ass, and she didn't turn him away. He leaned down to kiss her face — her forehead, her nose, her cheeks — her lips. The kiss fired an urgent need between them and they fell into the passion of the moment. But not for long. Coco began to feel panic rising in her chest and she pushed away from Chase, hating the growing sadness in his eyes.

"Chase, please stop. I can't do this. Not right now." And she backed away until there was some space between them. Space that didn't ease the tightness gripping her heart.

"Coco, I need you. I've spent the last two days trying to figure out how to get you back. What can I do to make this better? Please give me something to hang onto."

"Chase, you've spent the last two days getting your head back together, picturing us together going forward. An hour ago, I was still trying to figure out how I was going to make my head and my heart move ahead alone. Without you. I'm still hurt. And angry. And confused. I need a little time to see more clearly how things might work between us. I have a trust issue right now. I'm not sure I trust you or myself not to over-react to whatever comes up next between us."

"Coco, please don't send me away. If you make me walk out that door, I'll just camp out on your front porch until you come to terms with how our future is going to go. I'll set up my office out there. I'll pay you rent but I won't leave. Please don't make me go." And they both shed a few tears, and then a little laugh, picturing Chase, old and grey, practicing law while living on Coco's front porch.

"Chase, you make me crazy. And not necessarily in a good way. But okay, you can stay. We do need to talk some more. But please don't think that anything is going to happen tonight. I'm too tired, too raw, too close to the edge. And right now, I'm too hungry. There's nothing in the fridge that's safe to eat and the freezer is empty. You're going to pick up all the shit I just threw at you for scaring me and I'm going to order a pizza. And I have laundry to do. Then I'm going to call Gigi and talk for a few minutes. And sometime tonight I have to turn my phone back on and get back into my email and see who I've been ignoring the past week. If that doesn't sound too boring, you're welcome to stay."

"That sounds like heaven to me, baby. Thank you very much. I promise I won't get in your way until you're ready." He leaned in close in enough for a quick kiss, both of them noticing the spark of electricity that passed between them. And then he started picking up all the things from the fridge that littered the kitchen floor, thinking about the second 50 book, and wondering what that Grey guy would do in Chase's place.

24

*T*wo hours later, Chase and Coco had eaten pizza and drank the last of the beer from the fridge. Coco had finally turned her phone back on and was stunned by the number of messages and texts from Chase. Messages and texts that she decided she would read later. When he wasn't there. When she could process all of his messages in private. Her quick conversation with Gigi did nothing to help the current state of confusion and stress she was feeling.

In order to keep Chase from getting too bored, because she really did feel more comfortable having him in the house with her, she undocked her laptop and brought it to the living room where she could read and respond to emails, and still watch a little TV with Chase while he read what she considered a dangerous book.

"Chase, I have other books you could be reading. I'm a little concerned that you're going to let that book put ideas in your head that I can't follow through on tonight. Maybe **War and Peace** would be a better read for you tonight."

"Seriously? **War and Peace**? Have you ever actually read that whole book? That is one fucking long, boring book. I like this 50 book much better. And I still think I could teach this guy a thing or two."

Coco checked to see how far he was into that second book and said "Keep reading." And she shook her head and went back to her laptop to finish up the work that absolutely had to be done before morning.

At 10 PM, Coco was yawning, ready to put her laptop away and go to bed. But what to do with Chase? She wanted him to stay but she wasn't prepared to make love to him yet. And she wasn't sure how to broach that subject. But Chase did it for her.

"Coco, you're really tired, and so am I. But I don't want to leave you alone. I think we should go to bed, maybe talk for a little while until we fall asleep, and see how things look in the morning."

"Chase, I'm not sure that's a good idea. I'm not ready to…"

"Coco, it's okay, I understand. But I just need to have you in my arms, start to rebuild the connection between us, pretend things are at least a little better between us."

"I think, considering we're sitting here side by side, and I haven't tried to bean you with a ketchup bottle in the past few hours, we can assume that things are at least a little better between us. But we just talk. Maybe cuddle a little. Until I fall asleep. Part of the reason I didn't sleep well over the weekend was I missed being in your arms. And I didn't think I'd ever be there again. But I can't just jump right back into the deep end. So, baby steps, okay? Give me a little time. Maybe even make me beg a little before you devour me. Okay?"

"Coco, there's nothing I like more than the sound of you begging, baby. Okay, it's a deal. Let's go to bed." And he stood, pulled Coco up off the sofa, and led her to her bedroom. He put on the sweat pants she threw at him, and he admired the tee shirt she had on when she came out of the bathroom.

When Chase came out of the bathroom after her, she had a question for him. "Did you put the seat back down, gorgeous? I don't want to go swimming in the middle of the night again." And he made a face, went back into the bathroom and put the toilet seat back down.

As he turned off the bathroom light, and got into bed, he said "Coco, I promise, I'll get the hang of that eventually, but you're going to need to be a little extra vigilant for a while until I get in the habit."

"Oh Chase, what will I ever do with you?"

"For tonight, just let me hold you."

Once they were settled in bed, with Coco spooning comfortably against Chase's solid chest, he started talking. "Coco, when I realized you'd run away on Saturday, I panicked. The weather was so bad, I was afraid you'd have an accident if you were out driving in it. And then my imagination really took off. I even asked Gigi if she thought you might do something like Martin had done. Even after she assured me that you would never do that, I was still afraid you might not come back. Where did you go, baby?"

And she told him about her plans to drive to Marco Island. And about the horrible storm that stopped her in Savannah. She laughed a little about how much wine she drank and how much junk food she ate. And how the room service waiters spent less and less time in her room the longer she was there. She couldn't smell herself, but she was pretty sure they could smell her – and didn't intend to stay any longer than it took to wheel one cart in and another one back out again.

Coco wanted to ask Chase how long he'd been at her house before she got home, but her yawns were becoming non-stop. She planned to just rest her eyes for a few minutes while Chase answered, but within a few minutes, she was sound asleep. Chase kissed Coco on the top of her head and laughed a little to himself – he had formulated a plan to win Coco back, based on what he'd read earlier in the evening. Then he cried himself to sleep, thankful that she had allowed him this much contact her first night home.

Coco woke up Tuesday morning alone in bed and was disappointed when she thought Chase had left without telling her goodbye. Then she heard loud noises coming from the kitchen and wondered what the hell was going on. She spent a few minutes in the bathroom, pleased to see that the toilet seat was down, and then headed for the kitchen.

She found Chase dressed, putting one plate of eggs and sausage on the table with a cup of coffee, and she frowned at him.

"Coco, I'm glad you're up. I was just about to come in and drag you out of bed."

"Chase, it's 6 AM. What the hell?"

"I made you breakfast but I don't have time to make sure you eat. I have to go, I have an early meeting. Sit. Eat everything on the plate. You'll have time for 30 minutes of yoga and a shower before you get back on line and get back to work. Make sure you stop for lunch, there's a salad in the fridge for you."

"Chase, where did this food come from?"

"I went to the store this morning, but I only got the essentials. You'll have to go tomorrow and get stocked up. Sorry I left the mess for you to clean up. I really have to go, baby, have a great day."

"I don't understand…"

"Thanks for letting me stay last night, baby. I really have to go. Eat!! I'll call you later today and see how your day is going." And he brushed a quick kiss across her lips and headed out the door.

And to the Universe, she asked "What the fuck?"

By 9 AM, Coco had eaten breakfast, did her yoga stretches and took a shower. She'd also cleaned out the remaining emails that needed her attention, and she'd talked to two of her clients. It was time to look at the emails and texts she had found from Chase on her phone. Most of the messages were the same thing – "Coco, where are you? Call me!!" The last two messages were the ones that made her cry, made her regret everything that had happened in the past ten days.

The text, sent at 6 AM Monday morning, was short and sweet – "Please forgive me, Coco, I can't make it without you."

The email he sent her at Noon Monday took her breath away – *"Dearest Queen of My Heart, it's been 47 hours since you left my house. I don't think my heart has beat in all that time. My blood still flows through my veins somehow but my soul is so empty without you. My future seems faded and grey without you. If you don't forgive me, if you don't come back to me, it will go on that way until I die, an old, lonely shell of a man. Even if you never speak to me again, I will always be yours, nothing will ever change that. Please tell me we can fix this, tell me you forgive me. Please come back to me and let my heart start beating again."*

Coco sat at her desk and sobbed until there were no more tears left in the Universe. She knew how she felt about Chase, but she just didn't know if she could trust him again. She didn't know if she could trust herself again. All he had to do was look at her and her heart rate sped up like a Formula One race car on a fast track. That wasn't a good thing for someone with trust issues. But then, who could really trust any other human being, who could be sure that even someone who professed love could be counted on 100%. And neither of them had said 'love' yet.

Coco closed her eyes and saw Chase's face, felt the touch of his lips on hers, felt the slide of his fingers over her body. She could hear her own screams as he drove her to the madness of orgasm. She could hear his moans as she drove him to his own madness. And in that moment, she knew that she had forgiven him, and herself. She knew that no matter what he did in the future, she would always forgive him. Because she loved him. And nothing else mattered.

Late that afternoon, Chase called Coco to see how her day had been. He didn't talk long but apologized that he could not be with her for dinner, and said he would come to the house after his evening business meeting. At 10 PM, he called to tell her that the meeting was not going well, and that it would be late before he came to the house. She had so much to tell him, but he ended the call before she had a chance. At 11 PM, she figured it was too late and she wouldn't see him that night, and she went to bed.

At midnight, Chase let himself into Coco's house, quietly stripped and climbed into her bed. He snuggled next to her and she leaned her naked body into him in her sleep. His instant erection almost convinced him that he should wake her up and make sweet, slow love to her, but that wasn't part of the plan to win her back. She had said he should make her beg and that was what he intended to do – even if it killed him.

Wednesday morning, Coco woke up to the sound of the shower running. She felt the heat of the bed next to her and realized she'd had company while she slept. If the shower was running, Chase was in the bathroom naked, and she intended to join him.

She walked quietly into the bathroom and slipped into the shower behind him while he was washing his hair and put her arms around him, pressing her nakedness against his back and those sexy ass cheeks. He didn't react at all, almost as if he had expected her to join him.

"Good morning, baby, did you sleep well?"

"Apparently I had company and didn't know it, but yes, I slept very well. Can I help you with anything this morning?" And she reached around to grasp his cock. But he had other plans.

"No, Coco, we shouldn't do that. You haven't had enough time yet, you're not ready."

"How the hell do you know what I'm ready for? I'm ready for you! Now!"

"No, I don't think you are. But I can at least help you out a little if you're in need." And he turned quickly, turning her with him, so that her back was now against his front, with his cock pressed against her back. He reached down between her legs and began a slow torture, his fingers lightly swirling around her clit, just enough to bring her to the edge but not enough to let her slip over. And he made her hang there on the edge, panting and moaning, trying to push her clit closer to his hand. Every time she pushed forward, he pulled away just far enough to maintain the light touch and nothing more.

And then he stopped. And left the shower with an evil little laugh. And she protested.

"Chase! Come back here! I know you're doing this on purpose, you asshole! You think I'm going to beg you to fuck me and that is so not going to happen! Anything I need, I can do myself!"

And he turned toward her as his towel dropped to the floor. "I'm sure you can, baby, you're a very capable woman. I just don't want to rush you into something you'll regret later. Now I really have to go. Your coffee is ready in the kitchen, and there are cinnamon rolls in the oven, they should be ready in about 10 minutes. Have a great day, I'll call you later." And he blew her a kiss on his way out of the bathroom.

"Buckingham, you suck!!" And in a much quieter voice, she said "At least I hoped you would."

By the time she finished her own shower, the cinnamon rolls were ready and Chase had left. She was pretty sure she was going to have a really hard time concentrating on work with that feeling between her legs making her crazy.

25

Chase called Wednesday evening, saying that he was at a group therapy session with his Army buddies and probably wouldn't get to her house to see her that evening. She went to bed at 11 PM with her favorite vibrator but after 30 minutes, she was exhausted and unfulfilled. She drifted to sleep, dreaming of Chase's hard cock in her hand and his hot breath on her neck. Chase crawled into her bed at midnight, gently removed the vibrator from her hand, and laughed to himself, thinking that, based on the somewhat frustrated look on her sleeping face, she had probably been unsuccessful in her attempt to find relief. She was close to the begging point, and he hoped that they would be able to spend the weekend in bed together, catching up on all the moaning and panting and screaming orgasms they'd missed in the past two weeks.

Thursday morning, Coco woke up to the sound of the shower again, but she stayed in bed this time, waiting for Chase to come out of the bathroom. Two could play at his little game. She had apparently slept naked again the night before and wondered if Chase had something to do with that. When she heard the shower turn off, she threw off the bed covers, propped herself up on all of the pillows and reached down between her legs. She started circling her clit with a slow steady motion, and in less than a minute, she was writhing against her own hand. Two fingers of her free hand slipped into her wet pussy, just as Chase was walking out of the bathroom. He already had an erection, but the sight of Coco pleasuring herself made his cock actually point toward her, trying to drag him along behind. He couldn't hide the growl that escaped his chest at the sight of her.

The look of desire on Coco's face was like a siren's call to Chase but he was stubborn enough that he wasn't going to let her win this battle. So not part of the plan. Ignoring his own obvious needs, he slowly dried off and got dressed in full view of her, teasing her with his stunning body, resisting her attempts to lure him back into bed.

"Coco, you seem chipper this morning. I hope you slept well. You're on your own for breakfast today but I did start the coffee for you. I have to run, sweet thing, I'll call you later. Have a good day, baby." He blew her another kiss as he left the bedroom, wondering if he could get back home before he had to take care of his own horny demands.

"Buckingham, I know what you're doing! You're a bastard, you know that?!?"

And she heard him laugh as he left the house. She threw herself back onto the pillows and thought to herself that Thursday was going to be another shitty day.

By 5:00 PM Friday, Coco's work week was done, and her thoughts were on one thing – just one thing – getting that fucking Chase Buckingham back inside her somehow. He'd been a bastard all week, teasing and taunting her, a few times in the shower bringing her to the edge but never helping her over. And she hadn't been able to get herself there – Chase had stolen her 'O' and didn't seem interested in giving it back. Mostly he'd been treating her like his friend and not his lover, which she desperately needed to be again. She decided if it was begging he wanted, it was begging he was going to get.

At 5:30, Coco texted Chase and inquired about dinner plans.

"Chase, I was thinking I'd make dinner for you tonight. Are you available?"
"One call left to make and then I'm done. 7:30?"
"7:30 is great. See you then."

Coco had restocked the cupboards and fridge a few days before, and she had everything she needed to make a quick, easy, fabulous dinner that she knew Chase would love. By 6:00, she had everything prepped and ready to go. The stuffed chicken breasts would go in the oven at 6:45 and the bacon wrapped asparagus bundles would go in at 7:15. She had coincidentally made Peach Crisp the evening before and it was sitting in the fridge waiting to be enjoyed. It could warm through while they ate their dinner and she'd serve it with ice cream for dessert. Assuming they actually got to dessert! She put three bottles of Moscato in the wine fridge to chill, thinking if she couldn't get Chase into bed by luring him with her dinner and her sex appeal, she'd get him drunk and take him that way.

By 6:30, Coco was out of the shower, dressed in a black strapless calf length silk number that showed off all her curves. Paired with her black snake skin stilettos and Chase's favorite perfume, she was sure he would be drooling within five minutes of entering the house. And the drooling wouldn't just be for the food.

By the time Chase arrived promptly at 7:30, the house smelled so good, Coco couldn't wait to eat. But she would gladly hold off on eating if Chase was in an amorous mood. Unfortunately, he was the perfect gentleman. And she was pissed. So they ate dinner, struggling with conversation about their individual days, as Coco got hornier and angrier. Every time she served Chase something, she practically shoved her boobs in his face, let him smell her perfume up close and personal, even bent over to pick up something off the floor, giving him a pussy shot he should not have been able to resist. And yet he did resist. And she couldn't take it anymore. She was up on her feet before she realized what she was doing, her index finger pointing right in his face.

"Buckingham, you are one fucking bastard!"

Chase got out of his own chair and asked "Coco, what has you so upset, baby?"

"You do, you big prick! I've been trying to seduce you into my bed for four days and what do I get? Nothing!"

"Coco, I've slept with you every night this week."

"Oh, yes, you've been IN my bed, but you haven't DONE anything in my bed. You've been more chaste than the freaking Pope! I can't even get myself off anymore and don't think I haven't tried! I've gone through two vibrators and three sets of batteries and all I get is exhausted! And it's all your fault! My 'O' is broken and you're the only one who can fix it! And stop smirking at me!"

"Now, Coco…"

"Don't you 'Now, Coco…' me. You want me to beg? Fine! At this point, I'm not above begging." And the tears started to roll down her cheeks.

"Coco, please don't cry."

"Chase, are you punishing me for needing a little time to get past last weekend? Because it really feels like you are. I'm so nervous, I can hardly breathe. Nervous that you still want to make love to me, and more nervous that you don't. Are we back together or are we not?" By the time she finished the last sentence, her voice was barely a whisper and she wondered if Chase had even heard what she'd said.

"Coco, I haven't been trying to punish you – well maybe the tiniest little bit. I can see how you might have felt that I was. Baby, I just need you to be sure that I'm what you want. I don't want you to wake up in a month or a year, and be miserable, and decide this was all a mistake."

"Chase, I don't know if we can get back to where we were before, but maybe we can find a different place that's just as good? I don't want to just walk away and know that the best thing that ever happened to me is gone because I pushed you away. I need you to hold me and make love to me and tell me you'll be around for a while. Chase, I'm begging you. I just need to know we're okay."

And he grabbed Coco and hugged her tightly, and she wrapped her arms around him and held on for dear life. "Oh, Coralee, you don't know how hard it's been the last few days, pretending I don't want to bury my cock deep inside you, wrap my arms and legs around you, and never let you go. Right now, baby, I can't think of anything I'd rather do in the world than make love to you all night. And then sleep a few hours, and make love to you all day tomorrow. Until neither of us can walk or speak in complete sentences."

"I think I'd like that, Chase. I think I need that."

And he picked Coco up and carried her to her bedroom, whispering naughty nothings in her ear, promises of all the things he planned to do to her.

When Chase set Coco down on her feet in the bedroom, he noticed she was crying again, gentle tears streaking down her cheeks.

"Coco, don't cry. And don't be scared. It's just like our first time again. Remember that first night? We were both a little scared and so attracted to each other. And everything was perfect. Spectacular. We're like magnets, you and me. Drawn to each other, such a strong bond. And it will always be like that. No matter what happens in the future, the one thing you can count on is that we will be together. When you do something pig headed, I'll still be here. And when I do something stupid, you'll always forgive me. Right?"

"Right. Chase…"

"Shhh, Coco. There's nothing you need to say. Just let me make love to you. If you can still talk when I'm done, you can talk then." And she nodded and smiled a very shy, un-Coco-like smile. Chase reached up and wiped the tears off her face, lowered his head toward her lips and then stopped, millimeters away.

"Chase…"

"Shhh, Coco. Give me a minute. I'm savoring the calm before the erotic storm of emotion I'm going to feel as soon as my lips touch yours again. I've been dreaming of this moment all week and I want to make it last as long as I can."

Seconds or minutes or a lifetime passed and finally, he couldn't wait any longer. Instinctively, they both took a deep breath, and then their lips touched, the spark ignited, and the tension of the past few weeks was burned away in the inferno of their passion. This night was better than that first night because they already knew what each other's responses would be. Chase knew that Coco would suck his tongue deep into her mouth, her hands would reach down to caress his cock through his suit pants. And she knew that as soon as her hand touched his pants, his cock would grow, almost pushing out to touch her, to welcome her back. The two lovers became one spirit, breathing out and breathing in, lost in the intensity of the moment.

Coco barely noticed when Chase unzipped her dress and pushed it to the floor. What she did notice was his hands on her naked breasts, gently touching, smoothing his hands over them, rubbing his palms over her nipples like they were precious gems. While his hands roamed her chest and then her ass, Coco reached between them and unbuckled Chase's belt and pulled it through the belt loops of his pants. When she dropped it on the floor, she unbuttoned and unzipped those sexy suit pants and reached inside to claim what was hers.

As she pushed his pants and jockeys to his knees, she dropped to her knees on the floor, focused on something she'd missed very much in the past two weeks.

Chase looked down at her and started to speak. "Coco, no, it's not time for that yet, baby."

"Chase, please let me do this. I really need to do this for you – for me. I've dreamed of it for too long."

"Okay, baby, but when I say you're done, and it's my turn, then you just lay back and enjoy. I've been dreaming of things too." And he tangled his hands in her hair and guided her mouth to his cock, knowing that they'd never be apart again.

She wasn't sure just how long she had played with Chase's cock in her mouth, but finally he did take control. "Coco, stop! When I come, I don't want it to be in your mouth, baby. I want to be buried in your tight pussy. I want my cock to feel all those tiny little muscles as they squeeze the orgasm out of me." And he pulled away from her, rather enjoying the combination of grumble and whimper that slipped from her throat as he pulled himself free. When she looked up at him, Chase expected to see a little fight in her eyes. But what he saw there was the peace and contentment she had needed so desperately, that she had finally found by lavishing his cock – and him – with her love.

Love. Neither of them had said it yet, but he knew they both felt it. And he needed to show her that no matter what had occurred between them recently, what he felt for her would continue to grow. For the rest of their lives.

Chase pulled Coco to her feet, and in the process, they both realized he still had his shirt and tie on, not to mention his shoes and socks, along with his suit pants and jockeys around his ankles. And they both laughed a little at the sight. So Coco reached up and pulled his tie loose, and started unbuttoning his shirt while he slipped off his shoes. Once she had his shirt off, he pushed her back an arm's length and almost franticly extricated himself from his pants, underwear and socks. He kicked everything away with a flourish and pulled Coco back to him, where they embraced for a few minutes, feeling the spark between them burst into flames.

They shared a kiss that was well suited to any erotic romance movie, filled with tongues and moans and gasping breaths. Chase broke the kiss to pick Coco up and almost throw her onto the bed in his unbridled lusty enthusiasm. On her back, Coco started scooting toward the pillows at the head of the bed and Chase followed, stalking her with an evil laugh bubbling from his throat. She started to spread her legs for him, but he grabbed her knees and pushed them back together, surprising her. Instead of climbing between her legs, he straddled them so that he could play with her swollen breasts and pebbled nipples, all the while rubbing against her clit and belly with his cock.

Coco's moans intensified as Chase played and she seemed unsure what to do with her hands. So she clutched his shoulders tightly, her nails almost digging into his skin. Which amped up his enthusiasm and the devilish flick of his tongue against her hard nipples.

With a quiet breathy voice, Coco said, "Chase, I still have my shoes on, gorgeous."

"I know you do, baby, those stilettos are for me – for later."

"Are you going to wear my shoes, gorgeous?"

"No, but they're going to look spectacular on my shoulders, teasing me – when I say it's time."

"Does that mean I'm going to feel you inside me at some point tonight? Or are you going to play until I pass out, short of breath and unfulfilled?"

"Oh, baby, you have no idea how long I plan to play with you. Bring you to the edge, let you rock there until you scream, and then back off until you can breathe again. And then start all over again. You'll be fulfilled, baby, but not until I say it's time."

"Such an evil son of a bitch you can be!"

"Yes, well, be that as it may, eventually my cock won't allow me to play any longer and I will be forced to take you – deep and hard – until we're both fulfilled, with those sexy stilettos riding around my neck. I know it's difficult for you but you'll just have to be patient and wait until I'm ready. This is for both of us. But mostly for me. Feel free to scream my name as many times as you need, baby." And Chase descended on Coco's mouth with a crushing kiss, fingering her breasts and rubbing against her clit until she screamed his name into his mouth.

An hour later, Chase finally couldn't hold off any longer, and Coco was almost comatose with pleasure and desire. He let her settle just a little so that she would know what he was doing, and then he raised her legs so that her heels rested on his shoulders, her stilettos looking like giant earrings in Coco's muddled brain. And he grasped her hips and drove into her – deep and hard – just like he'd promised. And her tears started to fall again, quietly, almost peacefully, as a new desire washed over her. And he stopped thrusting and looked deep into her eyes.

"Coco, you're crying again. Am I hurting you? Or are you just really emotional tonight?"

"I'm sorry, gorgeous, my emotions are all over the board tonight. I just never thought this was going to happen again, and having you back in my arms, back inside me again, is overwhelming me a little. It's all good. Just let me cry if I need to."

"Maybe you need a safe word so I know when I really need to stop. What do you think?"

"I don't need a safe word, Chase, and I don't want you to ever stop. Ever again."

Coco's words set Chase on fire and he started thrusting into her again and again, like their very lives depended on it. They were reforging the connection they'd both thought was gone forever, making it strong and sure with the force and the heat of their passion. They both knew that someday, way in the future, their passion would temper a little, would take on a different intensity, but the bond would always be there, a bond that would keep them together forever. Fulfillment came to both of them in a huge orgasmic explosion that made them both scream, sucking the last of their energy. It was all they could manage to shuffle around on the bed so that they could cuddle, with Coco leaning into Chase's welcoming chest. As sleep finally came, they rested peacefully in each other's arms.

26

Saturday was a haze for Chase and Coco. Some primal need was driving them and they made love everywhere – in bed, in the shower, in the hot tub, on the sofa in the basement family room. They stopped only to eat breakfast and a late lunch, and each time, just as they thought the magnetic pull between them had eased, there would be a stray look or an innocent comment and they would be at it again. By the time evening came around, they were both – finally – too sore, too stiff and too tired to do more than just touch each other, holding hands as they sat in the family room theater chairs watching a movie on the big TV.

And it was time to eat again. Being too tired to actually get dressed enough to go out somewhere to eat, even too tired to make an effort to cook something, they decided on having something delivered. They bickered back and forth about what it was going to be, and who was going to pay, and then finally settled on Coco's choice of wings and beer, with all the extras, and she agreed that Chase could pay.

"Alright, Coco, we'll go with the wings, the fries, the cheese sticks, the onion straws and the beer, but I pay! You made dinner last night – that was just last night, wasn't it? I think my brain is sex-addled. Anyway, tonight I pay." And Coco picked up her phone and placed the order, quickly, before Chase changed his mind.

"Okay gorgeous, I'll let you pay. I'm not sure I have the strength to climb the stairs to answer the door anyway. And when you come back down with the food and the beer, could you bring the Advil from the bathroom? I'm so stiff!! I just don't understand! I feel like I worked in the yard all day!"

"I think I've been tricked into climbing the stairs! But I guess you're worth it. And you're right about needing some Advil. After all, I'm the one who did all the 'planting' today! All you had to do was just lay there and be the 'garden'!"

"I was a lovely soft 'garden', wasn't I? So agreeable, so pliable. Feel free to 'plant' again any time – starting tomorrow! I think the 'garden' is closed for the night!" And her slight movement to change positions in the chair made her wince enough to make Chase laugh.

"I guess we'll just have to see about that, won't we?" He raised her hand to his lips and kissed it gently, but neither of them had the strength to make any further moves. Chase had kept an eye on the time, and crawled up the stairs, finding his wallet and some sweat pants just as the delivery driver was ringing the doorbell. He took all the food to the kitchen and went back to the bedroom to grab the Advil and his dress shirt for Coco to put on. He grabbed the food and the beer from the fridge, but before he went back downstairs, he yelled down to Coco.

"Coco, is there anything else you need me to bring down? Because I'm only making this one trip. If you decide you need something else, you'll have to get it yourself."

"There's a bag hanging on the hook in the laundry room. Throw the Advil, the beer and a few bottles of water in that. It'll make it easier to get everything down here."

To himself, he muttered "She can be so fucking bossy! I think I love that about her." And he stopped at the use of the L word again, feeling much more comfortable with it than he would ever have imagined. Then he grabbed the bag, threw everything in it, including his shirt, grabbed the food, and headed back downstairs.

Coco looked at Chase, carrying a bag full of beer and all that food, and smiled her most seductive smile. "Gorgeous, you look so hot right now. And it's not just because I'm starving and you're carrying a bunch of food. You're just really freaking sexy with your bare chest and your slightly too long, curly hair and those just tight enough sweat pants. Some day when I can actually move again, I'm going to show you just how sexy I think you are."

"Yeah, well, baby, I ought to make you crawl over here and get your own damned food, but I'm too much of a gentleman to make you do that. You do, however, have to slide your little ass off the chair and down here onto the floor with me, because I'm not going to spend the next hour handing you whatever food you think you want. Now take some of that Advil and hand me the bottle so we don't both wake up sore and grumpy tomorrow. And here, take my shirt and put it on. You're way too distracting naked. You really think my hair's too long? I'm kinda liking it this way. Some of my clients seem to like it this way too."

"Which clients? Do I have to hurt someone? Because I can, you know. You just tell me if someone puts a hand on you, and I'll take care of it!"

"Coco, you should know I never flirt and tell. But maybe I should get a haircut on Monday."

"No, gorgeous, I'll let you know when it's time for a haircut. Everything about you is perfect just the way it is. Just work on that arrogant thing for me and I'll be happy." She laughed as she took the shirt Chase offered her and slipped it on, looking like a teenager wearing her dad's clothes. Then she slid down out of her chair onto the floor and dove into the large tray of food sitting between her and Chase. For the next hour, they stuffed themselves and washed the junk food down with beer and water. When they couldn't eat another bite, they left the half full tray on the floor and climbed back into their theater seats to get comfy. The movie they started watching didn't hold her attention long – the last thing Coco heard was her mantle clocking chiming 10:00 PM and she was out. Chase smiled at his sleeping lover, then got up and covered her with a soft sofa throw blanket. Then he climbed back into his own very comfortable chair and snuggled in with his own blanket. He managed to stay awake a little longer than Coco, but he wasn't awake to hear the clock chime 11:00 PM.

At 3:00 AM, Chase woke up and turned off the TV and the lights, then coaxed Coco up out of her chair and up the stairs to finish the night in bed. She never really woke up and when he cuddled up behind her in bed and pulled the covers over them, she leaned back into his chest and put her arm protectively over the one he had around her waist. And they never moved for the next 6 hours.

Coco woke up at 9:00 AM, almost blinded by the damned Myrtle Beach morning sun streaming in around her bedroom drapes. She leaned back and realized that Chase wasn't in bed, and he wasn't in the bathroom either. She started to think maybe her mind was playing tricks on her and she hadn't just spent the last two days with him. The thought tugged hard at her heart. And then she heard familiar racket in the kitchen and her heart lightened again.

Coco pulled on a tee shirt and took care of some business in the bathroom and then headed to the kitchen. By the time she got to the living room, Chase was on the sofa, his long legs stretched out, feet propped up on the coffee table, with a cup of coffee and the Sunday newspaper. He looked up at her and said "Good morning, sunshine. Need some coffee? I was going to bring you some but the last time I checked on you, you were still dead to the world. Did you sleep well?"

Coco plopped down on the sofa on her knees next to Chase and kissed him on the cheek, gently running her hand up and down his sexy muscular arm. "I slept very well, thank you very much. I was a little confused when I first woke up. I fell asleep watching TV downstairs last night and woke up this morning in bed. I started thinking I'd dreamed the last two days. Then I heard familiar noises in the kitchen and decided you weren't a dream after all. Just a dream come true."

"Oh, baby, you say the sweetest things. Let's get dressed and I'll take you out to breakfast."

"No, I'm going to make breakfast for you. As long as eggs, sausage and fruit are okay with you. I'd whip up some pancakes, but I'm out of milk."

"Whatever you make will be just fine, sunshine."

"Good. You stay here and enjoy your newspaper. I'm off to the kitchen to get my own coffee and make breakfast. Fifteen minutes okay? I'll call you when everything's ready."

"That will be perfect." And he took her hand and kissed her palm, winked at her and then went back to reading the paper.

By 11:00 AM, they had eaten breakfast and cleaned up the kitchen, and Coco had talked Chase into 30 minutes of yoga stretches to work out some additional muscle stiffness their hours of passion had caused. A quick – boring – non-sex shower and they were dressed and ready to go. Wherever.

"Coco, there's somewhere I'd like to take you today, is that okay?"

"I'd be happy to go wherever you want. Where is it we're going? Do I need to change?"

"You look fabulous, but I would recommend bringing along some flat shoes to do a little walking off road."

"You've piqued my curiosity. You know that's not a good thing!"

"Patience, Coco. Let's go. I need to stop by my house and change my clothes."

Coco grabbed her topsiders and a sweater to wear with her little knit dress, snatched up her purse and keys, and they were off.

The drive to Chase's house took hardly any time at all – or maybe she was just excited to see where he was taking her. While he was changing clothes, she called Gigi to say hello.

"Coco, where the hell have you been? I haven't talked to you since Friday. Did you make dinner for Chase? What did you make? Were there orgasms involved? Tell me!! Tell me!"

"Yes, I did make dinner for Chase on Friday and it turned out very well. I just haven't had time to call you since then. And you know I don't orgasm and tell!"

"I call bullshit on that! You talk more about sex than Maggs and me combined! But I see that you're at Chase's house right now so I won't nag for details just yet."

"Wait. How do you know where I'm at? Are you stalking me?!?"

"No. I'm tracking your phone. There's an app for that, you know. Haven't I ever mentioned that before? I started when you moved back home. It took you awhile to settle in and I was worried about you. Then of course you took off last weekend, proving my point just a little bit. You really have to stop leaving your phone at home like that! It's not safe! Anyway, I talked to Bob and Monica the other day and told them I was doing it. Bob is tracking your phone, too."

"I think I'm really pissed at you right now. Your nosiness knows no bounds, woman!! But I'm not going to let you and your intrusive behavior ruin my day with my man. Expect to be yelled at later!"

"Your man? I guess things did go well this weekend. So what are you doing today? Is more sex involved?"

"Stop!! We're going somewhere but he won't tell me where. Now leave me alone. I'll call you tomorrow if I have time. AND STOP TRACKING

MY PHONE!!" And she disconnected the call just as Chase was walking into the living room.

"Who's tracking your phone, Coco? Isn't that illegal without a court order?"

"It's that nosy bitch, Gigi. She says there's an app for it?"

"Really? I'll have to talk to Robert and check that out."

"No! You won't! Now where are we going?"

"I told you, it's a surprise. Let's go." And he hustled her out the door and into the jeep, and they were off.

Chase had headed down Hwy 17 South and Coco was enjoying the Sunday drive. But not knowing where they were going was driving her just a little crazy. Just about the time she thought he was taking her to Brookgreen Gardens – one of her very favorite places – he turned in the opposite direction and headed toward the shore. He had Coco drive through the fence gate he had just opened, then he closed the gate again and got back behind the wheel. Chase drove for about 15 minutes down a long winding lane, and finally parked next to a burnt out shell of a house that had probably once been a lovely home. The lot was full of trees that blocked the Eastern view, but Coco could hear the waves on the shore and knew they must be close.

As they walked around the property, Coco asked "Who lived here, gorgeous?"

"This was my grandparents' house when I was growing up – my dad's parents. My grandfather died when I was in high school, and then my grandmother died during my first tour with the Rangers. We were off base for three or four weeks at a time back then, and when I finally found out she had died, she'd already been buried. When her will was read, everyone was surprised to hear she had left me the house. I got a 30 day leave to come home, and I ended up spending it with my mom and dad, cleaning out the house. I think my parents wanted me to sell the house and the property, but I decided I wanted to keep it, and it sat here empty for all the time I was in the Army. Dad would stop by now and then to make sure the house hadn't collapsed or anything, but they never did anything with it, waiting for me to come home. I had just about decided to fix what needed fixing and move in last year, but it got hit by lightning during a storm. There was no sprinkler system and the fire department is volunteer down here, so by the time the fire trucks got here, there wasn't much left."

They had stopped in the middle of the trees, admiring the view of the shore below them. As Coco looked back at the house, she said "Chase, I'm sorry to see this. It looks like it was a comfortable home at one time, I'm sure your grandparents were very happy here."

"Yes, they were. I'd like to be happy here someday too. I'd like to be happy here with you."

"Chase…"

"You don't have to say anything right now, Coco, I know this has been a real whirlwind romance. But I can't honestly see myself with anyone else – only you. Just tell me you'll think about it."

"Chase…"

"Coco, we could be very happy here."

"Chase, let me talk."

"Sorry, I'll shut up."

"Chase, I know the last three weeks have been more than I could ever have dreamed, you're such an amazing person, I wonder sometimes what you see in me. But I can't see myself with anyone else either. I had a dream the other night about the two of us as really old people, sharing a room in a nursing home, still sharing a bed, still getting frisky now and then. And when I woke up, I had such a warm feeling in my heart. I'd like that dream to become reality someday."

"Coco, I promised your Aunt Monica that when I was sure how I felt about you, I would tell you right away. Coco, I'm going to say the 'L' word. If you don't want to hear it, that's too bad, I can't help it, it's true. Coco Brighton, I love you. You don't have to say it back, I just needed to tell you how I feel. I may have loved you as my dance instructor, I'm sure I love you as my crazy, sexy partner for life. We can get married, not get married, I don't really care, whatever you want. I just want to be part of your life for the rest of my life. Coco, baby, will you build a house and a life with me?"

"Chase Buckingham, I do love you. You make me absolutely crazy sometimes and I know that's never going to change, and that's okay. You complete me in a way I never dreamed would be possible, and that's the most important thing. You've made me see that I don't have to be the quintessential single business woman – I can be just as happy and just as fulfilled being the other half of you. I would be honored to build a house and a life with you – here or wherever else you go. I'd follow you anywhere, gorgeous."

And they embraced and shared a sweet, tender kiss – that morphed into white hot passion in just seconds. Clothes flew off as they sank to the ground and made sweaty, sexy love in the grass that would someday be their back yard. As Coco lay there after their joyous coupling, wrapped in Chase's arms, thinking how peaceful everything was, Chase's hands started wandering across her ass cheeks toward a destination he hadn't visited yet. As a single finger swirled around that tiny hole, teasing and taunting her, Chase whispered in her ear – "Coco, let's get dressed and head to your house. I believe there's a fox tail butt plug there with your name on it, baby. I can't wait to see you on your hands and knees, sucking my cock, with that plug stretching your ass, teasing me with that long tail hanging down between your legs. I hope you have lots of lube, baby, I think we're going to need it."

"Fuck, Buckingham, what is it with you guys and anal??" And he just laughed that laugh.

Yes, it was going to be a very interesting life, a very full life, and Coco and Chase were going to enjoy every freaking minute of it – the ups and the downs, the struggles and the joys. These sweet second chances rarely came around, and they needed to be treasured and savored like a decadent treat. Fate had taken years to bring them back together again, and they were going to live life together with all the gusto that love – and a fox tail butt plug – could bring.